SOUTH
OF EDEN

SOUTH
OF EDEN

EARL
MURRAY

A TOM DOHERTY ASSOCIATES BOOK

NEW YORK

This is a work of fiction. All the characters and events portrayed in this novel are either fictitious or are used fictitiously.

SOUTH OF EDEN

A Forge Book
Published by Tom Doherty Associates, LLC
175 Fifth Avenue
New York, NY 10010

www.tor.com

Forge® is a registered trademark of Tom Doherty Associates, LLC.

Design by Lisa Pifher

Library of Congress Cataloging-in-Publication Data

Murray, Earl.
     South of Eden / Earl Murray.—1st ed.
        p. cm.
     "A Tom Doherty Associates book."
     ISBN 0-312-86923-1 (acid-free paper)
     1. Conservation of natural resources—Fiction. 2. Fathers and daughters—Fiction. 3. Forest conservation—Fiction. 4. Environmentalism—Fiction. 5. Cattle trade—Fiction. 6. Colorado—Fiction. I. Title.

PS3563.U7657 S67 2000
813'.54—dc21
                                                                    00-029337

First Edition: August 2000

Printed in the United States of America

0 9 8 7 6 5 4 3 2 1

to my good friend, Larry Yoder—
thanks for "not leaving" the bookstores

SOUTH
OF EDEN

S he rode behind the strange man on his horse, asking him questions, curious about their final destination. He said that it was hidden somewhere in the mountains along the Continental Divide. At first she was worried, but he had insisted that it was all part of a great adventure, one that she would never forget. He had reassured her, even asked her if she had changed her mind and wanted to go back. But of course she hadn't wanted to go back.

So far it had been interesting. She hadn't expected to travel out so far from any known habitation, but he had paid her a great deal of money, many times more than she could make in an entire week working at Trixie's. And the idea of sitting on a mountaintop, watching the clouds drift overhead, had been far too tempting to pass up.

The scenery had been spectacular, despite the fact that the mountains were in a period of drought and the greens weren't quite as green and the flowers weren't as thick as she would have liked. It seemed that the series of dry years had brought natural changes to the area.

Smoke rose from the side of a mountain in the distance, a series of thin plumes that sifted skyward. Her companion didn't appear to be bothered. When she asked if they were going to fight fire, if that was the big adventure, he laughed at her.

"Let it burn," he said. "There's way too damn many trees up here anyway."

Lottie Burns hadn't expected that answer, not from a man who had seemed to be so nice. The remark made her wonder now just who he was—that and the fact that he kept fondling the big hunting knife in the sheath at his side. For hunting, he had told her. They had already seen a lot of elk along the way.

They continued on, following some lost trail through what she knew to be the western Colorado wilderness, drawing ever closer to the smoke in the distance. She had only been in the area for a couple of months, having taken the train from San Francisco, searching out a new life amidst the high peaks west of Denver. Not a new life, necessarily, but the same life in a different location. She had thought of it as a new start in new surroundings, and hopefully a workable means by which to leave past problems behind. She had convinced herself that she would do very well. A lot of miners and cattlemen and railroaders looking for a good time, she had heard. And they paid well.

Trixie, the large madam with her own place in Glenwood Springs had welcomed her and had outfitted her in fine gowns and dresses. She was young and, except for the crooked knife scar above her left breast, thought quite attractive by all of her patrons. She had become a favorite of many who frequented Trixie's and the big madam had begun working her harder, giving her less time off for rest. Everyone knew that in the profession she had chosen, women came and went on an almost daily basis. Getting the most from the most popular was only good business.

Her companion had come into Trixie's the day before, his eyes searching through the women, measuring them for his wants and desires, as all the men did that came in for pleasure.

He had selected her and at first she had found it difficult to look straight at him. He had such unusual eyes, gray and glassy, almost mesmerizing if you stared at him for very long. But his voice was soft, a soothing purr that relaxed her and made her feel at ease. He had made a point of telling her that he had never seen a woman who appealed to him so abruptly and so completely, a woman with whom he could relax and be himself.

Of course he would say that. At first she had thought that he wanted what all the others wanted but likely at a bargain price. But as he had continued to talk with her, there had been more flattering remarks, seemingly heartfelt compliments regarding her personality, which none of the other men had ever cared about. He had told her that Trixie's could be a cold and lonely place when all men ever came for was to use her body and move on. How many of them, he had asked, had ever showed the slightest interest in her for who she was. He would be good to her, he had promised, and give her a comfortable place to live, and he wouldn't force her into anything as a routine. This had all sounded so good to her and she had decided she would give him all the pleasure he would ever want and more, just for being so kind.

But that's where this man had seemed different, this man with the unusual eyes, the unusual glassy gray eyes. Their first night together at Trixie's had been one of sleep only. He had told her she needed to rest for their journey, not to worry about his needs for the time being. It was the first time she had ever encountered that. Perhaps the mark of a nice man, she had thought. He had told her that they were headed into a mountain paradise, and that he would show her a special place that he had come to call his very own.

He told her about a special mountainside where no one ever

went, an unspoiled piece of the wilderness that held many secrets. "You'll see every flower there that you could ever imagine,"
he had promised. "In every color and shape and size."

Lottie Burns couldn't wait to reach this mountain paradise
with all its beauty and grandeur, and she didn't give a damn
that Trixie had been angered at losing her. During the train ride
north from Glenwood Springs toward the Eden Valley he had
told her many times that she would be far better off with him
than she had been, being used for nothing more than profit at
the hands of the big madam.

"The fire won't burn the paradise you talked about, will it?"
she asked.

"No, not my paradise," he replied. "It will create a new
paradise."

"How do you know that?"

"Take my word for it."

They drew ever closer to the fire, him remaining stoically
silent. Nothing she said now could bring a single word from
him. They stopped briefly to water his horse and to have something to eat. She approached him, lowering the front of her gown
even more than the revealing cut already allowed.

"Maybe you would like to sample some of what you've invested in now," she suggested. She hoped it would make him
happy, ease the tension that seemed to be building within him.
But he pushed her away, saying, "We'll do things my way, when
I say. Don't ever do that again."

Her hurt and surprise quickly turned to concern. "Take me
back, please," she said. "I'll gladly refund your money."

"You can walk back, if you'd like."

Frowning, she looked in all directions. Surrounded by
mountains, the sun falling ever closer to the horizon, she knew

that she had absolutely no chance of finding her way out.

"Well, what do you want to do?" he asked.

"I'll go with you, I guess. But I don't understand you."

"Don't worry about understanding me," he said. "Just do as you're told."

Riding slowly in the early twilight, they arrived at the open meadow he had told her about. She wanted to stop and walk through the flowers, a carpet of reds and yellows and blues. She wanted to touch something soft and pretty, to make herself feel better. He told her they wouldn't be stopping, but continuing on instead to his "real paradise."

She had to wonder at his idea of paradise, as they had entered a burn area from some bygone year, where once-huge pines had been badly scarred, left as blackened trunks with sharp and shortened limbs, looking like an endless mass of giant headless scarecrows.

In the distance the new fire burned brightly, the flames licking up into the approaching darkness. He pointed into the distance and said something about rain likely coming and ending the fire before it could do its rightful duty. He said it would be a long rain, that it was too dry for something that would stay and soak the land. Just enough to get everyone's hopes up.

But she didn't care what he was saying, and was, in fact, not even listening. The burned and jagged trees were decorated with women's clothes and the ground around her looked disturbed by digging.

"We're here, now. We've arrived in paradise. Do you like it?"

She didn't answer and he urged the horse forward. The shadows were growing heavier and the twilight deeper, and she continued to say nothing. Instead, she stared wide-eyed into a field of bones and skulls with huge antlers rising, twisted and jagged into the waning light, like so many cornstalks after a howling wind.

"Aren't you even going to ask about this place?" he said. "Don't you want to know what you're seeing?"

Lottie's stomach began to knot.

"No," she said. "I don't want to know."

"They're elk skeletons," he told her. "It's a burying ground for old bulls. When they know the end is near, they come up here and just lay down and die."

"Why are we here?" she asked. She trembled slightly, trying to hide it from him.

"I told you, it's my special paradise. Here, I'll show you where the last bull that died is buried."

"I don't want to see it."

"But I insist."

He dismounted and pulled her down after him.

"What's the matter, Lottie? You're shaking." He stared at her with expressionless eyes.

"Please, can we go back?"

He ignored her and forced her to a spot where a huge bull elk lay in death. It smelled badly. It had been only partially buried, its head and back exposed, along with the ribs on both sides, the front legs spread out in front as if it were trying to climb out of the hole. Its massive antlers rose skyward and strings of long blond hair were tied to the upper tines.

She realized that the animal was not fully decomposed, but had fragments of hide and hair still attached to the bones.

"What do you think?" he asked.

She noticed something protruding from the ground, sticking up at an awkward angle from between two of the elk's ribs. At first she thought it was a small chunk of tree limb with short, oddly curled little branches at the end. In the shadows it was difficult to see. She leaned forward, then jerked back with a start, her hand over her mouth.

A skeletal face looked out at her from between the ribs. The chunk of tree limb was really a human arm, the oddly curled little branches, fingers.

"Her name was Jenny," the strange-eyed man said.

Lottie Burns turned to run, but he had anticipated her reaction and grabbed her quickly by the arm.

"It's all right to scream," he said. "No one can hear you way up here."

2

The late-evening forest rested, recovering from the flames. The saving rain had passed and the clouds had blown into twisted streaks of scarlet across the twilight sky. Below, lodgepole pines, like swaying soldiers in close formation, moaned in the wind, and the smell of drowned fires hung in the air like a rank fog.

Ellis Burke drove his newly purchased 1905 Buick up a remote and rugged wagon road, made treacherous by the previous night's downpour. He struggled to keep control with each uneven turn of the wheel, wondering how he had gotten himself so lost. He had accepted a position as a roving forest ranger in the newly established Routt National Forest, Eden District, and had sought help in the local town of Eden in finding a cabin that was to be his headquarters. He had been directed by Lee Miller, the town banker, to head south of town and take the first road to the west, past the local landmark known as the Devil's Grave, and travel up the creek to a line cabin, where he would be welcome to settle in for his work.

He had anticipated an easier time for himself and his new automobile, a grand machine, the class of its kind, with front- and backseats and a fold-down top for inclement weather. It was supposed to be a short drive along a gentle grade, Miller had said. Gentle compared to what? He could easily have rented a horse and saved his new car from the rigors of the northwestern Colorado backcountry.

The locals had been expecting him, the townspeople and the ranchers in the area. Many had stopped their horses and carriages in the late afternoon as he entered the proud town of Eden, born during the early days of the range-cattle industry, now thirty years past. They seemed to know all about him already. He had seen the newspaper article himself, while eating dinner in the town's hotel restaurant. GOVERNMENT WON'T GO AWAY, the *Eden Star* headline had read, subtitled *Eden and Surrounds Continue to Be Target of Changes, New Ranger to Arrive*, followed by his picture, taken in the brown and green of his forest service uniform.

The article had described how Burke would be replacing Mark Jones, the first district manager in the area. Jones had worked the area the previous summer, mapping different types of trees and grasslands within the forest reserves. Jones was said to have tired of the trying position and moved on, but to where no one knew. Burke would replace him and continue the job of surveying forest reserves to be included in a long-range management plan for the benefit of the resource. He would also be the acting district manager until a new one was selected.

Burke's main responsibility would be to assess the amount of grazing reserves so that a solid grazing conservation plan could be implemented. The plan would restrict the numbers of livestock allowed to graze within the boundaries of each reserve. To support the program and allow for sustained use of public grazing lands, allotment fees would be collected on a regular basis.

It was no secret that traditional ranching practices would soon be a thing of the past. Burke had already read comments by irritated stockmen in the Denver papers, expressing their tensions and worries regarding grazing rights on the newly established national forests. They had been pasturing their livestock on public lands since shortly after the Civil War and wanted no changes. It appeared that each and every ranger assigned to the various districts along the West Coast and throughout the Rocky Mountain West was definitely not welcome.

Burke had been surprised his first day in Eden. Lee Miller had been more than cordial, meeting him in the street and offering to provide him with a special account, should he decide to deposit money with him. Miller had introduced him to the town's postmaster, where Burke had sealed some letters he had written to his superiors in Denver and Washington, D.C. during dinner. He had wanted everyone to know where he was and his immediate plans.

Those who appeared to care less about his arrival merely went their own way and made no comments to him about being in a position to turn their world upside down. The hotel personnel had been most cordial, as had the dinner crowd. He had even detected a smile or two from among the local women. Perhaps they had found him attractive in the new clothing style he had brought out from the Ivy League, his baggy trousers with a short suit coat, complete with a fashionable brown derby, sitting comfortably in his new Buick, the first automobile to arrive in this remote mountain town.

He had named the Buick Emily, after his deceased sister. She had been a year younger than him and had died of tuberculosis at the age of five. In those early years, she had been his best friend and they had shared a lot together. He would always miss her.

Now he concentrated on what lay ahead. As nightfall settled, the rising full moon appeared veiled and murky in the smoke-laden darkness. Burke grew ever more frustrated as the grade grew steeper and more treacherous. Nervous coyotes yapped from a nearby hilltop and from the high rocks above came the screaming yowl of a mountain cat.

How much farther could it possibly be? He was certain he had heard the directions right. But the way was far too difficult and the muddy slopes too trying.

He decided to walk the remaining distance. He would venture on for a short distance and should no cabin appear, return to his Buick and spend the night, or make his way back down the mountain, an option he wanted to avoid if at all possible. The shadows held too many traps and surprises.

He parked at a ninety-degree angle to the hill, the front tires wedged against clumps of sagebrush. Satisfied there would be no downhill movement, he pulled a lantern from the floorboards on the passenger's side and struck a match to the wick. It flared to life, throwing shadows that flickered across the grass and sage-brush. He patted Emily's shiny hood and started up the hill, facing into the mountain wind, which now cried in the night like a lost soul.

How much farther was this place? He was beginning to wonder where he was, and whether he would even find the cabin he belonged in.

Burke made his way up a small hill and noticed a campfire burning brightly along the trail. Four riders rode out of the shadows, each one holding a lantern. They were dressed in dirty cotton shirts, heavy working chaps, and low-crowned working hats. Each one was armed with a revolver.

The leader urged his horse a few steps forward.

"Been expecting you," he said to Burke with a small grin. "You're a little late."

"Who are you?" Burke asked.

"You're on Eden ranch property. We don't take kindly to trespassers."

"I was led to believe I was welcome."

"You were led wrong."

The leader's face held a muscled toughness that set off strangely vacant eyes like dark glass embedded in leather.

"So why did you think you could drive that pile of metal crap up here?" he asked.

"I told you, I was directed to this gulch. There's supposed to be a cabin up here I can use as my headquarters."

Glass Eyes said, "There's no cabin up here, my boy." He turned his horse and motioned to one of the others, a young blond cowboy who rode over and took Glass Eyes's lantern. Saying nothing, Glass Eyes quickly untied a rope from his saddle and threw a lariat over Burke's head and shoulders.

Before could react, Burke found himself facedown, bouncing along the rough ground. He was immediately covered with grass and mud, his coat and trousers ruined. His face stung with each whip of sagebrush and he bit his tongue as his chin bounced into his chest. He tried to pull himself up with the rope but Glass Eyes kept turning his horse, causing him to roll over and over.

Glass Eyes finally reined his horse and Burke struggled to his feet, breathing heavily, clawing at the rope that bound him.

"Just settle yourself down," Glass Eyes told Burke. "We're going to have a little meeting."

Lottie Burns awakened in the darkness of a small shed, gagged and bound hand and foot, amidst the smell of Neets foot oil and saddle leather. She felt groggy and disoriented, vaguely aware that she was in a strange place, the captive of a very strange man.

Slowly, her head cleared and she remembered that he had given her a drug, had forced her to drink whiskey tainted with something bitter. He had held a knife in her face, giving her a choice of the drink or the blade.

Before hauling her to the shed, he had spent a good deal of time with her in the graveyard, the "special paradise" that he had told her was his to enjoy. He had told her to go ahead and scream and had laughed when she fell silent.

"That's what they all do," he had told her. "There's nothing up here but us and the wilderness, my own wilderness, where I shall give you a chance to become immortal with me."

He had gone on to say something about a favor that he wanted her to do for him, something very special that she would feel proud to take part in. He said they would share something cold and hard and that would make them both very happy, so deep inside. He hadn't said what it was, and she hadn't asked.

Then, for the next hour, he had taken her on a tour of the graves, introducing her to the women he had killed, telling her their names, where they were from, and even their last words.

"They usually beg me not to kill them," he had told her. "But one said she would have done the favor if only I had asked her nicely. Can you imagine? It was too late by then. We couldn't have made it work."

During the tour, he had forced her to touch the bodies of the dead elk, to caress their mangled, rotting fur, to touch their dried and sunken eyes and whisper words of love to them. After a while she had barely been able to move, so frightened was she at wondering what he might do to her. He had waved his knife around often, circling her and the dead elk and the dead women, saying gibberish as if in prayer at each site.

He had forced her to take each dead woman's hand, often little more than skeletal remains, and place it first to her heart, and then to both eyes, and finally to her mouth.

"You will be sisters, all of you," he had told her. "Just think of it."

She had vomited repeatedly, but that didn't seem to bother him.

"They forgive you," he had told her, "for they all did the same thing."

When they had finished at the last gravesite, she had collapsed completely, barely able to function.

"Perhaps you would like to choose our gravesite," he had said.

"*Our* gravesite?" she had managed.

"Yes, ours."

3

Burke stood before Glass Eyes, who had taken a seat at a rough table in front of the campfire. The table had a small, round top with what appeared to be detachable legs. He was drinking from a bottle and toying with a deck of cards in front of him, all the while whistling the tune "My Darling Clementine." A large hunting knife with a bone handle was stuck in the right side of the table. Glass Eyes would occasionally reach up from the cards and caress the knife. He would stop his whistling and allow his tongue to hang down from his mouth.

He finally looked up at Burke and smirked.

"You don't look so good," he said. "Too bad about your new duds."

The three men chuckled. They stood or sat around the campfire, two of them passing a bottle of their own back and forth.

Burke fought a headache and intense pain in his shoulders and ribs. He noticed Glass Eyes glaring at him.

"Did you hear me?" Glass Eyes took a drink and shuffled the cards. "You look like you soiled your new clothes."

Burke tested a loose tooth with his fingertips. "What a remarkable observance," he said.

"A little edgy, are we, Mr. Burke?" Glass Eyes said.

"How do you know me?" Burke asked.

Glass Eyes ignored him and dealt himself a hand of solitaire.

"I'm Sid Preston, foreman for Eden Land and Livestock," he

said. "These three work for me: Mr. Len Keller, Mr. Jeb Mason, and Mr. Burt Gamble. Now that we all know one another, we can be friends." He snickered, his dark eyes dancing.

Keller, a tall man with thinning gray hair and a set of piercing gray eyes, glared at Burke and looked back to Preston. "Why all the formalities?" he asked. "He's not welcome."

"Settle down," Preston said. "I need to talk to him."

Mason was young and blond, barely out of his teens, with a strong build and a wild, cold look. He had a cocksureness about him, a constant sneer on his fuzzy face, the blond hair never having turned to hard whiskers.

"I'd like to take him around the sage a time myself," he said. He laughed, dribbling tobacco juice from his mouth.

Gamble was also shorter and strongly built, by far the oldest of the four. He leaned against a tree just back from the fire, away from the drinking, drumming his fingers nervously on the handle of his Colt's pistol that protruded from his belt. Obviously more cautious, he watched Burke closely.

"What's the matter, Burt?" Preston asked. "You look worried."

"Maybe we'd ought to let him be," he suggested.

"Why would we want to do that?" Preston asked.

"We've got other things to do."

"We've got this to do first," Preston said. "I'm telling you that."

"You're the boss," Gamble said. The men turned silent. The wind continued to blow.

Burke studied the men around the campfire, coming to the conclusion that all four were deranged, Sid Preston being the worst.

"What's the reason for this?" Burke asked him.

Preston played cards as if he were all by himself. Keller and Mason made snide remarks and snickered, while Gamble just stared at Burke.

"Too bad nobody here speaks English," Burke said.

The laughing stopped. Preston leaned across the table. "You're a little uppity, huh? But what would you expect from an Eastern dandy?"

"How do you know where I'm from?" Burke asked.

"I saw your school picture in the papers," Preston replied. "I always heard Yale was a long ways from here, to the east."

"You can read a map," Burke said. "I'll give you that."

Preston turned back to his cards. "I guess you can't read one," he said. "This is Eden land."

"Like I told you," Burke insisted, "I was directed up here."

Preston smiled while he played cards. He reached over and petted his knife, as if it were a cat laying close by. Suddenly he stared up at Burke, his face contorting. A thought came to him as though arriving from far away.

"Don't I know you from somewhere?"

"Not hardly," Burke said. "I've got much better taste in friends."

Keller stepped forward. "Maybe he needs another go-round in the sage."

"Put the rope around him again," Preston agreed.

Preston watched only partway while Keller and Mason struggled to get the rope over Ellis Burke's head and shoulders. Though tired and badly bruised, the ranger put up a good fight until he was overpowered.

This amused Preston, but he was thinking more about the woman he had captured and that now awaited him up on the mountain, at his own secret place. He knew that she would do very nicely, and in the hours that had passed since he brought her up, he had grown more and more excited about the possibilities. Should she do him the complete favor—and he in turn, do her the same complete favor—a paradise far beyond what he had already discovered awaited them both.

But now he must deal with a man who could disrupt his paradise, and he couldn't have that.

Yes, this Ellis Burke had the potential to really cause problems. If only he could remember where he knew him from.

"Stop messing with him," Preston told Keller and Mason. "Bring him over here."

"I thought you wanted us to teach him a lesson," Keller protested.

"Just bring him over here."

Burke again stood in front of Preston, struggling to remain on his feet. He breathed heavily, tasting fresh blood in his mouth.

"Come closer," Preston told Burke. Burke took a few steps forward and Preston said, "I'm sure I've met you. But where?"

"I told you, you're wrong," Burke replied.

"No, I've seen you somewhere before. I just don't recall where." He set the deck of cards down. "You wanted to know why you're here?"

"Yes, I asked that," Burke said.

"We thought we'd throw you a party. Invite you to leave

this country, right now. Ever have a going-away party before you even got settled?" Everyone laughed.

"Is this how you treated Mark Jones?"

The room quieted and Preston frowned. "We're talking about you, Mr. Burke—Mr. Burke who's going to turn right around and leave Eden the same way he came in."

"If you get rid of two rangers, one right after the other, you'll have officials showing up to check on you," Burke said.

Preston cleared his throat. "Mr. Burke, we *are* the officials here."

"You're not listening," Burke told him. "I'm talking about officials from outside of the area. Forest service personnel. Federal marshals."

Preston turned back to his game, matching cards where he could. He touched his knife and made odd noises, suddenly lost in his own world.

Burke continued. "Federal marshals will come and talk to you, Mr. Preston, because Mark Jones never made a final report to the forest service national office. No one knows where he is because he just disappeared. I'll bet you know something about that."

"You trying to be a lawman?" Preston asked. "Don't talk to me about the law. I used to be a Pinkerton detective."

"Then you should be better informed about rules," Burke told him. "I can see you're not used to regulations."

"We've already got a system that works, Mr. Burke. It's worked for a long time. We don't need you here."

"You've got grazing problems in this country, and they're getting worse," Burke said. "Without a plan you're going to ruin the forests and grasslands here."

"None of us want you meddling."

"Are you telling me that all the ranchers here think like you do?"

"The ones who count," Preston replied.

Burke pointed to the cards spread on the table. "You missed a play, the ten on the jack." He had seen an opportunity to unnerve Preston and took advantage of it.

Preston stood up and flipped the deck of cards into the fire. He grabbed his knife and stepped around the table and stood in front of Burke.

"You're ruining the party. You can't even be grateful to someone who wants to be your friend. What's the matter with you?"

"It's not my party, it's yours," Burke said. "And nobody asked me if I even gave a damn about it."

Preston turned to the others. "That's a fine thing. Throw a party and the guest of honor isn't polite."

"You might as well release me," Burke said. "I wrote letters to friends before I came up here. Sent them just this afternoon. If they don't hear from me again soon, they'll all come looking. And they'll bring the law. You can bet on it."

Preston wanted no outsiders involved. He turned to the three men. "Get him out of here. Take him to his car and make him drive away." He turned back to Burke. "The next party I throw for you, you'll get a written invitation. You can bet on that."

Burke left and began the hike back toward his Buick, fighting the pain in each step. He could hear Keller and the other two behind him, exchanging words with Preston in front of the fire. Soon they mounted their horses and rode up beside him.

"You're lucky I'm not in charge," Keller said. "I'd have hanged you for what you said."

Burke ignored him.

"You hear me?" Keller said.

Burke remained silent. Keller took his rope from the saddle and Burke stopped walking and faced him.

"You won't touch me and live to tell about it."

"We'll see," Keller said.

Gamble rode up. "Don't make no trouble, Len. We're to see him off. That's all."

"He needs to learn some manners," Keller said.

"Maybe, but you heard Preston." Gamble was visibly nervous. "He said to leave it be for now."

Mason rode up and said, "I'm putting in with Len. Let's stop this thing before it gets started."

"If you two figure to do that," Gamble said, "I'm riding back to the cabin. I want no part of it."

"You afraid of this Eastern dandy?" Mason asked.

"You missed the point," Gamble explained. "This ain't the time nor the place."

Keller coiled the rope and tied it back to his saddle. "Just so there comes a time and place."

Burke walked with the three riding to one side, still arguing. When he had finished the hike to his car, he struggled with the crank before finally getting the engine started. He climbed inside and Keller rode up to the front and smashed both headlights in with his boot.

"The moon's full and the smoke's cleared a little," he said. "You don't need 'em."

Burke put the Buick in gear and started back down, struggling to see the shadowed road. He had to go a long way before the laughter from Keller and the blond cowhand died out.

4

Burke neared Eden, struggling to make out the road in front of him. Clouds had covered the moon and the air had thickened with drifting smoke. Finally, he rejoiced in the raucous sounds of nightlife that filtered out through the darkness. He drove down into town and noticed a small group of cowhands dancing in the middle of the street, hooking arms and swinging one another in circles to the scratchy sound of an old, badly tuned fiddle.

Burke parked his Buick in front of the hotel and gathered himself before limping to a nearby stock tank. The water was cool and refreshing. He was aware the fiddling had stopped and that a crowd was gathering. He washed the blood and dirt from his face and neck, ignoring them. His cuts and bruises had swollen even more and in the night chill, his muscles were as stiff as old springs.

One of the cowhands, bottle in hand, stepped up to the tank. He was small, with quick eyes and an abbreviated chin, his grizzled face seemingly ending just past his lower lip. He encouraged the other hand to continue playing his fiddle, but his grin faded when he saw Burke's angry face.

"Maybe you could use a drink," he said, holding the bottle out.

"I've had enough hospitality for one night," Burke said.

"No, no, I didn't mean nothing by it," the cowhand said.

"We would like to make friends, since we're going to be dealing with you."

"What do you mean?" Burke asked.

The cowhand introduced himself as Chick Campbell, late of the Eden Land and Livestock Company, now in the employ of William Conrad, owner of the town's newest establishment, the Flat Tops Hotel, and also owner of the Rocker 9 Cattle Company, with headquarters south of town, just across the valley from Eden Land and Livestock.

"We're celebrating the fact that Rube Waddell just lost their two best hands today. Us!"

Campbell and the other cowhand clapped one another on the back and shared a drink, laughing and whooping.

The other hand, tall and rangy, missing his right thumb, stepped forward. "I'm Art Gilroy, at your service."

"Why would you take my side?" Burke asked.

"We've all known changes were coming," Gilroy replied, "and they've been needed for a good long time. Waddell wants things his way and Sid Preston does his bidding. We were told to keep quiet about everything that was to be done to stop you forest reserve people. We can't stomach saying one thing and doing another, so we quit. Besides, Mr. Conrad offered us a lot better pay."

"It's good to know that not everyone wants to rope and hog-tie me," Burke said.

"You get yourself some rest, Mr. Burke, and we'll see to it your auto-mo-bile stays safe," Campbell told him with a pat on the back. He studied Burke. "You can trust us. Be certain of that."

.   .   .

Sid Preston rode through the silent forest, whistling "My Darling Clementine." He had left Keller and Mason and Gamble beside the fire with explicit instructions to watch the new ranger's every move and to report to him in three days at the same place, six miles up the gulch past the large mesa known as the Devil's Grave.

It had been their meeting place for nearly a year, ever since he had decided to take up residence in the old abandoned wolfer's cabin near the headwaters of Eden Creek. He had moved out of the main bunkhouse on the Eden ranch to be a part of his paradise and to prepare for the day when the right woman would make all his dreams come true.

He thought again about Lottie Burns, wondering if she was the one. Though she hadn't enjoyed the bonding process with her sisters, she had managed to finish the ritual and hadn't begun to babble, as a few of the women had.

This had caused him great disappointment. He had given them both a couple of days to regain themselves, but it hadn't worked. They had both gotten worse. And both had refused to perform the special favor, and that had been too bad.

They had both become completely submissive, up until the very end, when they had suddenly gone crazy, flipping and flopping around. It had been difficult for them, but more difficult for him.

And the special person who always watched certainly hadn't been happy.

He tied his horse near the cabin and went to the door of the shed and listened carefully. Crickets sang their night songs and in the distance, thunder boomed—the ever-present sounds of the sky, adding to the pounding that he always felt inside himself whenever he thought of that special time that could come very soon.

He continued to listen, knowing that Lottie Burns realized he was there but was not going to move.

He burst through the door and she jumped.

"It's too dark in here for you," he said, and struck light to a lantern. "Have you been waiting for me?"

He knelt down and touched her face, his fingers sliding down to her neck, feeling her throat.

"Very nice," he said. "Do you want me to take off the gag?"

She nodded and he carefully untied the knot. It was one of the sleeves to her dress, velvet-lined and now shredded to pieces. She drew in deep breaths and began to weep.

"Why so sad?" he asked.

She continued to weep, covering her face, turning on her side and curling into a ball.

He pulled her back up and pushed the hair away from her eyes.

"Are you going to do the great favor for me?" he asked.

"What favor?" she managed.

"Didn't I tell you?" he said. "I want you to put a knife in my stomach."

Burke told Chick Campbell and Art Gilroy that he had enjoyed meeting them, then grabbed his bags from the Buick and entered the hotel. He was greeted by the night manager, a nervous man impeccably dressed, who stared at him.

"I'll get you a doctor."

"Never mind," Burke insisted. "Nothing's broken."

The manager instructed a porter, a young black man, to show Burke to his room and left. The employee personally took Burke's bags and led him to the second floor.

"I didn't check in," Burke said. "How can I have a room?"

"Mr. Conrad's been expecting you."

"But I don't even know this Mr. Conrad," Burke said.

The porter said, "Sir, I do what I'm told. No questions."

"I didn't mean to take it out on you," Burke said. "I'm sorry."

"Think nothing of it, Mr. Burke," the steward said, handing him the key. "Be glad Mr. Conrad is on your side."

"That man behind the desk was Mr. Conrad?"

"No, Mr. Conrad's a very big man. You can't miss him. He'll be along soon. Until then if you need anything, let me know."

"What's your name?" Burke asked him.

"Jackson Mills, and I won't take your tip," he said. "Mr. Conrad has paid me special to take care of you."

"I can say that you certainly have thus far," Burke said. "And you don't have to bow to me."

"I wasn't," Jackson said. "I was looking at your shoes. A nice pair that got ruined, but maybe I can clean them up for you."

"We'll see," Burke said.

Burke thanked him and unlocked the door. He dropped his bag next to the nightstand, then lit the lantern and sat down on the edge of his bed. His face felt like he had taken a thousand lashes from a very ugly whip.

He heard someone climbing the stairs. The doctor, an older man named Simmons, knocked on the open door before entering the room. After introducing himself, he closed the door and set his bag next to the bed. He moved the nightstand and lantern out from the wall, then grabbed a nearby chair and sat down in front of Burke.

His eyes were deep blue and discerning, his beard silver-tipped, like a young grizzly, and in his prime he might have been nearly as strong.

He studied the pupils in Burke's eyes and asked him if he was nauseated.

"A little," Burke said. "And a little dizzy."

"Do you know the name of this town?"

"I thought it was Eden. They might want to change it."

Simmons smiled. "The word around town is that you had an accident in your new automobile."

"Word travels fast," Burke said.

"Well, it appears the car dragged you some distance," the doctor commented. "I'm glad to see that you got out from under it when you did."

"I get the feeling you've seen this before," Burke said.

Simmons didn't answer. He felt both of Burke's arms and shoulders and stated that there were no signs of separation or serious bone damage. He then placed a stethoscope to his chest.

"You're breathing normally," he said. He probed Burke's lower ribs and nodded when he grimaced. "Likely a crack or two in there, but nothing serious. Do you want something for the pain?"

"No. Thanks, anyway."

"A stout fellow, you are," the doctor said. "Do you plan on staying?"

"Without a doubt."

"You must have a passion for your work."

"There's a lot of it to be done," Burke said.

Simmons turned his attention to Burke's battered head and face. He searched through his satchel. "I'm going to take a stitch or two along your right eyebrow."

Burke endured swabs filled with alcohol and the prickly sting of the needle. There came a knock at the door and Burke allowed the entry. Bill Conrad appeared in the doorway, a well-dressed man of very large stature in early middle age. He held a cigar in one hand and a basket of fruit in the other, which he placed on a table along one wall.

"I see you've arrived, Mr. Burke." To the doctor he said, "How is he?"

"Mostly bumps and bruises," Simmons replied. "He's lucky."

"Mr. Burke, your stay here is on the house."

"That's not necessary," Burke said.

"I insist," Conrad said. "Perhaps we can talk, at your convenience. I insist."

Conrad left and Burke felt the stitches in his eyebrow. "I've gotten decidedly different receptions tonight," he said. "That confuses me."

"There are a lot of opinions available here, as you will see," the doctor said, closing his bag. "A good number of ranchers, especially the newcomers, believe in your cause for grazing restrictions. The old guard, however, is feeling a bit pressed."

"What do I owe you?" Burke said.

"Mr. Conrad is taking care of it."

"I'd rather pay myself," Burke said.

Simmons stopped in the doorway. "Allow Mr. Conrad to befriend you," he said. "You're going to need him."

5

Burke stood in the window, watching the sun edge up over the mountains. The fire haze had been fully eliminated by the evening's rainfall. The sky overhead, rapidly turning from gray to blue, held no clouds whatsoever. The drought had not actually ended.

His sleep had been fitful at best, having succumbed to exhaustion for a few hours just before dawn. The pain in his body had subsided considerably when the steward had insisted he use the new bathtub reserved for special guests. The warm water had been soothing, the antiseptic soap cleansing. Following the bath he had enjoyed a late dinner of rib-eye steak and potatoes, with vegetables and mushroom gravy, brought to his room on a silver platter.

A full stomach had felt good but Burke had laid in the darkness, thinking about his reception and about Sid Preston. Chick Campbell and Art Gilroy, the two cowhands who had defected to Bill Conrad, would certainly know a lot that could help him. He already knew that Rube Waddell would soon announce his plans to run for the state senate, and would stand a good chance of winning the seat. Waddell had already gone on record to state that he didn't believe the federal government had any business interfering in Colorado's livestock industry.

Burke had done his homework on the big ranchers, pulling his information mainly from Mark Jones's monthly reports.

Jones had kept meticulous records of his dealings with the land-owners and their responses to his efforts to map the forest reserves. His last report had mentioned that Preston and his men were watching him constantly, and had begun harassing him. He had written that he had gone directly to Waddell for relief from Preston's men, but had been turned away without even so much as a short meeting.

He had also stated that he had uncovered something that could affect relations between two major cattle operations, but hadn't described his findings. Burke couldn't help but believe that Waddell and the Eden brand had to be part of that discovery. Now Jones was missing and Burke wondered what the next report might have said.

Jackson Mills knocked on the door and entered with a breakfast platter of elk sausage and scrambled eggs, together with orange juice, hot coffee, and rye toast. To Burke the young man seemed out of place. Almost setting himself up for problems. But he had to have a connection to Bill Conrad and would likely have no serious problems.

The sight of Burke's face, swollen and dark from the cuts and bruises, made him shrink back.

"You look a lot worse than last night," he said. "I just don't know why someone would do that to you."

"There are some bullies in the neighborhood." Burke handed Jackson a golden railroad spike.

"It's not a tip, but for your collection."

Jackson's eyes bulged. "Where did you get something like this?"

"My secret. Don't lose it."

Jackson smiled on his way out the door. "You're an interesting man, to be sure."

.   .   .

Lottie sat tied in the shed, wondering when the man would return and what he would say to her this time.

He had told her that he wanted her to thrust a knife in his stomach, his own special knife. She was still having trouble processing his request. At the same time he would stab her with another knife, a "twin" of the first knife. They would bleed together and empty their insides side by side and then enter a special place reserved for them and only them.

He had retied the gag back in her mouth and she was having trouble breathing. He hadn't given her any food or water, so she was also weak.

But at least he hadn't forced her to take any more drugs.

She still struggled against her bonds, but found it futile. Saving what strength she had left would be the best thing to do. Maybe, if she played it right, she might find a means of escape.

At this point, her emotions ranged from plateaus of strong determination to deep lows, a certainty that he would come at any moment and take her back to the graveyard. She believed if he did that, she wouldn't survive. It didn't take much imagination to reconstruct what he had done to each of his victims up there.

She had met any number of strange and violent men while working her profession, but she was ordinarily protected from them by tight security, especially in the best and most expensive of locales. She had also worked in places where her life had been in danger. Something had always happened, though, that had kept her alive—another patron coming to her aid, or as in one case, a troupe of angry school teachers bent on shutting down the establishment she worked in who had taken their wrath out on the drunken miner who was assaulting her.

Most of those occasions involved men with a "mean streak" as they were known, men who slugged and kicked, often for the thrill of watching a woman crawl. She had met a number of them in the gold and railroad camps across the West, finally tiring of the danger and seeking more secure confines of the better houses in San Francisco.

But never had she met a man such as this gray-eyed, silver-tongued monster who delighted in doing things she could not even conceive of as being real.

But, she now realized with clarity, this certainly was real.

Burke finished his breakfast, his mind still dwelling on Rube Waddell and Sid Preston. He had dressed himself in his green-and-brown uniform, with the insignia of a tall spruce tree on the left sleeve. His favorite suit had been ruined and his derby hat lost. He wouldn't be dressing up in this town again anytime soon.

The sun had risen fully and wagons filled Main Street, lined up in front of the two dry goods stores. The spring work season had begun and the cooks from the various ranches were in town for supplies. Most of them paid Burke no attention, so busy were they jawing with one another about the upcoming roundup, all wondering whether the following year would find most of them out of work.

Burke wanted to stop and tell them they would all be on the payroll, but their jobs would be just a little easier. Fewer cattle on the range would make for a shorter work period, saving money for the owners. In addition, the steers would be larger, affording higher profits. Burke had already decided how he would convince the landowners that by reducing their numbers, each animal got more forage to consume. But trying to sell the idea to a group of hotheaded kooks would just alienate him further. He would save it for another time.

Burke made his way to the Valley Bank and Trust, located on the corner of Main Street and Roosevelt, three blocks from downtown. Made of red stone from local quarries, it was an impressive two-story structure with rows of large windows and a frontispiece of local wildlife carved midway up the building. A bear and a mountain lion stood facing a large bull elk in the middle.

Burke entered and walked past the receptionist to a private office along the east wall. A middle-aged man in a brown suit that fit too tight sat busily turning the pages of a ledger, fretting over figures, chewing the end of a pencil to shavings.

"Mr. Miller," Burke said, "I hope I'm not disturbing you."

The man looked up, his stern features holding no expression. He closed the ledger and placed it into a desk drawer.

"I told you before, my name is Lee," he said. "We're all friends here in Eden."

"That's good to know," Burke said.

Miller stood up and walked to a small cookstove in one corner of his office. He lifted a blackened coffeepot and asked, "Need something to wake you up?"

"I'm awake," Burke said.

Miller filled his cup and took a bottle of bourbon from a table near a window against the back wall and poured generously into the coffee. He tipped the cup toward Burke and took a long drink.

"Good for what ails you," he said.

Burke ran his fingers over Miller's new desk, smoothly finished in an oiled, red mahogany surface that gleamed with the morning sunshine washing in through the window. The wall behind his desk was covered with pictures of Miller on hunting trips with Rube Waddell, holding big-game rifles and standing over or kneeling beside fallen elk, bear, and mountain lion. More photos showed Miller with other livestock owners, taken in their ranch homes and in various Denver locations.

"It makes for good relations," Miller said.

"Yes, I suppose." Burke sat down in a chair. "So, Lee," he said, "it doesn't seem like you're too surprised to see me like this."

"What do you mean?"

"Well, look at me. You haven't even asked what happened. You must already know."

"I heard you wrecked your automobile. I told you this country was a little rough for that kind of new contraption. I can't imagine taking one of those crazy things into the mountains, especially after dark." Miller added more bourbon to his coffee and lit a cigar. "Where is the damned thing, anyway? Did you leave it with the blacksmith?" He laughed.

"You're not nearly as friendly as you were yesterday," Burke said.

"Neither are you," Lee responded.

Burke pulled a piece of paper out of his pocket. "Why did you send me up the wrong creek?"

Miller turned and stared out the window, puffing on his cigar. "You must have taken a wrong turn in the dark."

Burke stood up and tossed the paper on the banker's desk. "This is the map you drew for me. Maybe you don't know the country all that well."

Miller turned quickly. "Don't ever say something like that to me."

"Good, then I'm right. You set me up. I need to know why?"

"I have a lot of things to do, Mr. Burke."

"I suppose you thought I'd just fold up and call it quits," Burke said. "You don't have any idea what you've done."

"If you intend to stay," Miller said blowing cigar smoke, "you would be wise to take a little advice. The sooner you understand the importance of having Rube Waddell and the other big operators on your side, the better off you'll be."

"You've got that backwards," Burke said. "They should have known to treat *me* right. Too late for that now."

"That's ludicrous, Mr. Burke."

"Is it? The changes are coming. It doesn't matter who tries to stop them, they're coming."

"It's not that simple," Miller argued. "You can't just overturn everything overnight."

"I'll tell you what I believe," Burke said. "You've made a lot of money off the big cattle outfits around here. I'm not here to challenge that, but I won't be pushed or paid off, either one."

Miller stared hard at him. "You're stepping over the line."

"What are you going to do, drag me through the street?" He motioned out the window. "I understand there's going to be a groundbreaking ceremony across the way in a few days. Bill Conrad is building a bank. That so?"

"I believe he intends to," Miller said. "I can't see how he'll compete."

"I believe he will," Burke said. "And I, for one, am going to put my money on him."

"I suppose he'll be getting some favors from you when the grazing allotments are decided," Miller said.

"Nobody will be getting any favors from me," Burke said. "Everybody is going to have to share in the cutbacks. Even you."

Just after noon, Burke arranged with the porter to have a large pail of hot, soapy water and a rag brought down to his car. He asked to have his bags brought down as well, and then paid cash for his room. Initially, the manager wouldn't take the money, but Burke insisted that he had already told Bill Conrad of his plans at breakfast. He and Conrad had discussed a number of things during the meal, but the tab for the room hadn't been one of them. When Conrad learned Burke had paid for his stay he hurried out to where he was loading his Buick.

"I thought I told you last night was on me," Conrad said.

"And I told you at breakfast that I couldn't take sides with one operator against another," Burke said.

"I don't know why you'd turn down my friendship."

"It's not your friendship I'm turning down," Burke corrected him. "I just can't accept favors."

"I don't understand why you won't allow me to help you."

"You can help me by speaking publicly in favor of the new grazing policies, Mr. Conrad. That's how you can do the most good."

"I still insist that you accept my help getting you established here," Conrad said.

"I can do that myself, Mr. Conrad."

"I'm giving you my grazing land to build your headquarters on. You could be a little grateful."

"Mr. Conrad, I'll be building my cabin on the forest reserves that have already been plotted. You and the other operators here have been making use of public land for a long time, and have gotten pretty rich off it, but that doesn't make it yours."

With his bags packed inside, Burke began washing the mud and grass off his Buick.

"I'll have someone do that for you," Conrad said.

"I can handle it," Burke insisted.

Conrad walked around the car and stopped in front of the headlights. "There's nobody here that can fix those, you know."

"I'll get them fixed in Denver one of these days."

"It will just happen again," Conrad said.

"No, it won't."

"How do you intend to stop Sid Preston and his goons?"

"I won't do it alone," Burke said.

"I don't follow you. Are there more rangers coming up here?"

"In time. But more to the point, Sid Preston has overstepped his bounds here. You said that yourself. If the Eden brand makes it hard for me, they'll be making it hard for everyone else. I can legally shut the reserves down. No grazing for anyone."

"Do you really think you could do that?"

"If need be." Burke scrubbed hard at a spot where mud had collected under the bumper. He knew that would be difficult to impossible, but he had to make his point to Conrad.

"I thought you knew that Rube Waddell was going to run for the state senate," Conrad said.

"This is bigger than Rube Waddell," Burke told him, "or the state of Colorado."

"Mark Jones told me the same thing. He's not around here anymore," Conrad pointed out.

Burke stopped his work. "Do you know what happened to him?"

Conrad looked away toward the mountains. "Nobody knows what happened to him, except Sid Preston and his men."

"Do you know that for a fact?"

"It can't be any other way," Conrad said.

6

Burke continued his break from washing his car and patted a saddle horse named Lancaster that he had tied to the bumper of his car. Burke had just purchased the red gelding at a blacksmith and livery stable in Eden, having been assured that the horse wasn't over five years old. Upon a thorough inspection of the animal's teeth, Burke said he would pay two-thirds the asking price and no more. "He's between eight and ten years old," he told the owner. "Granted, he's a strong horse and in good shape, but his younger days are behind him."

The owner, a large man named Lars Skoglund, had shrugged. He'd been caught trying to outfox an Eastern dandy who supposedly didn't know a lot about life outside the big city. At least that's what Sid Preston had told him. Damn Sid Preston, anyway. He usually spoke with his head up his ass and his assessment of the new ranger had been no exception.

Preston had come to the livery stable a few days before with a lot of orders about how to handle Ellis Burke. Skoglund had taken the instructions with mixed feelings. Granted, the Eden brand did a lot of business with him, but they didn't own him like they seemed to think. Preston had known that Burke would be outfitting himself for his job and had told Skoglund to sell him an older horse, one that had seen better days. Lancaster had split a hoof during a high-country hunt but had healed well. Burke had even asked about that. Skoglund had flexed his powerful muscles, developed from years at the forge, and had told Burke he would stand fast in his price. Burke had pointed out that the red gelding wasn't the only horse for sale in the area. The blacksmith needed the money and had agreed to the terms, so to hell with Preston.

Skoglund had come to admire the new ranger. Having taken a beating at the hands of Preston and his men—and still being around—he obviously wasn't one to be easily intimidated. He might have come into town wearing fancy clothes and driving one of those new-fangled things they called automobiles, but he was no shrinking violet. He wasn't the same kind of man that the first ranger, Mark Jones, had been, either. Where Jones had spouted off about his position as a forest lawman of sorts, Burke had spoken little and had an air of authority that he didn't push. He would be a hard one for the Eden brand to handle.

Burke began once again to wash his car from a pail of clean water that Jackson Mills brought for him. Bill Conrad had left momentarily to assist a hotel guest.

"Why would you want to live here, Jackson?" Burke asked.

"Mr. Conrad is teaching me the hotel business," Jackson replied. "He intends to make me a manager some day. Not here, but elsewhere."

"I think you'll be a good one," Burke said.

"I appreciate that," he said. "If I can be of any more help, let me know."

"Do you know where they sell automobiles in Denver?" Burke asked.

Jackson smiled. "If you're asking me where you might get your car fixed, I can assist."

"It won't be for a while," Burke said. "I've got other concerns right now."

"Just say the word." Jackson left as Bill Conrad came out of the hotel and lit a cigar.

"You've certainly made a friend in that boy," Conrad said. "I wish I could make those kinds of inroads."

"I wish you'd stop trying," Burke said.

Conrad studied Burke. "You're a lot better prepared than Mark Jones was, I'll say that. You're not just another college boy."

Burke smiled. "I'm sure you've checked me out."

"Yes, I took the liberty of doing just that," Conrad confessed. "I know your father was a railroad tycoon from Helena, Montana, who entered politics and used his influence to get what he wanted. You didn't exactly see eye-to-eye with him, so you became a bit of a maverick. But you accepted his offer to get you into Yale and then paid for your education yourself. Very interesting."

"I'm not the only one who paid my way through school."

"An Ivy League school? You must have had a good job somewhere. Maybe before you left." He eyed Burke. "Then after you graduated, you seem to have vanished for a while. I just don't know where you were between the time you left Yale and accepted this job down here. Nobody seems to know about that."

"Everyone has their secrets, don't they?" Burke said. He began drying his Buick with a clean rag.

"A man in my position has to know who he can count on and who's going to come after him," Conrad said.

"I have to treat everyone the same," Burke said. "That's my job."

"A few of us don't see it that way," Conrad said. "We see

you as an equalizer for us. It's no secret that some of the bigger operators have been hogging the range for some time. Waddell and his Eden brand are the worst. They run way too many cattle and they've effectively pushed out every small operator who ever tried to get a foothold here. The Forest Reserves Act is going to cut Waddell down a notch or two. I for one am not going to be shedding any tears over it."

"You're not exactly a small operator, yourself," Burke told him. "Four thousand head of steers is nothing to sneeze at."

"It's a start," Conrad said.

"I hope you don't think I'm going to allow you to increase your numbers at Rube Waddell's expense," Burke said. He threw the rag aside and dried his hands.

"I just want a level playing ground, Mr. Burke."

Burke cranked his Buick over and the engine began running with a smooth putter. "I've done a little checking of my own," he told Conrad. "Your father made a fortune in the gold fields at Cripple Creek and he invested wisely, including livestock herds across the western half of the state. He put you in charge of moving in here and you've ruffled some feathers along the way, including Rube Waddell's. You've got plenty of resources to draw from and you can stand toe to toe with Waddell when it comes to finances. But not politics. Your father had no desire to run for office."

Conrad smiled. "You've unturned a few stones yourself, but just the same I'm sending some of my men to help you get organized, whether you like it or not. Let's just call it looking out for Rocker Nine interests."

Burke climbed into his car. "You can't fight my battles for me. I'm not going to be the cause of a range war here."

"Mr. Burke, like it or not, you're already the cause of a range war. And it's just about to start."

Lottie Burke awakened to the sound of someone walking around the outside of the tack shed. It was him; she recognized his footsteps.

He would walk a short distance and stop. Then she would hear a gritty metal-against-metal sound, like a knife being honed against a whetstone. When he had finally made it all the way around, he unlocked the door to the cabin and opened it slowly.

Lottie looked through the open door. No one was there.

He suddenly jumped into the cabin, holding his knife up, laughing.

"How's Lottie today?" he asked. "Getting thirsty?"

He hadn't given her food or water since putting her in the cabin. She had grown weak and dehydrated, and could barely stay on her feet when he pulled her up.

"I'm going to take you to the creek and give you a chance to clean yourself up," he said. "Don't be too long, or you'll miss your meal."

"Could I have some food now?"

"Clean up first, if you would. You don't smell so good."

He left her at the creek and walked back toward the cabin. She watched him disappear into the timber along the trail.

She didn't care. She drank deeply, slurping it in, washing her neck and head, removing her dress and immersing herself in the cold water. It revived her some and even though she detested the thought of being anywhere near him, she hoped he wasn't teasing her about the food.

She decided to stay at the stream a short while longer, at least until her head cleared some. She dug a root from the bank. It tasted bitter, but she wolfed it down like it was a rare delicacy.

She ate another and drank more water and washed herself. She knew he was watching her, toying with his knife. She could see the glint of the afternoon sun off the blade.

After drinking more, she dressed herself in the wet clothing and made her way toward the cabin. Partway there, he came out of the trees behind her.

"You don't need to stay in that wet dress."

"It's fine. I don't mind."

"No, it has to dry. You can wear this."

He produced another dress and insisted she put it on, right there and then. He watched her change clothes, whistling "My Darling Clementine" and toying with the knife.

"Why is it so important for me to change clothes?" she asked.

"That good dress of yours with all the fancy lining has to look good for tomorrow."

"For tomorrow?" she asked.

He smiled. "Let go inside."

The cabin was small and one-roomed and old, constructed of pine that had begun to weaken at the corners. A sloppy bunk rested against one wall, covered with pieces of tattered women's clothing. The walls were barren for the most part, but for more remnants of clothing hanging on a few nails.

Lottie noticed all the women's clothing and asked, "Does someone live here with you?"

"Yes, but she won't talk to you," he replied.

Lottie realized that trying to befriend him wasn't working. Her only out was to eat something to restore her strength and look for a way to escape.

A small wooden table sat against one wall and above it was a long shelf covered with whiskey bottles. They appeared filled with solids mixed with a dark liquid, but it was impossible to see them very well in the shadows.

"Want a drink?" he asked.

"No, no thanks," she said. "Maybe some more water. And food."

He ushered her to the table and pulled out a chair for her.

"Make yourself comfortable."

She sat down. Some kind of insect was emerging from a hole in a log near her arm. It plopped onto the table and scooted in zigzag patterns across the surface. As her eyes became better adjusted to the dim light, she noticed many more—dozens of them—skittering along the walls and floor.

"Pine beetles," he said. "They don't eat humans." He laughed.

"You said something about food," she reminded him.

"In a minute," he said. He went to a small wooden box that rested atop an empty whiskey barrel and returned with a piece of paper.

"Our contract," he said. "Sign it."

Lottie studied the paper. The few lines written in scriggly longhand were impossible to read.

"Sign it," he repeated.

"What is it?" she asked.

"I told you, our contract. Your good faith to carry out the special favor for me."

"Tell me again about the special favor. Please."

He removed his knife and laid it on the table. "Why are you playing games with me?"

"Games?"

"You know the special favor. We talked about it. We'll be together then, in that special place."

Lottie began to shake. "Please, that's not what I want."

He leaned into her face. "You promised me." He pulled her hand against his stomach. "You promised to do this for me . . . for us."

She jerked away. "No, I didn't."

"Now you're lying to me. What's the matter with you?"

"I never told you I would do that," she said, fighting tears.

He stood up and began to pace. "You could have had food and plenty of water. You could have rested for our special day. But I guess you don't want that."

"I don't . . ."

"You aren't saying the right things."

She began to shake uncontrollably.

"You hear me? You're telling lies, just like the others. I didn't think you were like the others."

"Please, just let me go. I'll leave the area, I swear I will."

He began to pace again. "I just wish you had kept your word. I really do."

7

Burke picketed the gelding to graze nearby and unloaded supplies from his car. His muscles ached and he struggled with each load, finally taking fewer and fewer items. He had wanted to unload everything, erect his tent, and drive back into town for the remainder of the supplies. He had also purchased a mule from the blacksmith and had arranged for a week's worth of bacon, beans, flour, and coffee at the Eden mercantile. But he wasn't going to get things done nearly as fast as he had planned, so he sat down and took a deep breath.

No broken bones, the doctor had said, but they ached like they were all broken. And there were other complications: He was pissing blood, not a lot but enough to be concerned about.

He knew it was his right kidney. He had felt the deep pain when he had been dragged over the rock. He would drink a lot of water and wait a few days, see if things cleared up. Though Simmons seemed to be good at his profession, Burke didn't care for doctors.

After getting his cooking utensils unpacked, Burke carried a pail of water from the creek and set to boiling coffee.

"That smells damned good, it does," yelled a voice from the trail.

Chick Campbell rode into camp, leading a large yellow mule packed heavily with supplies. With him was Art Gilroy, the tall cowhand missing his right thumb. They tied their horses and the mule to some trees nearby and walked to the tent.

"Guess I kind of expected you," Burke said. "Did Bill Conrad send you?"

"We're just good-natured folk," Chick said.

Burke smiled. "Bringing the pack mule up was a nice gesture. I appreciate it."

We thought we'd save you a second trip," Campbell said.

"You brought way more supplies than I ordered from the mercantile."

"We won't tell you no lies," Art put in. "Mr. Conrad had us load up some more goods for you, just in case you ate faster than you figured on."

"That man just won't give up," Burke said.

"He means well," Chick said. "But you already knew that."

"People are starting to get the wrong idea," Burke said.

"He wants you to get things going as soon as possible," Chick said. He pointed to the coffeepot. "It smells like you're a damned good cook."

Art said, "Don't be flattered. He thinks everyone's a good cook. You can't trust him to boil water."

Burke handed them each a tin cup filled with coffee.

"I'll bet you do cook pretty good," Chick said. "It says in your college paper that you served some kind of fancy duck at a party."

Burke nearly dropped his cup. "How did you know about that?"

Chick laughed and pulled a copy of the Yale school paper out of his pocket. There was a story profiling the 1902 Yale School of Forestry graduate students. "It says that you boys had a good time celebrating the Yale bicentennial," he said, "and that you fixed, what does it say, *duck all orange?*"

"Duck *a l'Orange*," Burke corrected him.

"Yeah, that's it. All orange," Chick said, still grinning.

"What in the hell is that?" Art asked.

"It's duck with orange and usually currants or berries of some kind."

"Orange duck, huh," Art said. "Who'd think of that."

"You look here like you'd cook orange duck," Chick continued. "There's even a picture of you and your class, all dressed up like Robin Hood." Chick pointed to Burke's picture. "That's you, or I'm a bald-faced frog in a skillet."

Burke blushed. "We wanted to win the best costume contest, and we did."

"Damn, are those tights you're wearing there?" Art asked.

"Yes," Burke said. "And that's a jerkin and hood. And we had bows and arrows. That's how they dressed in those days."

"Damn," Art said.

Chick nodded. "And I suppose those tights were green, just like the real Robin Hood."

"Yes, they were," Burke said. "I'd better get started putting the tent up."

"One more cup of coffee," Chick said.

Burke poured and Art asked, "Were you wearing those tights when you cooked the duck?"

"No," Burke said. "We wore them for the celebration. I don't know what happened to them after that."

"I'm glad to hear that," Art said. "I'd hate to think you'd wear them at your new job up here. You're going to have enough trouble as it is."

The three set to work erecting Burke's tent, pounding the stakes solidly and tying them off with strong rope. Chick mentioned that the wind could be ferocious, and could come up at a moment's notice. They placed a small woodstove in one corner and fit an insulated stovepipe through the canvas side.

"At least you'll stay warm until your cabin's done," Chick said.

They moved past the tent flap and stood outside in the evening's coolness. The sun had found the horizon and the sky was turning crimson, the clouds sitting still, their underbellies glowing red.

"Wish it would rain again," Chick said. "And for longer."

Art had taken it upon himself to make more coffee. He poured all around.

"Wish we'd have brought some duck up for you to cook," he said.

"Will beef and beans do?" Burke asked.

Chick said, "I can fetch us a sage hen pretty quick." He and Art were both laughing. "Can you *a l'Orange* it? We brought the oranges."

"If you want that kind of food," Burke said, "you'd better try the White River Hotel in town."

"They don't have orange duck," Art said. "Or orange sage chicken, either."

"Guess we'll have to settle for beef and beans," Chick said. He looked at Burke. "We did bring up some wine and oranges, and picked some red currants for you to make a sauce."

Art added, "And I already got three sage chickens, just in case you wanted to show off."

"I'll see what I can do then," Burke said.

Art brought the three grouse over and he and Chick watched while Burke began the meal.

"You're working a little slow," Chick observed.

"I am a little stiff," Burke acknowledged.

"Tell you what," Campbell said. "For being so nice and cooking this fancy meal, come tomorrow, we'll haul you down to Glenwood and dunk you in the hot springs,"

"That sounds like something I could go for," Burke said.

"You're forgetting one thing, Chick," Gilroy said. "We can't go in the hot springs without proper dress."

"I forgot," Chick said. "Mr. Burke, here, will have to go by himself, I guess."

"Maybe I could help you," Burke suggested.

"Would you do that for us, brand new duds?" Campbell said. "We'd be obliged forever, both of us."

"If you're willing to take me down there, it's the least I can do," Burke said.

"You need to soak for a while, get yourself back together from last night," Gilroy said. "Keep yourself strong for when Preston and his men come back."

"I'm not sure they will," Burke said.

"Of course they will," Campbell said. "Why wouldn't they?"

"I told them they would be inviting an investigation by running me off."

"He might think about that for a while," Gilroy said. "But not for long."

"His judgement is what you could call clouded," Chick said. "He's gotten away with a lot over the years. But green tights or not, we figure you can take care of yourself."

Burke continued to cook, browning the three sage grouse in the pan and then deglazing with the wine, adding the currants and juice squeezed from the oranges at the appropriate time.

"You've taken on quite a job," Chick said, drinking his coffee and watching Burke cook. "You'll have other problems besides the big outfits who want you out."

"What other problems?"

"You'll likely have to deal with some grizzled old farts in the high country, the type who were out here in the early days and don't like society," Chick replied.

"I thought you were one of those," Burke said.

"Art is, not me," Chick said.

"Damn tootin'," Art said. "Ship them all back where they came from."

"But we're serious," Chick said. "There are a few up there who will give you what for if you try to tell them they're on Forest Service land, or that they're poaching elk and deer illegally."

"Old Buck Gentry comes to mind," Art said.

"He's as crusty as they come," Chick said. "Even worse than Art."

Burke thought a moment. "I'm glad to know that."

"We just don't want you worrying to much about their kind and not enough about Rube Waddell and Sid Preston."

"I get it," Burke said. "Forget about everyone but the Eden brand and those of the same ilk."

"That's kind of fancy, but yes," Chick said. "Bill Conrad will do anything he can to break Rube Waddell. And that's a good idea."

"Waddell can follow the regulations without being broken," Burke said.

"Maybe you're more of an Eastern dandy than we thought," Art said. "You either break Rube Waddell or he breaks you.

And you should get to it as soon as possible, while Waddell has his mind on other things."

Chick explained that the Waddell household had been in minor chaos for some time, a chaos that had been escalating of late.

"His wife's taken ill," he said. "He spends a good deal of time with her down at Glenwood, in the hot springs."

"What's the matter with her?" Burke asked.

"Waddell told us she has a cancer in her breast. He takes her into Denver to see some doc there. She might not have much longer."

"That's too bad," Burke said. "Do they have children?"

"One," Chick replied. "Cassie's due home any time from school. She's an eye-popper, that one."

"She been back East for a good long spell," Gilroy added. "She grew up out here a-horseback but her daddy wants her to find a rich boy back there. He told her he didn't raise no outlaw daughter."

"Sounds like they have their problems," Burke said.

"Plenty of them," Chick agreed. "They both came out of the chute a-kicking and it's a toss-up whose heels go higher."

Art added, "With Cassie here old Rube's going to have a lot on his mind. He'll likely put his management plans off to Sid Preston."

Chick shook his head. "Preston don't manage things, he forces them. He gets a kick out of dealing pain. Real pain. Sure, he took out some horse thieves and cattle rustlers in the country but when they were gone he didn't stop. He tied into the homesteaders, set them up and then called them thieves. No one knows for sure if he did the actual killing, or had his three sidekicks do it. Either way, he's got a lot of blood on his hands."

"Is some of that blood Mark Jones's?" Burke asked.

The two were silent.

"C'mon, you must know something about what happened."

"Jones caused most of his own troubles," Art said.

"What he means is Jones had an attitude," Chick explained.

"He had a job to do," Burke said. "You have to stand your ground."

"He stepped over the line," Art said. "He threw his authority in everyone's face."

"That wasn't a reason to kill him," Burke said.

"We don't know that for sure," Chick said. "We heard some bunkhouse talk about the ranger getting lost in the woods for good. Nobody ever asked any questions. You don't ask Sid Preston questions."

"Why hasn't there been an investigation?" Burke asked.

"No proof," Chick said. "No body, no case."

"There should have been cause for someone to go looking for a body," Burke pointed out.

"There's not enough lawmen around here to take care of the troubles as it is," Gilroy said. "They won't be going on no wild-goose chases."

"That gives Preston a lot of power," Burke said.

"A crazy man with power," Chick agreed. "That's the worst kind."

Sid Preston sat at the rough table in his cabin, his boots up, honing the blade of his hunting knife. The lantern's bright glow filled the tabletop, illuminating an empty whiskey bottle with the cork removed, an oaken cutting board, a bottle of wood alcohol, and a small chunk of fresh meat—a special selection that he had taken earlier, at the midnight hour. Now he wanted to preserve this special selection and keep it with other, similar, selections he had made since his coming to work for Rube Waddell at Eden Land and Livestock.

He had various bottles of different sizes and shapes located on a ledge above the table. He had noticed Lottie Burns staring at them, wondering. But she hadn't asked anything.

At various times, when he felt the need, he would take one or more of the bottles down, so that he could stare through the glass at the contents and remember the events surrounding that special selection.

Now he was preparing this special memory of Lottie Burns, to be included with the rest and remembered from time to time.

He worked the steel against the stone and inspected it, his tongue hanging partially from his mouth, moving along his lips as if he were sampling fresh honey. His eyes were large and filled with a distant glee, an all-engulfing rapture, as he tested the knife's keen edge on a piece of paper, slicing it easily with a raspy hiss, like that of a newly awakened snake.

It was his favorite possession, this blade of tempered steel, this tool that had created his life's most memorable moments. He wore it throughout each day in a handmade sheath and slept with it under his pillow each night, reaching often in his sleep to allow his fingers to caress it, willing his mind to embrace it, filling his dreams with visions of serrated blades and rivulets of blood that wound their way through empty darkness, like little streamers on a soft black wind, spreading and floating and coursing their way into the mouths of sleeping women, where they collected into bubbling pools.

The dreams never awakened him, never frightened him, but

gave him spasms of passion instead. He realized that the enjoyment could not come each and every night, but he tried his best to make it so, nonetheless.

He took the small chunk of meat and placed it directly in the center of the cutting board, then began a systematic carving process that rendered the flesh into thin ribbons that lay in little pools of blood, like tiny stillborn snakes. He took his time, in no rush to end the delicate carving.

He wanted to show his work to Lottie Burns before he finished with her. He wanted to show her her own tongue, sliced and diced to his own brand of perfection. Then, in a few days, he would complete his time with her and she would join the others in the elk burying ground.

While he worked, his mind turned to Ellis Burke. Since the ranger's coming, Preston had grown ever more concerned. Burke was a determined man in his own right, with plans of his own, and it made Preston wonder what it would take to make him go away.

He saw Burke's face again and wondered what it looked like without the cuts and bruises of that first night, without the redness and puffiness. He had decided to wait a length of time, until the healing process was complete, before he paid the ranger a little visit. He wanted to know more about this man. . . . He *had* to know more about him.

He had dreams about him.

Late the night before, Burke's veiled features had invaded his dark tranquility, facial image out of focus, distant, yet staring intensely at him. Preston had tossed and turned in his bunk. Even holding the knife tightly hadn't turned the vision away.

He had gotten up to pace the floor, had taken a walk in the darkness of the forest, trying to remember where he had met this man. He was altogether certain he had at some point in the past.

But that was a problem to be dealt with at another time. There was no need to trouble himself with the thought of Burke now. No need to disturb this segment of his pleasurable evening, or the following evenings when he allowed Lottie Burns to fulfill his desires.

Lottie Burns's tongue, with its rough upper side and its smooth, slick underside, had at last been dissected several times. The carving complete, he took each individual tiny strip of meat and dropped it into the empty whiskey bottle. One after the other, he slid them carefully down through the bottle's open mouth. He liked the way they dropped and lay across one another in the bottom, piling up, like little dead snakes in a glass den.

Preston placed the last slice of tongue down into the bottle and then stuck a small funnel into the top. He began pouring alcohol into the bottle, a little at a time, until he had covered the little snakes.

He corked the bottle. "There," he told himself. "I'm done."

He was ready to show Lottie Burns her tongue, but first he must show it to someone else, someone he had showed every one of his collections to.

He walked over to the empty whiskey keg.

"Mother," he said. "It's ready."

8

Cassandra Jean Waddell stepped down from the train, her deep blue satin dress shining in the afternoon sun. The Glenwood Springs station was alive with activity—the bustle of travelers and tourists anxious to see the little western town that Theodore Roosevelt had made famous the previous year. He had been in the area before the turn of the century but his most recent hunting trip into the Flat Tops area had convinced him that the intermountain forests of the American West should be managed properly for the enjoyment of future generations.

Cassie hadn't been home in over two years. Her studies at the newly established Institute of Musical Art in New York City had kept her both busy and content. But in breathing the fresh air and gazing upon the steep slopes of aspen and brush oak, ablaze in autumn scarlet and gold, she realized how much she had missed the wide open spaces and the glory of the mountains.

As she walked among the travelers she heard conversations in German, French, Spanish, and even Russian, as well as in English. The entire world now knew about the hot springs, the *yampa*, the big medicine that the Ute Indians said lived in its bubbling waters, along with the interesting nightlife and the day tours afforded to those with an interest in the scenic Continental Divide. Nestled against the brushy pine and oak on the western slope, the little town born of gold fever was enjoying an international popularity.

Cassie had been born in Denver and had been educated there, but had spent her summers on the family ranch where she had learned how to manage horses and keep courting cowpunchers at bay. She had visited Glenwood Springs many times in the company of her parents and had watched the little town attain its growing reputation with interest.

In her mid-thirties, Cassie could well be considered a died-in-the-wool spinster by all existing standards, far past what most would consider her prime and certainly in the waning light of her man-snatching years. But anyone who knew her would instantly argue that Cassie Waddell could catch any man she wanted and would be able to do so even if she chose to wait another ten years. Some might argue, in fact, that she could catch any man of her choosing, from any locale she wished, in any country in the world.

Cassie had been engaged previously to a Denver lawyer's son, a young man named Lincoln Prescott, who had given her an ultimatum: Do as he said without question or do without him. The week prior to the marriage, Cassie had learned that young Lincoln would be taking her to Boston with no plans of returning for a visit in the near or distant future. He would be joining his uncle's law firm and had no desire to see Denver or the mountains ever again. Cassie was to remain beside him and have no thoughts of traveling back on her own. She could accept that fact and be his dutiful bride, or forever be a backwoods woman with no future in polite society.

Cassie chose the mountains with few tears shed. Her father had wanted the union desperately and had been enraged at the news of their breakup. Rube Waddell shared the view that Cassie cared more about horses and the wilderness than she did about the established norms of a genteel woman and that her behavior reflected back upon him. Upon Lincoln Prescott's departure for Boston, he didn't speak to Cassie for a month. She quickly decided that she wanted to follow in her mother's footsteps and made plans to attend music and acting school in New York City. Her father had finally broken his silence with her just long enough to say that he hoped she might find a new life on the East Coast and remain forever out of his.

With her talent, Cassie had established herself immediately. She had forgotten Lincoln Prescott and there had been no one else in her life, her studies and concern for her ailing mother taking center stage. She had no shortage of suitors but her present concerns did not center on men, or how she might be perceived in regards to them. She had received a letter from home that had left her worried. Her mother's normally steady hand had left jagged points on her letters and her usual straightforward style was lacking.

Cassie had written her father and had informed him in no uncertain terms that she would be returning home for an indefinite period of time. His reply had suggested that her mother wasn't as bad off as she perceived. But Cassie instinctively knew better and wrote back that her education and her standing in polite society would remain on hold until she alone made the decision to resume her life in music and theater.

Now, as she prepared to meet her mother, she agonized over a situation she had created for herself, a lifestyle she had chosen. She had juggled this secret pastime with her schooling, growing more and more interested in this sidelight over her studies.

She hadn't stopped to think why she had gotten herself into the situation in the first place, except to realize that it had been a reaction to a desire within her, a desire to get back at her father for the troubles between them over the years.

But now, with the news that her mother was dying, Cassie realized that her secret would have to come out.

From the milling crowd of people, Cassie saw a woman lift a handkerchief and then hurry toward her. Seeing her mother there at the station, easily twenty pounds below her regular weight, brought tears to her eyes. They embraced and Cassie, noting the obvious physical pain, could hardly keep from breaking down.

There was no way she was going to share any secrets with her mother right now.

"I'm so glad to see you, Mother," she said. "I wanted to come sooner."

"I know, but it was best that you finish the summer session first."

Charlotte Ann Conley Waddell had been born in Denver to Lester Conley and Janette Markham, parents she had loved and been very close to until her father's death from a heart attack in the year after her marriage to Rube Waddell. Lester Conley had made a fortune in the Central City gold fields and Charlotte had spent considerable time there, performing in plays at the various theaters. Her call to the stage had been preempted by her marriage and her move to the wild country of north-central Colorado, where the open range was providing a fortune for cattlemen raising beef for the burgeoning markets both at home and in the East.

Her life with Rube Waddell had been challenging at best. Unable to make it back to Denver as often as she had liked, she had brought her mother to the ranch for extended periods, until her mother had tired of the turmoil her presence created in the household. Finally, she had moved to Chicago to be with another daughter and Charlotte had never forgiven her husband.

"Where is Father?" Cassie asked as they waited for her luggage.

"Need you ask?" her mother replied. "He's with a group of cattlemen at the hotel. He said he would join me before your arrival. But you know how that goes. I had to come to the station without him or I'd have missed you."

"How are you feeling?" Cassie asked. Then she said, "How stupid of me. You can't be feeling well."

"Some days are better than others," she said. "Today, of course, is far above average."

They took a carriage to the hotel and Cassie met her father near the registration desk. He stood as tall and stern in his dark three-piece suit as she had remembered him, his hair slightly grayer under his dark fedora, his gray-green eyes as vacant as ever. She had always thought of him as forever pretending to be there in person, but always far away in thought, as if he had precious little time and should be somewhere else.

"Forgive me," he said. He leaned over and kissed her cheek fleetingly. "These are troubled times and our meeting ran over schedule."

"Troubled times?" she said. "I've been thinking about Mr. Burke. I'm wondering if he might not improve things a bit."

"You can't be serious, Cassie. The Forest Reserves Act is the single greatest threat ever to the freedom of this country."

"Aren't you overreacting?" Cassie asked. She watched his neck grow red. "You certainly won't be put out of business by it."

"Cassie, you can't possibly know the ramifications of this legislation."

"I'm beginning to wonder if it isn't long overdue," Cassie told him. "We've always argued about your longhorn pasture. You've never cared what I thought. You just kept putting more and more steers in that meadow."

"Cassie, there is no problem with the grass."

"Maybe that's why Ellis Burke is here," Cassie said. "Men like you don't give a damn about the land. Just what you can take from it."

"Perhaps there's another subject we might pursue," her mother suggested.

"Forgive me, Mother," Cassie said. "I know better than to discuss politics with Father."

"But you never learn, do you?" he snapped. "Your ignorance is astounding."

"Just like old times," Charlotte Waddell said with a sigh.

Burke departed the train at the Glenwood Springs station, followed by Chick Campbell and Art Gilroy. Chick and Art were laughing, adjusting their brand-new three-piece suits and bowler hats, courtesy of Burke's generosity. They had eaten well and their present good nature had been bolstered considerably by the train's fine bourbon.

"Don't we look *dee-bone-air*?" Chick asked. "That how you say it?"

"Yes, debonair," Burke replied.

"Just plain good to look at," Chick said with a broad smile. "*Dee-bone-air.*"

Art Gilroy stuck out his chest. "I look that way myself, don't I?"

"Listen, Art," Burke said. "You can't look debonair and drool tobacco."

"Yeah, you're right," he said. He took the handkerchief from his suit coat and wiped away the brown trail running down his chin, then stuffed it into his back pocket.

"Art, you're going to have to work on debonair," Chick observed.

"I've got a knack for it," Art argued. "You could see it right off when we got on the train."

"Really?" Chick said.

"Yeah," Art told him. "Did you see how those ladies watched me? They thought I was something special."

"No, they watched *out* for you," Chick corrected him. "They wanted to stay out of your damned way."

"You always was the jealous type," Art said.

They loaded their luggage into a carriage bound for the Hotel Colorado. During the ride, Chick and Art pointed out various saloon and gambling halls along the way. Chick told Burke about the time he had watched the famous gunfighter, Doc Holliday, face a man down at a poker table.

"He was cool as you please," Campbell was saying. "This tinhorn gambler knew that Holliday was sick with consumption and so he decided to push his luck. But what did Holliday have to lose? I thought he was going to blow that tinhorn's eyes out of the back of his head. That's just what he told the tinhorn would happen if he didn't do just what he said. He made that guy put both hands down the front of his pants and whistle. I saw it. Then he made him back out the door with his hands still down his pants." He pointed to a high hill that overlooked the town. "Old Doc's buried right up there in that cemetery."

.   .   .

The hotel was alive with activity. Burke led the way to the desk, noting that a lot of cattlemen were present. Chick and Art stood behind him, appearing important. They registered and after a quick cleanup in their respective rooms, they met in the warm waters beside the fountain that adorned the pool.

Chick frowned and said, "Art, what happened to the clean pair of long handles I gave you?"

"They were supposed to fit me?" Art said.

"They might have been a little short, but at least you wouldn't have looked like you rolled on a barn floor."

"It's that bad?" Art said.

"It's worse. Look what you're doing to the water. You don't look so *dee-bone-air* now."

Burke swam over to the north wall, where streams of steaming hot water poured from pipes into the main pool. He laid back and allowed the heat to relax his sore muscles. Art and Chick soon joined him and continued their discussion regarding which of the two was more worldly.

Burke paid them no mind. He was eavesdropping on a conversation nearby. A glaringly attractive woman, dressed in a daring bathing suit, conversed with two people who he had decided must be her parents. There seemed to be no love lost between the woman and her father.

Art and Chick stopped their discussion and turned their attention to Burke.

"I see what you're looking at," Chick said. "That's the renegade beauty we told you about, Cassie Waddell."

"She marches to her own drummer, that's for sure," Burke commented.

"Yeah, I like her swimwear, too," Art said. "Yes, I really like it."

"It's not polite to stare," Chick said. "Besides, you'll scare her."

"She ain't scared all that easily, from what I hear," Art said.

Burke noticed the three of them looking at him—the father, mother, and Cassie, who seemed interested in what her father was saying. No doubt, Burke thought, they realized that he was the new special ranger in the area.

9

Cassie listened attentively while her father discussed the reasons he didn't like the man resting against the side of the pool not far away. Besides being in the company of the two rebellious ex-hands, Chick Campbell and Art Gilroy, he was the new ranger who had arrived to assess the grazing limits within the forest boundaries, and as such would destroy the range-cattle business in the entire region.

"He's nothing more than vermin," Waddell said. "He needs to be sent away."

"Rube, you don't even know that man," Cassie's mother said. "How can you say such vile things about him?"

"Just look at him, Charlotte. He's already gotten himself into a saloon brawl somewhere."

"He's built pretty well," Cassie observed out loud. "And his face doesn't look all that bad, even with the bruises."

"If you think that kind of talk bothers me," Rube Waddell said, "it doesn't."

"Yes, it does," Cassie said.

"If you would listen to me for a moment, you might not be so infatuated," her father said. "You can count on selling Megan now that we have her back."

He definitely had her attention. Her pet horse, a beautiful chestnut mare, had been missing since before she had left for New York.

"Megan's back?"

"She was stolen by thieves. Sid Preston got her back. But the point is, we'll just have to sell her, and you can blame that man right there." He pointed toward Burke.

"I don't understand," Cassie said.

"Would you explain that, Rube?" her mother said.

"Charlotte," Rube Waddell said, "I'm talking to Cassie."

Despite not feeling well, Charlotte Waddell bristled. "And I'm talking to you, Mr. Rube Waddell. I'm Cassie's mother and you won't bar me from this conversation."

"I just want you to stop talking and listen," Waddell said. "If this fellow, Burke, has his way, he'll cut grazing so far back that we'll have to sell a lot of our horses."

Cassie frowned at her father. "Nice try. We won't have to sell all of them, and we'll keep Megan for sure. Why didn't you write to me that you'd found her?"

"You're not listening, Cassie. He's going to destroy us. That's why he's here."

Cassie continued. "I really think that *you* took Megan and hid her somewhere, just to spite me. And now you want me to help you with your battles."

"Don't be ridiculous, Cassie. When the allotments are decided and the permits handed out, Burke will try and scale us way back."

"You're just trying to be sensational, Rube," Charlotte said.

"And, as usual, you don't know the issues," Waddell told her. "He's after us, and that's a fact."

"There's one way to find out for sure," Cassie said. "I'll go ask him."

"Don't do that," Rube Waddell said. But she was already gone.

· · ·

Burke watched Cassie Waddell ease through the water toward him. She appeared very sure of herself, intent on some mission.

She didn't mince words.

"Mr. Burke, I've heard a lot about you, and not all of it good, I'm afraid."

"I'm hardly surprised," Burke said.

"I understand that you've come to take over the grazing lands and the grazing rights of all the established ranchers."

"That's a lot of responsibility for one man."

"Don't make jokes, Mr. Burke. It *is* Mr. Ellis Burke, isn't it?"

"It is. And you're Miss Cassie Waddell, I presume?"

"I would shake your hand, Mr. Burke," Cassie said, "but first I need to know some facts."

Burke noticed that they had become the center of attention. Women talked in whispers, their hands shielding their lips, while the gentlemen discussed business as a front to quick glances.

"What are your intentions with regard to grazing allotments?" she continued. "Do you intend to prohibit horses from grazing on the forest?"

"Restrict, Miss Waddell, not prohibit. Just like the cattle."

"I have a horse that means the world to me, Mr. Burke, and I intend to let her graze near our home, whether you like it or not."

"Maybe I should explain," Burke said. "If she's all by herself, you have nothing to worry about. If she's part of a large herd, you're going to have to decide which horses you like best, based on allotment numbers. Does she eat a whole lot of grass?"

"What did I tell you about the jokes?"

"My apologies. It's just that this conversation seems a bit stilted, and for no good reason."

Cassie forged ahead. "How do you propose to come up with the numbers to base your restrictions on?" she asked.

"I'll assess the types and amounts of grass available in the various areas and we'll go from there."

"All very scientific, I presume."

"We're getting better all the time."

"I'm wondering," Cassie said. "Though my father is the worst, there are other ranchers like him. I suppose in time, their money will allow you to make decisions in their favor."

"Rich or not, your father's not going to win this one," Burke told her.

Cassie studied him. He seemed straightforward. He had a nice smile, despite his battered face. But he was a bit too confident.

"I'm still not certain of your intentions, yet, Mr. Burke," she said. "You don't dress like most men who ride the range and how many in your profession drive new cars, for heaven's sake?"

"I haven't polled the others."

"The point is, Mr. Burke, you have far too much to need this job. Why are you really here?"

Burke noticed that Cassie's father had left the pool, curiously without her mother, who made her way over to them.

"Mother, this is Ellis Burke, a man with some secrets, I believe."

"Come, now, Cassie."

"It's a pleasure to meet you, Mrs. Waddell," Burke said.

"Please, dispense with the formalities and call me Charlotte," she said.

Cassie frowned. "Mother, I don't think that's appropriate."

Charlotte Waddell studied Burke. "Cassie, I don't believe that Mr. Burke is an enemy. He has a difficult job."

"Thanks for the vote of confidence, ma'am," Burke said.

Charlotte coughed suddenly. "Please forgive me. I've been ill recently."

"I'm sorry," Burke told her. "I hope you'll be feeling better soon."

She smiled. "I'll do my best. It was nice to have met you."

"I'll be going with her," Cassie said. "Perhaps you can give me some instructions on rangeland management one of these times."

Burke rejoined Chick and Art, and they watched Cassie exit the pool and disappear into the women's side of the clubhouse. Nearly every other eye was on her as well.

"You get a date with her?" Chick asked.

"Hardly," Burke replied. "She wanted to scratch my eyes out."

"I'd let her do it," Art said. "And I'd even let her be on top."

"I mean it," Burke said. "Her father must have told her a whopper about me."

"Rube Waddell means to chase you out of the country, one way or the other," Chick said. "That's why you've got to let Bill Conrad do what he can in your favor."

"I've told you, Chick," Burke said, "I don't want someone saying I'm playing favorites."

Art leaned over and said to Chick, "Should we tell him about Vivian Cross?"

"We might as well," Chick replied, "if he's going to be this stubborn."

"Who's Vivian Cross?" Burke asked.

"She's a new widow, as of just a couple months ago," Chick told him. "She now owns Cross Land and Livestock, which is just south of Waddell's place. I'm here to tell you that she wants you out of here worse than Waddell."

"Why would that be?" Burke asked.

"Let's just say she has some plans of her own," Chick said. "Some very devious plans."

Vivian Alexander Cross tended the flowers carefully, a collection of mountain bluebells, blanket flowers, and white daisies, whose minute blossoms she referred to as her "tiny angels." They all bloomed gloriously on the mound of soil and rock that covered the remains of her late husband. She had begun her project in early spring, planting the seeds on the grave the day after her husband's interment, watering them religiously from a yellow pitcher.

With a feeling of accomplishment, she held the pitcher to her breast and sat down to stare at the stone marker.

BYRON RANDOLPH CROSS
b. 12-3-1852 d. 3-12-1906
Resting in Peace,
Absolved of all Toil and Trouble

She had been married to him for twenty-two of her thirty-nine years of life. Her feelings for him had changed over the course of their life together, and she wondered why he couldn't have tended to her needs, or even noticed that she had any. Why had he always been so busy?

Over the last ten years, much of her time had been spent in Denver's finest hotels, basking in the light of notoriety among the wives of other wealthy ranchers who, like herself, often allowed themselves the luxury of more comfortable confines while their spouses saw to the daily tasks of land ownership and livestock management. Normal winters—the previous four or five excluded—in north-central Colorado brought considerable snowfall and travel was oftentimes out of the question. And the little town of Eden, in its attempt to keep up with the changing times, fell far short of the offerings of Denver or even Glenwood Springs.

It was not uncommon to see Vivian, dressed in combinations of black or dark brown, accentuated by a fashionable hat, attending plays or parties, accompanied by her sister, Lenore Alexander Monts, and Lenore's husband, Raymond Monts, a prominent Denver attorney. She kept her black hair glossy, her neckline doused with perfume, and her dark eyes casually searched her surroundings for noteworthy people.

Byron Cross had never been one for fancy surroundings. He had always maintained that his place was on the ranch, tending to his investments. If he resented the fact that his wife felt differently, he never said a word to anyone. And as close as anyone could tell, he never allowed that it bothered him.

But among the people who discussed the happenings and the people in the valley, word was that Byron Cross had worked himself far too hard and way too long in an effort to keep his odd but pretty little wife comfortable, and had paid for it with his life. Years of stress and hard work had carved deep furrows in his brow and he had cleft bird's-foot wrinkles from each eye socket back to his heavy sideburns. Even a man of his size and strength must succumb to long days and short nights and nothing but more of the same to look forward to day after day, year in and year out.

It was a well-known fact that his heart had given out. Some said Vivian had broken it many times over the years and that he couldn't bear to live on wondering when she would return home. She had borne him no children and—when not with her sister—had been seen in the company of other men from time to time.

Vivian had been on the ranch a great deal during his last year of life, more than all the time during the previous years combined, causing many to speculate that she had changed her ways and decided that the man she married was worth being with. Others said that she had given him much too little of herself much too late to save him.

During that time she had read voraciously, gobbling up volume after volume on the structure and nature of vascular plants. At various times during her stay with him, she would attempt to read passages of taxonomic description at the dinner table, a trait that bored him and even after dark, sent him scurrying out of the house to attend to the stock.

This behavior would always leave her smiling and smug, content in her firm belief that Byron Randolph Cross would never take her seriously or endeavor to have a decent intellectual relationship with her. Never mind the sex—it was difficult and very unrewarding. Nonetheless, she fought her battles against guilt and once heard him say that he would be with her always, because that's how it was supposed to be.

With him buried, Vivian Cross held one of the valley's largest ranches, the Cross 12, in her sole possession and no experience in managing such an empire. She was given a lot of advice from the foreman, Shorty Walsh, her husband's closest friend and a man of impeccable loyalty. She would see him early every morning and late every evening, without fail, visiting the gravesite alone, hat in hand. She wondered if he talked to her deceased husband, as she often did, and she wondered that if so, how their conversations went.

Of late, Vivian Cross had developed her own ideas of how to manage the thousand head of cattle and two hundred horses. Shorty Walsh wanted to keep the operation separate from everyone and anyone else, while she had considered a move that would strengthen her position, especially in light of the coming grazing allotments. She had to protect herself, is how she saw it. Shorty Walsh could see to it that the day-to-day workload was handled efficiently, just as long as he realized that the major decisions would always belong to her.

10

Sid Preston took his table apart and tied it to the back of a mule. His mind was on Ellis Burke and the problems this man could cause if allowed to remain in the area. His claim to have documented his whereabouts to friends and coworkers elsewhere was certainly of merit; he couldn't ignore that. But something had to happen—an accident—something.

Len Keller stood near the fire, finishing a bottle.

"I'll take Jeb and Burt up the other draw tomorrow," he said. "When Burke gets back from Glenwood Springs, we'll be ready for him."

"Campbell and Gilroy with be with him," Preston pointed out.

"We'll take care of them too," Mason said.

Preston shook his head. "You'll never get it right, will you, Jeb?"

"What do you mean? I ain't scared of them."

"Never mind," Preston said. "Let's not rush it. We have to do it right."

Jeb Mason said, "Why don't you let us get it over with, Sid? And why do we always have to meet up here? We never go to wherever it is you stay. Why's that?"

Preston turned to him. "Don't ask me that ever again. Understand? I've told you before, I don't want any of you looking for where I stay. You'd never find it, anyway, but I don't ever want you looking. All of you, got it?"

Keller and Mason nodded. Burt Gamble was saddling his horse.

"Burt, did you hear what I said?" Preston yelled.

"I heard," Gamble said. "You'd better be sure and get that fire out before you leave. Awful dry, you know."

He rode away and Keller said, "I don't know what's gotten into him lately."

"It doesn't matter," Preston said. "We've got a job ahead of us."

The Eden Land and Livestock headquarters was located along Eden Creek, some ten miles south of town, past the Devil's Grave, at the base of a mountain Rube Waddell had named after himself. What the maps said made no difference to him. Waddell Mountain was his, as was all the land surrounding the building for seven miles in every direction.

He was partially right. Most of the land for seven miles in every direction did belong to him, with the exception of Waddell Mountain itself, which comprised some eight hundred acres, along with three sections of additional federal land on the north side of the mountain. Waddell's father, George Mason Waddell, had driven longhorn cattle into the region in the decade following the Civil War and later, as a result of a series of homestead acts granting land to those who could prove up on it, had acquired deed to three sections of land. The remaining acreage had been acquired by hiring miners and drifters from the saloons in Denver and various mining camps to file a homestead claim, stay long enough to prove up on it, and then relinquish deed to Eden

Land and Livestock when the allotted time had expired.

The Eden brand, *EDEN* placed on the right side, along the ribs, was among the best known in the region, along with the *Sevens*, the *Two Bars*, the *8 M*, the *Figure 4*, the *Reverse 4*, and the *0 V 0*, among others. They all grazed cattle in the forests and intermountain valleys along the west slope of the Continental Divide, clear across the vast open toward Utah. They had formed a large livestock association called the Colorado Western Livestock Association, to protect their interests and insure political power in the state capital.

Ranching reigned supreme, and would continue to reign supreme, even in the face of the U.S. forest service.

Lottie Preston's mouth was filled with pain. Not even the drug, laudanum, which she had read from the bottle he had brought in with him, could help her.

She had fought sleep most of the day, awaiting her death, but had succumbed to exhaustion late in the afternoon. Now, as she awakened, she hoped against all hope that this incredible nightmare would fade with her return to consciousness.

But the nightmare became ever more real and she struggled with the fact that she could have prevented this moment if she had only listened to reason.

One of the girls had told her in no uncertain terms not to leave with the gray-eyed man. Gracie Miller, another of Trixie's girls, often traveled up to Eden to stay with Bill Conrad, a local cattleman and owner of the Park Range Hotel. Gracie had said that she would be foolish, no matter how much he paid her to leave with him. She had said that his name was Sid Preston and that he worked for a cattle baron named Rube Waddell who cared only about gaining more wealth and power. Sid Preston, Gracie had told her, would do whatever it took to fulfill his boss's expectations.

She heard footsteps approaching the shed, together with the coarse whistling.

"Helloooo again, Lottie." Preston laughed and opened the door. He was holding his hunting knife in an odd manner.

It was too late to lament her poor choice now. Lottie Burns had forsaken all advice and had instead given in to her belief of a new life for herself with a man who had seemed like the answer to her dreams.

He stood over her, twirling the knife in his hand.

"Special night, Lottie."

She was so frightened that she couldn't even move.

"I'll take your gag off now," he said.

He knelt down but didn't remove the gag.

Lottie's eyes rolled as he touched the flat side of the blade against one side of her face and then the other. She held her breath as he put his face into hers.

"Mother's coming with us."

The spring stock growers' meeting was being held in Glenwood Springs at the Hotel Colorado. All the ranchers were in attendance, as the meeting was mainly to discuss the changes sure to come in their industry. The major change was represented by the forest ranger, Ellis Burke. Everyone wondered what he was thinking about his major meeting, taking place just a short ways away from where he sat in the hot springs, recovering from a severe beating.

Bill Conrad sat in attendance with a number of new members from the western part of the district, distinctly apart from Rube Waddell and the other large operators. There had already been some discussion about the Forest Reserves Act and the certain changes it would bring. The smaller operators welcomed the restrictions, as did many of the larger outfits. But Rube Waddell was not interested in giving up any of his perceived grazing rights.

Burke had not received a formal invitation, but believed he didn't need one. The meeting was in session when he entered the room. Everyone turned and Burke said, "I'd like to say a few words and be on my way."

Murmurs in the room swelled to protest. Rube Waddell spoke the loudest, followed by Lee Miller, who had become a member to hopefully draw new depositors to his bank. He anticipated Bill Conrad's competition to be stronger than he had first anticipated.

Oliver McClain, a rancher from the Meeker area, presided over the meeting. He quieted the men.

"Mr. Burke, what do you hope to accomplish here?"

"To bring some understanding of my mission," Burke replied.

"You make it sound like a quest for the Holy Grail," Waddell said. Some of the ranchers chuckled.

"I'll give you the floor, Mr. Burke," McClain said. "Don't overstay your welcome."

Burke began by stating that he hadn't come to end the livestock business in western Colorado, but to make it better. He explained that by trimming the numbers of cows and horses using the forest, he would be doing them all a favor.

Again, the men broke into an angry protest.

"Please, let's listen to the ranger," McClain said.

Burke cleared his throat. "Thank you, Mr. McClain. Gentlemen, I want to be clear and complete. The forest reserves are here to stay, and so is the forest service. You can do your best to railroad me out of here but someone else will come along and take my place. If there's too much trouble you just might attract the attention of President Roosevelt himself."

The talk began anew and one rancher spoke up. "I showed him around my place when he came out here to hunt. He said that he loved this country. Now you're saying that he's going to see to it that you crowd us out of business?"

"That's not going to happen," Burke said. "He's just my ace in the hole. He wants the forest service to succeed as bad as I do. Remember that."

"Should the president come out here again," Lee Miller said, "it will be to hunt with us, not to see you." More laughter.

"Are you sure you can bag your own game?" Burke asked Miller. "Or do you have somebody shoot for you?"

A strained silence followed, while Burke and Miller glared at each other.

Oliver McClain said, "We're straying from the issues here, gentlemen. Please continue, Mr. Burke."

"All I'm asking," Burke said, "is for cooperation from all of you. Nothing more than that."

"What kind of cooperation?" Miller asked.

"Mark Jones did some surveys before he disappeared and based on those, he came up with some temporary allotment figures. I'll use those figures during the spring shove-up into the forest reserves against actual numbers I count from your various herds."

"And that means these men will definitely have to cut their herd numbers," Miller said. "Am I right?"

"It's very likely that most everyone will," Burke admitted.

.   .   .

The shadows were long and twisted, the evening crisp and cool, as Sid Preston rode toward the burying ground, whistling "My Darling Clementine." He led his pack mule behind him, with his movable table tied over both sides. Bound and tied over the table was Lottie Burns.

She hung over both sides, bouncing gently with the rhythm of the mule as they made their way through the jagged trunks of burned trees. Her groggy condition had lessened, however, as the effects of the laudanum began to wear off. He had told her just before their leaving that he wanted her lucid for the upcoming special event.

On the pommel of his saddle rested a sack filled with a large, round object. Lottie had watched earlier while he tied it securely, talking to it, shedding tears.

They finally stopped and he untied her, then pulled her from the horse and laid her down against a tree. She had wanted the ride to never end, for she knew it would mean the end of her. But she could make no noise. Without her tongue, she had no ability to protest anything. He had singed the ragged back edge with a hot iron to stop the bleeding and when she had regained consciousness, he had shown her the remains, cut to ribbons, layered in the bottom of a whiskey bottle filled with wood alcohol.

He patted her on the head and began preparing for the event, taking the table from the mule and piecing it together. His breath, rapid and irregular, was broken by his coarse whistling. He grabbed her roughly and began to drag her toward a shallow grave. He had fed her very little over the past several days, so she had no strength to fight him when he released her bonds and began to strip her.

Right next to the grave lay the body of an enormous bull elk. He had turned the elk onto its back and had tied ropes to the legs, attaching them to four separate tree trunks, spreading the body cavity wide open. Lottie, naked and cold, offered as much resistance as she could as he positioned her inside the body and began tying her, hand and foot, to the elk's front and back legs.

He studied her for a moment, whistling in his odd way, his dull eyes completely vacant. He got up and walked over to his horse and took the sack from the saddle and returned. He opened the sack and pulled out a human head and placed it on the table, facing Lottie Burns.

"Don't worry," he said to Lottie. "She can't speak, either."

Sid Preston stared at the head for a time, whistling his tune, breathing heavily. He adjusted the head a couple of times, to be sure it rested with the shriveled eyes directly on the dead elk.

"I want you to be happy, Mother. I think this will make you happy."

It had been over ten years since Preston had killed his mother. He had threatened her for a number of years, ever since his sixteenth birthday, waving a knife in her face when the killing day arrived; first, he had told her she would never speak badly to him again. Then before she could react or say a word, he had wrestled her to the floor, knocking her senseless, and had removed her tongue. When she had gone berserk, he had finished her with his knife, filleting her like a trout.

He had felt badly afterwards, but couldn't undo her death, so decided he must decide how to keep her with him from that time on.

He didn't even remember where he had buried the body, but had decided to retain her head. He had placed the head in a cave way back in the high country and the dry air had mummified it nicely. Her skin had darkened and her features had withered, but he had propped her mouth open with a small stick so that it would remain that way, so that whenever he wanted, he could look in and see that she had no tongue.

It had kept nicely over the years in the empty whiskey keg that rested against an inside wall of his cabin. He only took her out for special occasions, those times when he consummated his union with the women he had brought up to his special paradise. She seemed to always be pleased.

This time would be the same as the others: There would be no special favors granted on either side. Perhaps the next one would understand and realize the greatness that awaited the woman who chose to become one with him.

Lottie Burns made herself go away, somewhere very far away, like she had done as a small girl in the dark bedroom where her mother had kept her and made her available to men with a desire for the young. She had found it easy to leave during those times.

On this last evening of her life she traveled as far away as she could, a long ways from the naked man with the knife, who stood over her, looking back and forth from her to the severed head. This man who was now touching her face and neck and breasts with the tip of his knife.

She allowed herself to go back to the views of the high mountains on that warm day the previous summer when she had first arrived in Glenwood Springs. That was a feeling she had wanted to have always.

So she would keep that feeling, seeing only the magnificent rising peaks and the endless stands of conifer and oak and aspen that grew along the steep hillsides. Yet she couldn't help but gasp in fear, if just for a moment, as he knelt down beside her and began his work. Soon it would be over, though, and she could float over the high mountains forever in peace.

11

The stock growers' meeting had carried on late into the evening. At one point, Burke had been asked to leave the room while the members discussed the issues he had brought up. Finally, a hotel worker had gone into the center-garden area to find him.

Once back in the meeting, he said, "I don't know why it's such an issue. Cutting back your herds will only improve your overall profits."

One of the ranchers stood up and addressed Burke. "Stock prices are down and the weather's not been cooperating, either," he said. "It's drier than a popcorn fart out there. Now you're telling us that cutting back is good. How are we supposed to make it?"

"Let me present you with something you no doubt already realize," Burke said. "If you lower your numbers so that there's more grazing for everyone, all the cattle out there will get more to eat and you'll have bigger, heavier calves and steers to take to market. If the numbers are too high and the forage isn't there, they all run weight off looking for food."

Rube Waddell stood up. "Here's my answer to your proposal. I intend to bring three thousand more steers in by rail." He sat down and lit a cigar.

Some of the other ranchers agreed, but they were in the minority. The organization had discussed different management ideas at their meetings before and had always ended up divided on the issue. Now that the forest service had entered the picture, there seemed little doubt that the matter would soon be settled for them.

"All of you who are with me on the issue of us running our own concerns, join with me," Rube Waddell said, standing up again. "We'll meet as soon as the general assembly is through."

This created considerable commotion, causing McClain's gavel to fall.

"Gentlemen, this shall remain an orderly meeting," he said. "Mr. Waddell, you're out of order."

"I'm starting my own order," Waddell said. "I can see that most of you want to cave in to this preposterous concept of bowing to government rule."

Again turmoil reigned and again, Oliver McClain pounded his gavel.

"Stop this!" he yelled. Everyone quieted and he added, "Rube, I can't stop you from forming your own organization, but as long as you're in attendance at this meeting, you'll abide by the rules set forth."

Waddell stood up and grabbed his hat off the table. "It's time for me to leave," he told the group. "I for one will not stand by and see my liberties denied. Those who feel the same way are welcome to join me."

Waddell started for the door, followed by three other ranchers, all stomping their heavy boots against the floor, billowing smoke from their large cigars. When they were gone the room fell silent in shock.

"I think your organization now faces a big challenge," Burke said. "If you want a fair and equitable distribution of grazing numbers, you're going to have to help me stop Rube Waddell and his followers from loading up the range."

Rube Waddell did what he pleased and didn't care who knew it. For an aspiring politician, he had made some controversial decisions, and he was continuing to make them. Breaking off from the main stock growers had further hurt his chances of successfully running for office, and now Sid Preston had informed him that Bill Conrad and his Rocker 9 ranch hands were catering to Ellis Burke.

He had informed Preston that he expected him to devise a plan that would get rid of the new ranger for good.

His main concern at present, though, was a new mansion he had begun work on the fall before. He had contracted for a new home of brick and stone and was overseeing the final stages, chomping on his ever-present cigar and watching the workers while they completed the stone inlays on the inside of his new mansion. He talked and pointed, as if directing their work, while they went about their business and nodded, ignoring his idle chatter for the most part. They were used to him bothering them, complaining about every detail, demanding changes at his own whim. Appeasing him over the months had taken a lot of the main contractor's time, but up to now there had been few complaints. The money had been spectacular.

Now, with the work nearly completed, Waddell was unusually edgy and combative about the final touches. He had wanted the stone facing from the main fireplace removed and replaced with pink granite he had imported from Montana. After a long session with the contractor, he had finally agreed to keep the original rock in place. The contractor had insisted that structurally, the house couldn't withstand that kind of remodeling. Waddell had agreed to allowing cuts of granite to be placed into the existing stonework. Today they would complete the job and the house would be ready for occupation.

As it stood presently, he would be moving into the new mansion himself. His wife and daughter would be staying in the massive log structure built four years earlier. No amount of persuasion could bring them to move. Cassie had argued that her mother was content where she was and had never wanted the extravagant new house in the first place.

Waddell did not particularly care about his daughter's point of view. He had made arrangements that he believed would eventually force her and his wife into the new place. If they couldn't see things his way and move, well, that didn't particularly matter either.

He stepped outside the mansion and lit another cigar. He noticed Cassie headed in his direction at a fast walk. He had tired of the endless arguments and didn't look forward to her onslaught.

Cassie arrived and wasted no time in getting to the point.

"I knew you were a selfish man, Father, but this is something beyond my wildest imagination."

"I'm surprised you didn't save it to spring on me in front of your mother," he said.

"She's having a difficult time with all this," Cassie said. "Her involvement in our discussions won't help her condition."

"I still don't understand your position," he said. "This is a beautiful house."

"But she never wanted it, Father. Can't you understand that?"

"You haven't been here for two years. You weren't privy to the conversations between your mother and myself, before she became ill."

"Are you calling Mother a liar?"

"I'm saying that I know what she said. You don't. She's very sick, Cassie. She doesn't remember much these days."

"Even if that were true," Cassie continued, "you have no right to force the cooks and the household help into the new house, leaving us by ourselves."

"You don't have to be by yourselves."

"I'm wondering, Father," Cassie asked. "Why did you really build this grand effigy to your ego? It couldn't have been for Mother. She doesn't have that much time left."

"You know why I built it," he said.

"I'm really not sure, Father. Please tell me."

From the near distance came the sound of a horse and buggy. Vivian Cross, the closest neighbor directly to the south, was seated next to her driver. Since losing her husband she had been a frequent visitor to the Eden Ranch, something that puzzled Cassie. Vivian and her mother had never been close friends. In fact, in the years past they had had tense words, on the occasion of a valley Christmas party, when Vivan had commented on Rube's ability to hold a woman closely and firmly while dancing.

Vivian Cross and her driver came to a stop and Rube Waddell helped her down.

"How nice to see you, Vivian," he said.

"I brought a couple of pies over," she said. "Just a little something. I hope Charlotte is feeling better."

"She's resting," Cassie said.

Vivian Cross suddenly turned to her and said, "It's nice that you could come home."

"Mother is resting," Cassie repeated. "She's very tired."

"I'm sorry to hear that," Vivian said. She turned her eyes from Cassie toward the mansion. "Is it finished yet?"

"The final touches are nearly in place," Rube Waddell said, smiling.

"May I have a tour?" she asked.

Cassie's father turned to her. "Why don't you take the pies to the house? I'll be along in a while."

Cassie knew full well that her world was changing in a terrible way. Losing her mother was going to be the single most tragic event of her life. No one had ever cared about her or supported her in the same manner. She had a close friend in Glenwood Springs who would always be there for her, and a few associates back in New York who had befriended her, but no one would ever be able to measure up to her mother.

Cassie's argument had always been that her life from the very beginning had been a blueprint for misery. The only pleasure she had ever derived from her existence was the time spent with her mother, and on her chestnut mare Megan, riding through the wilderness. The night she had lost her beloved horse had been the night she had decided to move to New York and pursue her own interests.

Her father had proclaimed the loss of the red mare to thieves. Cassie's horse and fifteen others had come up missing from the herd. After three weeks and no sign of her horse, Cassie had given up hope. Despite many attempts by her mother to talk her out of it, Cassie had made arrangements for an audition in New York. Her father had agreed to pay for her schooling and for the first time that she could recall, he appeared pleased with a decision she had made.

"You'll find yourself a new life there, and the proper outlet for your talents," he told her. But he had been too busy to see her off at the train depot.

The evening of her departure had been the last time she had seen her mother healthy. Notwithstanding her mother's tears, Cassie hadn't noticed anything wrong that was cause for alarm. Her disease had come on very quickly and as her mother had confided in a letter later that year, she had noticed a lump in her right breast.

Cancer was a disease everyone feared and no one knew much about, except that odd cells attacked the body from all directions and made the last months of life a living hell. Cassie's mother had also written that this terrible disease had also taken her own mother. Doctors were beginning to wonder if genetics played an important role in who was susceptible.

With little doubt as to the outcome of her mother's battle, Cassie had begun an immediate fight with depression. Despite her mother's insistence that she enjoy her time on the ranch, she found herself completely discouraged. And the more she thought about the new mansion, the angrier she became. This visit from Vivian Cross was testing the limits of her control.

She entered her mother's bedroom and watched her mother's eyelids flutter.

"Mother, can you hear me?" she asked.

Charlotte Waddell opened her eyes. "Help me up, Cassie, would you, please?"

"Are you sure?"

"Completely. Did I hear Vivian Cross's voice?"

"Father is showing her the new mansion."

Charlotte steadied herself on the edge of the bed. "He's doing what?"

"Showing her the mansion. I wish it would fall in on the two of them."

With Cassie's help, Charlotte made her way to the window and peered out. The driver, one of Vivian Cross's hired hands, had gotten down from the buggy and was watering the horses with a pail. Across the way, the workers were all outside the mansion, resting in the shade.

"I wonder why he's left them on break," Cassie wondered out loud. "I'm going over there."

Charlotte grabbed her arm with what little strength she could muster. "Don't."

"It isn't proper, Mother."

"Maybe not. But don't bother."

Cassie helped her mother back to bed and started out the door.

"Cassie?" her mother said. "Where are you going?"

"I'll be right back," Cassie replied. "I'm going to get rid of some pies."

Vivian stood in the main room viewing the massive fireplace. Waddell stood next to her, his arm around her waist.

"Does the pink granite meet with your approval, my dear?" he asked.

"It's very nice. But there isn't enough of it."

"It's very difficult to make the two types of rock form fit with one another," Waddell said. "One is granite and one is sandstone."

"Oh, I can see the difference," Vivian said. "I just wish there was more of the pink and less of the tan. I thought I told you that."

"Maybe you should have done the ordering, Vivian."

"Now, Rube, don't be difficult. You know that pink and black and brown are my favorite colors."

"Yes. Will the fireplace do?"

"I suppose it will have to."

"Otherwise, how do you like the house?"

"I would like it better, Rube, if I could move in."

"That wouldn't be prudent at this time, my dear."

"How much longer does she have?"

"Not much."

"I'm tired of being patient, Rube. Everything is moving faster than we had imagined. That new ranger is going to change things before we're ready for it."

"No, he's not going to change things, my dear."

"Who's going to stop him? You? The forest reserve people are not going to go away, Rube."

Waddell chomped on his cigar. "Perhaps not. But if we can persuade Mr. Burke to take a permanent trip out of the area, we'll have things in line."

12

Burke lifted a support log up to Chick Campbell on the roof and went back down the ladder for another. Art Gilroy straddled the peak, nailing the timbers to support beams. They had been working the better part of three days and with the help of two extra men had cut and notched enough logs the day before to get the cabin raised. Now the roof was in its final stages and Burke felt every bit as sore as he had before leaving for Glenwood Springs.

He had spent two full days with Art and Chick, soaking his sore bones in the warm mineral waters, revisiting the images, front and rear, of Cassie Waddell in her revealing bathing suit. A lot of people would not soon forget her appearance, especially him. His health had improved greatly and he didn't know whether to be more grateful to the *yampa* in the water or the hormones Cassie had flushed through his system.

But now he had little time to dwell on Cassie Waddell. In a few short hours, Chick and Art would be leaving to take part in the spring roundup, the branding and sorting of the calves and steers loose on the forest range. The cattle had already been pushed into the high country for the warm months, an operation they called the spring shove-up. Despite the dry conditions that had persisted over a number of years, grass had sprouted from minimal snow and a few thunderstorms.

Burke now had an opportunity to account for the numbers

of cattle grazing on the forest reserve during this narrow margin of time when all the cowboys from the area ranches were gathered together and all the stock were bunched in one place. When the roundup was over, the cattle would scatter everywhere again, until they were driven down from the high country in late fall. Burke had a lot of work to do if he wanted to accomplish his task.

As the roofing neared completion, Burke dwelled on the turmoil he had already caused in the area, and that he was sure to cause in the coming weeks. At this point he had no qualms about turning everything totally upside down. After all, that's why he had come in the first place.

Burke's new Buick appeared topping the rise at the edge of the meadow. Jackson Mills sat behind the wheel, smiling as he pulled to a stop in front of the cabin.

Burke had paid young Jackson to drive the car to Denver and have the damage caused by Len Keller repaired, and also to pick up one of the newest technological developments—a typewriter. He had read about their development and use while at Yale and had experimented on one of the earliest designs. He knew that once he had fairly mastered the keyboard, his time spent in correspondence would be greatly reduced.

Jackson had taken two of Bill Conrad's larger cowhands to Denver with him, just in case there were questions about a young black man driving a brand new automobile in a large city all by himself. They had gone back to Conrad's ranch to prepare for the upcoming roundup.

Jackson got out and stood with his hands on his hips. "Looks good, doesn't it?"

Chick and Art circled the Buick. "It looks brand spankin' new," Chick said.

Burke joined them and Jackson said to him, "I didn't have a bit of trouble. Not with them two big cowboys with me."

"Good," Burke said.

"But there is one thing," Jackson said. "I was playing faro and lost the gold spike you gave me."

"You lost it?"

"I got in pretty deep. I'm sorry. It was a gift from you, I know."

Burke had earlier regretted giving the spike away. Now it was too late for regrets.

"Don't worry about it. I appreciate your help, Jackson." He handed Jackson a wad of bills and pointed him to where three horses were contained in a corral. "Pick any one you'd like to ride back down. Just don't take Lancaster."

Jackson smiled. "But he's the best one."

"I know," Burke said.

Jackson had arrived without the two large cowboys, but had brought a woman along with him. She had already gotten out of the vehicle and was dancing around, humming to herself, picking flowers.

"That's Gracie Hill," Jackson said. "She's a friend of Bill's."

Chick and Art smiled. "A friend?" Chick said.

"A friend from Trixie's in Glenwood Springs," Jackson replied. "She came up to see Bill for a while and to look for one of her friends, who came up here with Sid Preston a few weeks back."

Gracie Hill was petite and brunette and filled with love for wildflowers. She brought a handful over and pressed them into Burke's face.

"Did you ever smell anything so sweet?" she asked.

"They're nice," Burke responded. "I'm Ellis Burke."

"Everybody knows who you are," she said. "Bill says that you're the salvation of the grazing lands around here."

Burke ignored the remark. "Did Bill get a count on his cattle for me?"

Gracie reached into the cleavage of her dress and pulled out a slip of paper.

"He said this was pretty close."

"Pretty close which way?" Burke asked, reading figures that totaled a thousand cow-calf pairs and three thousand steers.

"He's brought some more cattle in lately," Burke observed. He tucked the paper into a pocket. "We'll get an accurate tally soon."

"I've been meaning to ask," Art spoke up. "How are you going to count all those cattle yourself?"

"I won't count them myself," Burke replied. "I've hired two men to help me. They should be here sometime tonight."

"Anybody we know?" Chick asked.

Burke shook his head. "They're not from this area."

"So they're friends of yours?" Chick persisted.

"You'll meet them soon, Chick," Burke replied.

Gracie Hill had wandered off to pick more flowers. She returned and said to Burke, "Do you know Sid Preston?"

"As well as I care to know him."

"I understand that he's not a nice man."

"That's putting it mildly."

"Do you think he would be mean to women?"

"He'd be mean to anyone," Burke replied. "I can attest to that."

"That's what I was afraid of," Gracie said. "Do you know where he lives?"

"I assumed he lived in the bunkhouse at the Eden Ranch headquarters," Burke replied.

Chick Campbell said, "No, he lives way the hell and gone up in the high country. It's his secret."

"His secret paradise?" Gracie asked.

"I wouldn't equate him with paradise," Chick said. "Something else, but nothing particularly pretty."

"I warned her," Gracie said. "I told her he wasn't who she thought he was, but she just wouldn't listen. She wanted to live in the wilderness so badly. I need to find her."

Jackson Mills left, riding a horse from the corral. Gracie was once again picking flowers. She had insisted on riding back to town in the Buick, with Burke as her driver. Burke thought he had succeeded in convincing her that he hadn't the time or the inclination to do that kind of favor, that his job demanded his time fully. He had suggested that she ride back down with Chick or Art, if they were willing to drive her. But since neither of them wanted the responsibility, Burke agreed to take her, just as soon as he had finished one more pressing matter.

He removed the new typewriter from the backseat and placed it on a table inside the cabin. Chick and Art followed him, staring at the technological wonder.

"What won't they come up with next?" Chick said. He watched Burke place a piece of paper through the roller and try the machine out. "What are you going to do with that contraption?"

"There are a lot of ranchers in this district and I have to inform them that I will be counting their cattle during the roundup," Burke replied. "This little machine, with the help of my fingers, will turn out a letter for each and every operator. You see, these keys strike the paper and leave a letter mark."

Chick shook his head. "Hard to believe." He pointed to the letters on the paper and said to Art, "Bet if you wrote like that to some lady, and put flowers in the envelope, she'd want you forever." He thought a moment. "But maybe in your case, even that wouldn't work."

"I've had many more and a darn sight prettier women than you'll ever have," Art said. "Didn't you see how they was looking at me down there in Glenwood, in the hot springs?"

"They just wondered how you got in, is all," Chick said.

"No, they wanted to go out with me," Art corrected him. "But I just don't have time for each one of them personally."

"Are you saying you could work things out if they'd come to you in groups?" Chick asked.

"I'd consider it," Art replied. He looked out the window and said, "Where's Gracie?"

The three left the cabin and after calling for her several times, began a search. They split up and took different directions, each calling and watching and climbing hills, covering the area thoroughly. When it became too dark to continue, they reconvened.

"Where the hell'd she go?" Chick asked.

"I hope she hasn't decided to look for her friend," Burke said.

"That would be a damned fool thing to do," Art put in. "But we can't spend no more time looking for her, Chick and I. We've got to get to the roundup."

"Maybe she decided to walk back to town," Burke suggested. "Watch for her on the way down."

Burke set the typewriter on his desk and prepared to write letters to all the big operators. He rolled a piece of paper in, then sat and stared. It wasn't that he didn't know what to say; he was preoccupied with thoughts of Gracie Hill.

He left a note for the two men who would likely show up before long, then took Lancaster from the corral and threw a saddle on. The twilight glowed in the west and the calls of nighthawks filled the calm air. He rode silently through the timber, stopping and dismounting from time to time, leaving Lancaster tied to a branch while he sat beneath the rim of a hill and just listened.

The night was filled with sounds, but there was nothing to suggest a woman had become lost. He rode further in the darkness, crossing over into the next drainage. Eden Creek bubbled merrily, as if there was not a trouble of any kind in this high, forested world.

From atop the mountain came the call of a mountain lion, a form of scream, high and unnerving. It reminded him of his first night and he wondered what Sid Preston and his men were up to and how they planned to make life miserable for him. He smiled to himself. The two men who would arrive soon were no strangers to the likes of Sid Preston and Len Keller. It would be an interesting time when everyone said their hellos.

Burke had just tied Lancaster to a quaking aspen when he heard movement nearby. He crouched and took position, waiting to see if anything moved. He knew that mountain lions liked horseflesh, and that bears would eat anything that moved, especially grizzlies. All bears and cats were certainly at home throughout these mountains.

But instead of a growl, he heard a laugh.

"You afraid of the dark, Mr. Burke?" Cassie Waddell slipped from the shadows and took a seat on a nearby log. "I'm tired of hiking. Think I'll take a rest."

Burke relaxed and sat down, leaning back against the aspen. "Do you always hike this far away from home, at this time of night?" he asked. He noted her dress, but said nothing about it.

"I hike whenever I damn please," she replied. "Tonight I happen to be afoot because I gave my horse away."

She explained how she had been out riding when she had run into Gracie Hill. Gracie had been lost and had stumbled into Cassie.

"I told her to ride my horse down to the ranch and then take another one into town, that I'd be in town tomorrow."

"I often go riding in the dark myself," Burke said. "But tonight I was looking for Gracie Hill, also."

"Are you trying to get her away from Bill Conrad?"

Burke laughed.

"What's so funny? She said that you gave her flowers."

"She gave *me* the flowers," Burke said. "I've never had that happen before."

"So now you want her?"

Burke laughed again. "I don't have time to want anyone. Besides, she's not my type."

"What kind of woman is your type, Mr. Burke?"

"You can just call me Ellis."

"Sure, Ellis." She came over to where he was sitting and

nestled next to him. "You know, you're not all that bad."

"I'm glad to hear that."

"No, I've been thinking about it. I don't believe you ever suggested that my horse couldn't graze in our pastures."

"I'm glad you came to that realization." He couldn't help but stare at her dress, what appeared to be a modified evening gown, or possibly something like the garments worn by the women in establishments like Trixie's in Glenwood Springs. It was colorful and alluring.

"What do you think of my dress?" she asked.

"I like it just fine."

"I still haven't told my mother." She shook her head. "I don't know what's happening to my life. I'm wearing this dress because I decided to tell her that I wasn't just going to college in New York for the same education that she thought, that I was also pleasuring men in the evening. But I just couldn't bring myself to do it, so I put the dress on and went for a ride. I'm afraid she wouldn't understand."

"You might be surprised."

"Do you know what it's like to have the kind of power a prostitute has, the ability to control men as easily as you please? The connections to wealth and power it affords you?"

"How could money be an issue with you?"

"You certainly don't understand, either. My father has no intentions of including me in his empire. He never did have. Instead he's going to combine his holdings with Cross Land and Livestock, the nearest neighbor. He's going to marry Vivian Cross, I'm certain of it, just as soon as mother . . ." She hung her head and began to cry softly. "I'm sorry. I just hate my father so much. I want to get back at him any way I can."

"Nothing to be sorry for," Burke said. He rubbed her back

gently. She leaned into his shoulder and began to cry harder.

Burke let her cry for a short while and asked, "Are you certain of this union between Vivian Cross and your father?"

"They're blatant about it," she replied. "She doesn't even have the decency to stay away until Mother's gone." She wiped her eyes. "He's built a new mansion for the two of them. I can't believe it!" She turned to Burke. "The real reason I'm servicing men is to make enough money to buy the ranch."

"How can you do that?"

"I'm going to bring my father down. I'm going to ruin him."

"That's pretty harsh," Burke said.

"Well, he's ruined everything," she said. "I'm not going to have a mother for much longer and he simply doesn't care."

"Surely that can't be right."

"It is, and I know that for a fact."

Cassie was looking out over the mountains, into the far distance, where streaks of lightning were flashing.

"Another dry year," she said. "More fires."

Burke realized she was trying to keep her mind off her mother.

"Some years ago, a fire burned all summer long," Cassie continued. "No one knows for sure how it started. The powers that be want to blame the Ute Indians, but I say it was hunters who didn't drown their campfire."

"The fire that burned just before I arrived was a bad one," Burke said. "If it hadn't been for that lucky rain, it might still be going."

"Oh, well, let it all burn," Cassie said with a flip of her hand. "My father and people like him are going to destroy this country anyway."

"That concern no longer exists," Burke said.

"Want to bet?" Cassie challenged him. "My father is never going to adhere to a regulation of any kind as long as he lives." She thought a moment. "You don't have any ways of bringing big operators down, now do you?"

"Maybe."

"Then you could help me."

"I don't mean through the forest service." Burke immediately regretted the comment.

"How do you mean, then?"

"I shouldn't be talking like that," Burke said. "I don't like your father, either, but I can't let that interfere with why I'm here."

"Are you working for someone besides the forest service?" she asked.

"I'm a ranger, that's what I do," Burke replied. "Will your father be attending the roundup?"

"I doubt it," Cassie replied. "I'm sure he has plans with Vivian Cross. Len Keller will boss our reps, I imagine."

"I haven't seen Sid Preston for a while," Burke said. "Isn't he the ranch foreman?"

"Supposedly. He's a strange one and I don't like the way he looks at me. He was at the ranch the other day, talking to Father, and left again. They say he likes to be alone, but Father doesn't seem to mind what he does, just so he keeps his empire intact."

"I'd like to know where he is and what he's up to," Burke commented. "He didn't exactly give me a warm welcome."

"I don't like him. I don't like Father. I don't like any of them." She laughed. "I don't know why I'm telling you this. But I've got to tell somebody, and it might as well be you."

"Might as well."

"Everyone else is a stranger," she said.

"I know the feeling."

"You don't seem like a stranger to me," Cassie said. "I find it easy to talk to you."

She leaned over and Burke kissed her, gently at first, then stronger.

"My," she said. "I could enjoy more of that, but I'm sure you're not interested in a lady of the night."

"I don't see you that way."

"Well, I am that way."

13

It was late when Burke returned to his cabin. Cassie Waddell and their recent conversation played heavily on his mind. Afterward, she had abruptly gotten up and had insisted on finishing her walk, despite his repeated attempts to give her a ride back to the ranch. She said she had a lot to think about before the sun rose again and the walk would help her accomplish that.

She had mentioned getting the range ecology lesson he had promised her in the swimming pool at Glenwood Springs, so he had agreed to meet her the following morning where they had left each other. Burke realized that if she stopped to think about his comment about breaking big cattle companies, she might begin to wonder about him and have some questions for him then. He couldn't let that bother him now; he had too much to get done.

He poured kerosene from a can in one corner of his cabin into two lamps and set them on the table. He laid out his typing paper and put the first sheet into the typewriter. He hunted and pecked until he had drawn up the first letter. It read:

May 22, 1905

Mr. Ruben Waddell, Esq.
Eden Land and Livestock Company
Eden, Colorado
Subject: Head count of livestock on forest reserve

Dear Mr. Waddell:

This letter will serve to inform you that as of
next week, your herd will be subject to a head
count, being as accurate as possible, to commence
with the fall shove-down into the lower eleva-
tions. I will supply the personnel to complete the
count and would appreciate it if you would advise your hands to keep the cattle bunched at the
forest boundary until the process is complete.
This effort will benefit all the ranching concerns
using the reserves.

    I thank you for your cooperation.

                    Sincerely,
                    Ellis Burke
                    Acting Supervisor,
                    Eden District

Burke took the paper out of the typewriter and examined it,
then signed it. He had to type the same letter to all the ranchers
using the reserve, some thirty of them. He had gotten an even
dozen completed when he heard horses outside.

    He stood in the doorway, silhouetted by the lantern light,
as two men rode up and dismounted.

This was a visit he had hoped wouldn't come to pass.

"Evening, Ellis," one of them said. He was taller than his companion and raw boned, with hair the color of a rusty can.

"I wrote you not to come," Burke said.

"Aw, now you'd be foolish to think we'd turn this kind of opportunity down."

"I told you in the letter, I'm through with it all."

The shorter one said, "That's not how we see it, and we can make you stick with us."

"He's right," the taller one said.

His name was Red Maynard. Burke had met him while working as a cowhand in Montana and with the help of Dean Lane, the shorter one, had taken a strongbox from a train outside of Helena. The strongbox had contained railroad collectibles bound for a museum in the east.

One of the collectibles had been the golden spike he had given the young man who had helped him at Bill Conrad's hotel.

Burke wished now he hadn't done that. But he seemed to do a lot of things on the spur of the moment, without thinking them through.

Burke had made any number of mistakes during what Bill Conrad referred to as his "rebellious years." He had made a small fortune from robbing trains, enough to put him through college and provide a new automobile. And now he worried not only about Maynard and Lane, but Sid Preston as well.

The day would surely come when Preston would remember where they had met.

Burke had carried a grudge against the railroad from his days as a child. This came after the death of his mother, when he had been forced along on trips with his father and left to fend for himself every evening while his father drank and whored and gambled throughout the various towns, while Ellis was left in the company of railroad-affiliated strangers who made fun of him.

All the while, young Ellis Burke had sworn he would find a way to get back at his father, and the entire railroad as well.

Later, Burke's father had insisted he attend law school and go to work for the railroad. Instead, to spite his father, he had left home to become a cowboy in the Judith Basin of central Montana. There he learned the cattle trade and also discovered that he had a keen interest in the grasslands that were being overrun by Texas longhorns. He wanted to know the kinds of grasses that grew on the range and why there was such a difference in the amount of grass from one location to another, even though the soils and rainfall appeared to be the same.

He had met Maynard and Lane on a trail drive to Miles City. The two outlaws had rustled cattle together before and during the drive, and had stolen some twenty head of cattle from a ranch they had passed along the way, just for the fun of it.

Then Burke had made the mistake of inviting them to rob trains with him.

There had been a lot of close calls during the robberies and Burke had decided he wanted no more outlaw days, especially with Red Maynard and Dean Lane. He had left for college, thinking he would never see them again. But somehow they had gotten his address and had written him frequently, reminding him that he was still a part of their gang.

"The way we see it," Maynard said, pushing past him into the cabin, "you can show us where all the steers are and we'll take it from there."

"I told you, I'm not interested," Burke said.

"Oh, but you are interested." Maynard had turned and was glaring at him. "You'd better not push us."

"Another thing," Lane put in. "You should think twice before bedding down with a big rancher's daughter."

Maynard was smiling. "We saw you with her. Real sweet, is she?"

"You two were watching me?" Burke asked.

"Just stay away from her," Maynard said. "It causes complications."

"You two aren't going to dictate my life," Burke said.

Maynard walked up to Burke and pulled a picture from his pocket.

"This is your daddy, and he's real mad at you anyway, for going to school on his name and not becoming a railroad lawyer. What do you think he's going to say if he learns you also robbed his trains?"

Burke rode into town to mail the letters to the ranchers and then met Cassie on the slopes above the Eden ranch just before noon. She was wearing a dress similar in fashion to the one she had had on the night before, complete with a split skirt for ease in horseback riding.

"You seemed pleased with the way I looked last night," she said. "I thought you might be able to teach me some things."

"About grasses and grazing management?" he said.

"Of course," Cassie replied.

She wanted to show him a hidden pasture located a short distance from the main ranch. She mentioned that her father hadn't moved the cattle from the pasture to be included in the total count of Eden livestock using the forest reserve.

"He doesn't believe you'll ever know about them," she said.

As they rode, Burke showed her an area where the natural grass had been used minimally by elk and cattle, a location far from water. The grass made up nearly two-thirds of the composition while flowers and small, scattered stands of brush made up the rest. The grass was tall and lush, even though the mountains had suffered a number of dry years in a row.

"This is called 'pristine condition,'" Burke told her. "The types of vegetation growing here are at their climax, the best you can expect for the soils and rainfall, and other factors."

Cassie watched the stalks of various forms of fescue and wheat grass and native bluegrass blow in the wind.

"It is a beautiful sight," she said.

"You can't expect the grass to stay like this close to the rivers and streams," Burke pointed out. "Livestock hang out around water. But hopefully in the future, there will be ways to get water to locations like this and spread the grazing out."

The closer they got to Eden Creek, the more the vegetation changed. The high, lush grass was sparse and the amounts of sagebrush, especially, grew in density.

"The idea is to allow enough grazing to keep the grass harvested, but not overuse it," Burke said. "These areas evolved under grazing pressure from elk and buffalo, but they moved around, allowing the grass to recover after use. As more and more cattle come in, there's less and less space for them to graze in."

"Father should know this," Cassie said.

"I think all the ranchers know it," Burke said. "Most of them want what's best for the land, but there are those who really don't care."

"I wish Father would stop thinking he has to have the biggest ranch around and the most cattle," Cassie said. "He's definitely one who really doesn't care what he's doing out here."

"Have you ever spoken to him about it?"

"He wouldn't listen to me if his life depended on it," Cassie said.

They rode down off a high ridge through sagebrush that reached past their horses' bellies. The cover was extremely thick and very little grass grew underneath. The sea of blue-gray extended down across the bottom and up toward the timber on the other side, as far as the eye could travel.

Scattered across the slopes were spotted longhorn cattle, their tales switching at flies. They moved continuously in search of grass, finding very little in any direction they went.

"Those are Father's prize longhorns, from the early stock brought up from Texas," Cassie said. "Not really in the prize category, if you ask me."

"They look pretty lanky," Burke agreed, "but that's their nature."

"I've seen them when they were fat," Cassie said. "A number of years ago. But he's so worried about someone stealing them, his wonderful icons of the past. He keeps them locked in here with that jackleg fence and there's just not enough to eat."

Burke realized that the overgrazing problem was severe. It was evident to anyone who had two eyes and common sense.

"When I was a little girl, this area had grass as tall as the sagebrush is now," Cassie said. "Just like farther back along the hill. There was some sage growing here and there, only about one-fourth of what you see now. Now the area has been trampled so badly there aren't even any flowers."

"Think of it like a smorgasbord," Burke explained. "The big grasses are like steak, or even ice cream. Horses and cattle will eat them off first and if they don't have a chance to grow back, they die. Smaller grasses and flowers and sage take the place of the big grasses and if the grazing pressure continues, the smaller grasses begin to die out. Pretty soon, if it's bad enough, you have various kinds of brush and prickly plants and grasses that livestock won't eat. It's nature's way of covering the soil with something, anything. The trouble is, when the range is too bad, there's no way to stop wind or water erosion and you lose it all."

"Can it ever get back to pristine again?"

"There may be some seed source left," Burke said. "But it would take a long time with proper management."

"You can forget that," Cassie said. "We're talking about my father."

"This area is within the forest reserves," Burke pointed out. "He will be forced to remove his personal fence and herd the longhorns out of here."

Cassie smiled. "I can't wait to tell him that."

14

They rode further and Burke pointed out where the topsoil had washed away along the sides and bottom of the meadow, leaving gullies that were growing deeper with each passing year. They dismounted and he showed her where even the sagebrush plants were having a hard time. The problem was so severe that erosion had exposed parts of the upper root system.

"I'm sorry I even came out here," Cassie said. "I'm sorry I've been anywhere around here and had to see this. I should just stay home with Mother and forget about what's happening out here."

Burke selected a sagebrush plant where a tall grass was growing up from the middle, clinging to life.

"Maybe there's hope here yet," he said. "The cattle can't get their noses in there to graze. That's one way of surviving."

"No, in time he'll just ruin it all," she said.

"But it's important that you see this and understand what it means," Burke told her. "You can be of some influence when the allotments are discussed."

"If my father has his way, there will be no allotments."

"Oh, there will be allotments," Burke said. "For cattle and sheep as well."

Cassie laughed. "Haven't you heard what they did to the sheepmen who came in here?"

"I heard. There's always been trouble over sheep. They do graze a range harder than cattle, but that's no excuse for the big ranchers to claim everything for themselves."

"You're right, there are some ranchers who want the change," Cassie said. "But they won't speak up, not against their own."

"I attended a meeting not long ago," Burke said. "Your father attempted to divide the membership. Not many sided with him."

"But Lee Miller was one of them, wasn't he?" Cassie said. "Miller and Sid Preston will see to it that Father gets his way." She patted her horse's neck. "You've got quite a challenge ahead of you."

"I'll get it done," Burke said.

They rode out from Rube Waddell's overgrazed pasture, across the ridge and into rangeland in far better condition, through a segment of oak and ponderosa pine and then higher to a remote mountainside where a natural spring flowed out of a hill filled with quaking aspens. The branches were filled with birds, large and small, and of various colors, some of them very curious.

"Those are chickadees," Cassie said, pointing out the little hopping birds with the black-topped heads that chitted in the branches near them. "They love to talk."

She dismounted and led her horse to the spring. Burke followed her. When the animals had drunk their fill, Burke and Cassie removed the bridles and allowed them to graze on picket.

"This has always been one of my favorite places," Cassie said. "I can see that the grazing pressure has gotten heavier here over the years."

"The allotments will allow all areas like this to maintain a good cover," Burke promised.

"I hope you're right," Cassie said, gazing across the mountains. Tears began to form in her eyes. "Once Mother came up here with me, just before I left for New York."

"Maybe she would like to see this place again," Burke suggested. "It would do her good."

"That's a good idea," Cassie agreed. "She's been wanting to go for a ride."

Burke reached down and plucked a small flower, a mountain bluebell.

"Here's something to wear on your dress," Burke said, handing her the flower.

She took his hand and placed the flower in his palm. "Would you do the honors, please?"

Burke smiled and selected a buttonhole midway between her neck and her bustline.

She stopped him. "A little lower, if you don't mind. I think it would look better, don't you?"

Burke's eyes traveled down to her breasts. She placed her hands on his hips and smiled while he decided where to place the flower. He undid a few more buttons to expose more cleavage and leaned into her lips. She encircled him with her arms, pulling him tightly into her.

They moved to a grassy area within the aspens. The warm sun shone through the branches and Burke trailed kisses from her neck to her breasts, pulling her dress down, gently rubbing her back and stomach. She in turn began kissing him along his neck and chest, running her hands up and down his legs while she peeled off his shirt.

"Are you going to teach me more, professor?" she asked.

"Maybe we can teach each other," he suggested.

"This is the best class I've ever attended," Cassie said, pulling off his pants.

Gracie Hill lay in bed next to Bill Conrad, listening to his explanation of where her friend Lottie Burns had disappeared to.

"You know as well as I do that the girls from Trixie's come and go all the time. Who knows where she went."

"I told you, she left with Sid Preston."

"And my point is, why would she want to stay with him?"

"I don't know why she even left with him," Gracie said. "But she did. And I want to find her."

Conrad lit a cigar. "I don't want you out looking for her again. Understood?" He blew out a plume of smoke.

"You don't understand, Bill," Gracie said. "She was a good friend. I mean, *is* a good friend. I don't know why I said it that way."

"You stay with me from now on," he insisted. "You pull a stunt like that again and I'll send you back to Glenwood Springs."

Gracie climbed out of bed and began dressing.

"What do you think you're doing?" Conrad asked.

"What does it look like, Bill? I don't like what you're saying and I won't be told I can't look for Lottie."

"I mean it, Gracie," Conrad said. "I'll send you back."

"You can send me back after I find Lottie. We'll go back together."

Conrad climbed out of bed and grabbed her arm. "I won't allow you to go."

Gracie tried to pull away. "Bill, let go."

"Promise me you won't go looking for Lottie."

"Okay, Bill," she said, "If you don't want a lot of screaming and hollering coming from this room, you'll let me go right now. I'm serious."

Conrad became visibly angry, and clutched her even tighter.

"You're going to do as I say, and I don't care how loud you scream."

For the first time in their relationship, Gracie felt fear. She hadn't challenged him before this, about anything, and it startled her to see his reaction.

"Do you intend to hit me?" she asked.

Conrad released her and took a deep breath. "I just don't like back talk, is all."

Gracie rubbed her arm. "I never knew you could be like this."

"I'm sorry. I just don't want you doing this. Sometimes your judgement isn't all that good."

"Maybe my judgement isn't good, if I stay with you," she muttered. She realized that she had made a huge mistake. His eyes grew wide.

"But I'll stay with you, Bill," she said, "and we can start over. How's that?"

Bill nodded. "Good, we'll start over," he said.

Gracie looked into the ceiling and beyond, far into the distance of her mind, while Bill Conrad rode her, huffing and puffing and straining to reach a climax. She had gone over to Trixie's to be with Lottie again, back in time, when they had shared a fun evening off by themselves on the roof, counting stars and making wishes.

She wished she could be on that roof with her friend just once more, just long enough to have made a certain wish. Had it come true, Lottie would still be at Trixie's.

Gracie whispered into Conrad's ear, pronouncing him the greatest lover she had ever known. His breath quickened.

After their argument, she had shared a couple of drinks with him, promising to be good and do as she was told, and had gotten him aroused.

He had always taken good care of her and had paid very well, but she didn't want any part of a big man who lost his temper so easily, especially over a matter such as Lottie Burns. Had his friend been lost somewhere, he would go searching, no questions asked.

Gracie continued to talk to him and Conrad finally reached the top, letting out a huge grunt. Gracie worked her fingertips along his back and sides, urging him along. He fell on her, exhausted, and rolled to one side.

After a few minutes, when she was certain he was asleep, she dressed and eased toward the door.

He sat up in bed.

Gracie watched and waited. No need to panic. He often sat up in his sleep, as if he had forgotten to take care of something, but just couldn't awaken himself to get it done. When he had settled back down again, she unlocked the door and stepped through.

Sid Preston danced with tattered remnants of Lottie Burns's dress. Sticky with fresh blood, they adhered to his naked body as he waltzed through the dead trees and grave sites, holding his hunting knife tightly against his genitals. Although the event could never be as fulfilling as having the ultimate favor done for him, it was nonetheless adequate to sustain him for the time being.

Lottie Burns had been no different than the others, not after he had begun his work with the knife. At first she had acted as if she weren't there at all. He noticed this about nearly everyone that he had killed; they had gone somewhere before he had even started working on them.

He could understand it. He liked to go places, too, and did so a lot, especially when he spent time in the graveyard.

Far away or close by, he could go wherever he wanted, and take pieces of the women in the graveyard with him.

He often envisioned carrying a heart, floating through a dense black fog, headed toward a distant place where seats were filled with blurry images who applauded his arrival. He would carry the heart, actively beating, for all of them to see. They loved it, watching him come with the heart, but none of them ever stepped forward to touch the heart, not even when he tried to reach them.

They always remained a good distance away, in their opera seats, applauding, moving just enough so that he could never reach them. He had decided he would manage to reach them one day and find out why they didn't have any faces.

Preston continued to dance with the bloody clothing, remembering Lottie Burns's last moments. Like all the others, she had come back for the last few minutes of her life.

They had all come back eventually. They had to come back, to die. That's how it worked: They couldn't get off so easily as to float away without being forced to pull free of the pain first.

No, they couldn't stay away from what he was doing to them throughout it all. They had to come back and scream and moan before they actually left and went on their own separate journey.

It was this period of the event that he always waited for. The screams and moans and sobs were what brought him where he wanted to be. It was that realization that their bodies were holding to the last threads of life that urged him to finish his work quickly.

For it was after the work was done and they had struggled for the last time that he could finally reach that peak he looked forward to each time he made a special collection.

Vivian Cross stood at the edge of her husband's grave site and urged Rube Waddell to dig faster.

"I've hit the coffin," he said. "I just have to dig around it."

"Don't bother with that," Vivian said. "Just open it up and pull him out."

The sun had fallen completely and twilight had invaded the forest. Shadows moved with a slight breeze that touched the high trees all around.

Waddell looked in all directions as he pried the lid off the coffin with a hammer.

"I still don't think this is necessary," he said.

Vivian kneeled down and shone a lantern on her husband's dark and rotting face.

"See, I told you," she said. "He can see us."

Waddell turned away. "For God's sake, Vivian."

"Take the hammer and pry his mouth open," she said. "Hurry."

"Really, Vivian . . ."

"You promised, Rube, so let's get it done and be gone."

Waddell worked the claws of the hammer into Byron Cross's mouth and Vivian poured poisonous tea from her pitcher into the dark cavity. The liquid welled up and spilled out onto his molding clothes.

"Is that enough?" Waddell asked her.

"A little more." When she was finished, she said, "Get rid of the lid and we'll put this piece of hose in his mouth. Then you can fill the grave in."

As Waddell moved the coffin lid, he heard a noise from just under the hill.

"Blow out the lantern," he told Vivian.

"Rube, we're not finished."

"Blow out the goddamned lantern!" he hissed.

She obeyed and crawled to his side.

"Stay here and don't say a word," Waddell said. "I mean it."

Vivian lay still next to her husband's grave, trying not to breathe. She heard a horse come up onto the hill and a rider dismount.

No doubt it was Shorty Walsh, the foreman, who never missed a day visiting the grave, apparently even during roundup.

Vivian wanted to move, but was frozen to the spot. Shorty Walsh came ever closer and was about to strike a lantern when she cried, "Rube, where are you?"

Shorty Walsh dropped the lantern and said, "What the hell?" Before he could recover, Rube Waddell stepped up behind him and fired a .44 caliber Colt's Army revolver into his ear. He dropped like a stone.

"Don't ever leave me alone like that again," Vivian wailed.

Waddell wasn't listening. He stood frowning over Shorty Walsh's body.

"Are you listening?" Vivian cried.

"I told you this would be trouble," Waddell said.

"Just pull Byron out of the casket and set Shorty down in there. Then lay Byron on top. Do it."

Waddell had to admit it wasn't a bad idea. When the work was done and the tube inserted into Byron Cross's mouth, she held it in place while Waddell filled dirt in around the bodies.

He tamped the soil as firm as he could and said, "Are you satisfied now?"

"I don't want any more dreams," she told him. "Never again."

15

He watched from just beneath the top of the ledge, getting a clear view of the vast country below, yet certain not to be detected himself. He had lived in these mountains a good many years and had seen changes come, many that had brought him anger and sorrow, along with a feeling of helplessness. After all, he was but a solitary individual in a huge and remote wilderness where only the strong survived.

He could only hope that the bad was weeded out over time. From where he now rested, watching the very top of the high country above Eden Creek, he had seen the man bring a number of women up to that place and where they went after that, he had no way of knowing, for no one else ever went up there.

In his lifetime he had seen the open wilderness broken by mining and cattle trails—and now railroad tracks—bringing ever more people into an area that had once known only the Ute and then the mountain man. He had known the Utes well and had married one of them, and had come to realize that nothing but the earth and sky lasts forever. Who was he to tell them all to leave?

His concern centered on what those people might do to a pristine wilderness that bore so much fruit they didn't know what to do with it. Likely, after stripping it bare, they would move on to another pristine wilderness and follow the same pattern of destruction.

By that time he would be dead and gone. Until then, he would hold his own and weep.

Burke rode back to his cabin, wondering when he might see Cassie Waddell again. She had told him that she wanted him to come to the ranch and be with her and her mother. He didn't believe that was much of an idea and he told her he had to tally cattle at the roundup. He might come for a short visit after the work was finished, if her father happened to be away on business.

He dismounted and tied Lancaster to the same tree he always tied him to, an aspen just outside the door. Lancaster acted funny, his interest on something inside the cabin.

It was near dark and the shadows had lengthened considerably. Burke thought he heard a noise inside and stepped to one side of the door as it opened.

Out stepped Gracie Hill.

"Mr. Burke, I thought you'd never arrive."

"Why are you here, Gracie?"

"I want you to help me find Lottie."

Burke took her inside, lit a lantern, and sat her down in a chair at his table.

"You have a nice bed," she said. "I fell fast asleep."

"Gracie, you must understand. I don't have time to help you."

Gracie rubbed sleep from her eyes. "But you're the only one who can."

"What about Bill Conrad, or one of his hands? Chick Campbell or Art Gilory would be willing to help you."

"No, no," Gracie said. "Bill wants to send me back to Glenwood Springs."

"Not a bad idea."

"I won't go, not until I find Lottie."

"Did you ever consider that she might have left the area? Maybe gone to Rawlins or Bags, or down to the southwest country?"

"Lottie told me she wanted me to come visit one day," Gracie said. "She wouldn't do that if she didn't intend to stay."

"Did she notify you that she wanted you to come?"

"How many post offices are in these mountains?" Gracie asked.

"She could have mailed you something from Eden, if she'd wanted to."

Gracie stood up. "I don't like your attitude, Mr. Burke. I'll just find her on my own."

Burke settled her down. "You can't go anywhere tonight." He persuaded her to lie back down on the bed. "Get a good night's sleep and we'll talk again in the morning."

"Are you going to sleep with me?"

"No. I've got a sleeping bag, and my tent's still up." He sat down on the bed and took her hand. "You must care a great deal for Lottie Burns."

Gracie began to cry. "We came out from St. Louis on a wagon, Lottie and me and some other girls. We followed the railroads for a while and then we went to the cow camps. Lottie said we could do a lot better in a town somewhere, maybe get work at a good house with plenty of warm blankets. We went to Denver and then to Glenwood Springs. We talked all the time. We shared everything."

"I'm sorry," Burke said. "I hope you find her."

Burke and Gracie both looked up as the door opened. Red Maynard walked in.

"Don't you ever knock?" Burke asked.

Maynard smiled crookedly. "Three's a crowd? How about sharing?"

"What do you want?" Burke asked.

"Since you're the big ranger hereabouts," Maynard said, "maybe you'd ought to know that a lot of cowhands are looking for you right now. Everyone's in camp and roundup starts at three A.M."

The rangeland below the new forest reserves boundary was filling quickly with cattle. The major stockmen had sent their representatives to take care of the branding for them and cowboys from all over lounged around evening campfires, readying themselves for the following morning when the work would begin in earnest.

Burke sat with Red Maynard and Dean Lane in their own camp. The two men stitched loose stirrups and otherwise repaired their tack in preparation for the coming days in the saddle. While they worked, Burke organized his inventory supplies for the following morning. He had brought a number of pencils and notepads, and some wooden shingles to use as signs, each one with the brand of a different operator burned into it with a running iron.

Burke had devised a system by which he could get a reasonable count on the thousands of cattle that would be entering the forest. He had made a list of every brand and whether it was located on the left or the right side of the animal. Red Maynard would take position on one side of a small draw and Dean Lane would take the other. The banded animals would pass between them in single file and depending on which side the brand existed, one or the other would hold up a sign for Burke, and he would record it.

It was already obvious to Burke that Eden Land and Livestock, together with a number of other large outfits, had far more cattle than their permits allowed. This necessitated making a very accurate count and adjusting the grazing numbers for each permit before the fall shove-down. Burke realized that he would be too busy with his work to direct Maynard and Lane to any degree, so they would be free to steal whatever cattle they chose, and he would have to rely on them to give him his fair cut.

He wondered now why he hadn't parted with them after the train robbery near Rawlins, in southern Wyoming. The two had gotten careless, nearly costing them the loot they had stolen, plus being caught and jailed. Luckily, there had been but one man who had tried to stop them and when the shooting had started, his horse had bucked him off, nearly knocking him unconscious.

Burke had had to stop Maynard from shooting him needlessly. Later, while hiding in the Hole in the Wall, Maynard had said that he had been wrong in wanting to kill just for the sake of killing, and that he wouldn't make the same mistake again.

But Burke hadn't believed him. He probably had killed someone—up in Wyoming or Montana, or the Dakotas, and now they were on the run.

Lane had commented the night before that they were in good country, good and big, so no one could be easily found. When Burke had asked if they were being chased for something, he hadn't answered, and Maynard wouldn't even discuss the subject.

Now Burke's feelings about them grew from bad to worse. The two were spoiling for a fight. It seemed they had taken the stance that should the local cowhands threaten them in any way,

they would act in whatever fashion they saw fit to protect themselves.

In the beginning, his association with them had been his
own fault. Now he wanted to rid himself of them and they were
clinging to him like rotten meat.

Red Maynard set his saddle at the head of his bedroll and pulled
his pistol from its holster. He began cleaning it, staring at Burke
while he worked.

"You didn't tell us how hostile some of these outfits are
toward you," he said. "Maybe you'd ought to be better armed."

"I didn't come for a gunfight."

"It could turn out that way," Maynard said. "I wish I was
better prepared."

"You're carrying two revolvers and a rifle," Burke said.
"What more do you need?" And to Lane, "Why are you wearing
a bandolier of bullets?"

"I side with Red. I don't plan to take any chances with this
bunch, either," he replied.

"I want it made clear," Burke told them. "Under no circum-
stances are either of you to open fire on anyone."

"And just who made you the king?" Maynard demanded.

"We decided that I would set everything up and direct the
two of you to the best pickings," Burke said. "Remember?"

"I think things have changed some," Lane put in.

"Yeah, I agree," said Maynard. "Things were different before
you took up schooling in the East. Now things are a lot different,
since you became a big ranger and turned soft." Then he added,
"And just how many women do you need at one time?"

"What kind of question is that?" Burke said.

"It's legitimate," Lane put in. "We didn't figure you brought us here to do the work alone."

"And I didn't know you two had already decided how the work would be done," Burke said.

"We don't see a future in playing favorites," Maynard said. "The way it turns out, Eden is losing a lot of stock as it is."

Burke studied him. "What are you saying?"

Maynard moved closer, so no one in the surrounding cattle camps could hear him.

"Eden cowhands are stealing Eden cattle," he said. "You'd know that if you were out working instead of playing."

"Are you sure?"

Lane said, "We both saw it ourselves. Three of them. They came right from the Eden bunkhouse, because we watched them."

"We were going to pick some steers from the same bunch they did," Maynard added. "They beat us to them."

Burke sat and thought. "You sure there weren't four of them?"

Maynard raised his left hand. "I've been counting on these first three fingers all my life."

"Did they see you?" Burke asked them.

Maynard and Lane both shook their heads. "We stayed in cover. But they were right out in the open, as big as you please."

Len Keller sat with Jeb Mason and Burt Gamble, finishing their plates of beef and beans. The rest of the Eden cowhands had eaten earlier and were arranging their bedrolls for the night.

"I don't know if I can sleep all that well," Keller was saying, a smirk on his face, "knowing that Burke has brought a couple of gunhands in here to work with him."

"I didn't know the forest service hired that kind," Mason said. "But I ain't scared of them."

"Nobody's afraid of them," Keller said. "I'd like to see them try something."

"You don't want to go causing no trouble," Burt Gamble warned. "That's just what they want. It will give them an excuse to cut grazing numbers back even farther."

"That's not how they work," Keller said. "They count the grass, or something like that. It's got nothing to do with gunplay. Or it isn't supposed to."

"I wish Preston was here," Mason said. "He didn't say Burke would have a couple of gunhands with him. I wonder what he would do."

Burt Gamble poured himself a cup of coffee and said, "Preston's not been doing his job of late. He's been slack for over a year now, I'd say." He slurped from the cup, satisfied with his observation, settling back as if he'd gotten something off his chest.

The other two rarely agreed with Gamble and usually saw him as overbearing in his ways, too close-minded to be working with them. They had even suggested he look into getting off the range and spending his time with other broken-down cowhands in the saloons and hotels of Denver.

But this time they both turned to him and nodded.

"I wonder what he does with all his time," Mason said.

"That might be something to look into," Keller said.

16

Burke sat on Lancaster, tallying steers that passed by Maynard and Lane. They had discussed how their own operations would be carried out now that they were in competition with Sid Preston and his men. Maynard said he believed that the big outfits wouldn't be any easier to hit than the smaller operators and that anyone's steers should be fair game. Burke argued that they had to stick to a plan and not go off on a tangent. Losing focus would bring about mistakes, which would lead to their discovery.

And he was sticking to his viewpoint that the smaller operators in particular shouldn't be bothered. They would discover the stock missing almost immediately, and they would be more apt to go out looking for the culprits who had caused the damage.

With the Eden outfit losing stock already, it was going to be difficult to take more without causing suspicion, and the thought of whittling into Bill Conrad's Rocker 9 collection of fat steers seemed less and less a certainty, what with Conrad so interested in his past and Chick Campbell and Art Gilroy at his side a goodly amount of the time.

That should change after roundup. Not that he cared to take stock from Bill Conrad; the man had been far too generous. The end of roundup meant that Chick and Art would be busy trailing cattle to one of the stockyards along the main railroad line due south. That would give him time to do his range surveys and also scout out the areas that would serve them the best for easing into various herds.

But selecting the steers and moving them and doing it all without detection was going to be a huge challenge. Everything had seemed so much simpler and easier to arrange at first, when there had been no faces attached to the outfits, no Cassie or Chick or Art, no Bill Conrad with his detective mentality.

And no Sid Preston, with his little gang of thieves and his own little empire, and his secret ways that no one seemed quite willing to realize or look into. Someone was always up to something they wanted to keep private and everyone in these parts let well enough alone—live and let live, as it were—until a problem surfaced in their backyard.

Burke continued to mark brands down. They had been at it since just after dawn and Maynard and Lane had quickly tired of their work. Burke had to remind them repeatedly that if they wanted to appear to be forest service employees, they should act the part.

"How many more head do we have to count?" Maynard asked during a break.

"We'll be here until they get finished branding," Burke said. "That will be at least a week. But I told you that, so why all the complaints?"

Maynard leaned over the saddle. "I came here to count money, not a bunch of steers in a dusty draw."

"You'll have time for the money part," Burke said. "Just see this through."

By late afternoon, two of the larger outfits had pushed most of their cattle past Maynard and Lane. Burke had already counted over four thousand steers and he knew that easily eight to ten times that number were still left to be tallied.

A majority of the Eden stock had also been branded and Burke spoke to Len Keller about starting them through the draw for counting.

"I don't want to move them until Sid Preston gets here," Keller said.

"When's he coming?" Burke asked.

"Maybe by tonight, I don't know," Keller replied. "Why don't we just push them up on the reserves and count them another time?"

Burke shook his head. "They'll be counted before they go on."

"I don't know how long it will take Preston to get here. You don't want us to hold up the other outfits, now do you?"

"You won't hold anybody up," Burke said. "You'll just have to drive all the Eden stock back down."

"We're not going to do that."

"They're not going on the reserves without being counted."

"You're damned hard to deal with," Keller said.

"None of the other outfits have come to me with this kind of problem," Burke pointed out. "Maybe your bunch suffers from a lack of good management."

Keller stood up in the stirrups. "I don't take kindly to that remark."

"Are you going to get your cattle counted, or just waste time?" Burke asked.

"Get your men ready," Keller said.

Burke had been counting for ten or fifteen minutes when Maynard and Lane began yelling. Eden cattle began pouring down the gulch in large bunches, filling the draw and forcing Maynard and Lane to retreat or be trampled. When the steers had passed and the dust had cleared, Len Keller appeared with a smirk on his face.

"Damn! They got away from us," he said.

"That's your problem, not mine," Burke told him. "I estimate about a thousand head went by, and the number will go against your permit allowance."

"What! There weren't more than three or four hundred head in that bunch. We'll round them up and you'll see."

"Too late," Burke said. "There's other outfits waiting to be counted. A thousand head, Keller. Tell Preston and Waddell."

"You son of a bitch!"

"Easy, Mr. Stupid Stunt. You don't want to do something else real foolish. We're not as nice as Mr. Burke." Maynard had ridden up, along with Lane.

"I don't need you two here," Burke told them. "Get back in the draw and get ready for the next bunch."

"Yeah, you can handle this guy," Lane put in. "He's just learning to ride his first pony."

Keller was aflame with rage. "What are you trying to get away with here, Burke?"

"You should keep better control of your steers," Burke said. "I'll bet it won't happen again."

Keller was glaring. "There might be other things happening."

"You'd better get back with your outfit," Burke advised. "And I hope you didn't suggest running steers through the draw to anyone else. Any more stock that we can't count, the tally goes against your numbers. Got it?"

. . .

Gracie Hill wandered through the forest. She had long ago
stopped calling out for Lottie, realizing that the mountains were
far too vast and she would lose her voice before anyone heard
her.

She had slept late in Ellis Burke's cabin. She had been so
tired and the bed had felt so comfortable that sleep had meant
everything to her. She had awakened well into the morning and
after petting the horses in the corral for a while, and feeding
them handfuls of grass, she had decided to begin her mission to
find her friend. Burke wasn't going to return any time soon to
help her and going back to Bill Conrad wasn't an option.

She remembered the trail where she had met Cassie Waddell
and decided to take a different route, one that would lead more
directly into the remote back country. She hadn't found Lottie
during the first search and any paradise her friend might be
living in had to exist a good distance away from the main trails.

The sun was descending toward the west, making visibility
in the deep timber more difficult. She had no idea where she was
or where she was going, only that she had to be getting ever
closer to the paradise Lottie had so desparately wanted to find.
It seemed odd to her that a paradise should have so much rock
and dense timber, and seemed to be so alive with creatures she
couldn't see. Any number of elk and deer had stood and watched
her, as if asking where she thought she was going, and she realized that there were many more animals of different kinds that
must be aware of her presence.

The darker it became, the more she realized that her idea
had been a bad one. Yet somehow she seemed to sense that Lottie

Burns was somewhere near. The paradise couldn't be far ahead now and if she had to lie down and sleep through the night, she would, so that she could continue her search the next morning, no matter how difficult it became.

Rube Waddell stood with Vivian at her husband's grave site, holding the lantern. She had transplanted her collection of plants back on the grave, arranging them neatly around the area where the top of the hose stuck up through the dirt.

She had finished pouring the tea down the tube and now moved her fingers through the plants, caressing them, picking some of the stems and leaves and placing them in a small brown handbag.

"I want you to transfer these to your special black bowl when you get them home," she said. "Then go to your own garden and pick some more."

"How long do we have to be here?" Waddell asked her.

"Stop worrying and listen to my instructions," she said. "You must keep the soil damp at all times. That means watering daily, morning and night, without fail. You do have your garden in partial shade, don't you?"

"Yes, it's hidden up along the creek."

"That will help with evapotranspiration."

"Yes, I suppose it will." He had no idea what she meant. She was always rambling on about plants and their physiological makeup, information she had learned by continuously reading botany texts. He could see no practical application to any of it.

"You don't allow anyone else access to your garden, do you?" she asked.

"Are you asking if Cassie knows where it is? She hasn't found it yet."

"Good. Be careful, but just keep it watered."

"It's getting to be a burden, Vivian."

"Rube, it has to be that way, you know, for the little angels to work like they must. You cannot miss a watering."

"Maybe you should be over there, watering those plants instead of these," Waddell suggested. "Isn't this a waste of time?"

"Rube Waddell, do you know what you're saying?"

"Yes, I'm saying my plants need more care than these. That's the reality of it."

Vivian had become visibly angry. She stood up. "How dare you!"

"I thought we took care of things, with the tube and all."

"He's a strong man, Rube."

"I don't know what you saw, but I doubt if it was him."

"I don't care what you say or what you think. I know what I must do here."

"Vivian, like I told you the other night, this is not the same as pouring tea down him when he was alive."

"Listen, I thought I made all this clear to you."

"Nothing is very clear at this point, Vivian."

"What's the matter? Are you saying to want to call everything off?"

"Of course not. But I believe our time would be better served getting all the papers in order so that the wedding can take place as soon as Charlotte dies."

"I'm glad you brought that up," Vivian said. "So why hasn't she died yet?"

"She doesn't want to."

"Does she really have cancer?"

"I don't know for sure," he replied. "The doctor in Denver told her that she had numerous lumps in her right breast, and that's when I started mixing the plants for her tea. She started feeling more and more sickly, so I don't know if it's the tea or the cancer. But I've spread the news that she's dying."

Vivian smiled. "Good. But we have to continue being careful. We can't kill her overnight. I'm told that cancer can take a person quickly, so if you will just mix these leaves with some from your own little angel flowers, you will be set. Measure the daily amounts as I have instructed and then continue to serve your wife nice hot cups of tea, three times a day."

He had been watching her for some time, ever since he had noticed her far below, making her way up the mountain. Gracie Hill was a long way from Bill Conrad's swank bed. He hadn't expected her, but she would do.

He had noticed her earlier in the afternoon, while scanning the forest for movement of any kind. He never allowed his binoculars or his Sharps rifle to get very far from him, especially now that his collections were coming closer and closer together, now that his special paradise was growing in size. There had been a time in the past when the collections could be two or maybe three months apart. That wasn't the case any longer; now he needed to work on a woman at least once a month, and maybe more.

It was important that he find the right one, the one that would impart the special favor.

He had often dreamed of it, feeling the cold steel enter his intestines while plunging a separate blade into the woman's midsection. He yearned to be able to do that, to mix their blood and entrails together, to reach inside one another and become one.

That would be happening soon. The right one would be arriving and he didn't need people who had nothing to do with his desires coming up the mountain, looking around, wandering into his domain.

There were getting to be more and more of them, these wandering people, especially since the forest service had come into being. A few days previous he had seen two men watching Keller, Mason, and Gamble as they cut out fifty steers and started them toward a box canyon they used for holding. He had followed, watching the two men from a distance, knowing they had a good idea what Keller and the other two were doing.

He didn't know if the two strangers were forest service, or where they had come from. They couldn't have wandered into the area by accident. They were around for a purpose.

He fully expected Ellis Burke to show himself before long, but likely not until the roundup had finished. Then he would begin his grass and forest surveys in earnest, eager to accomplish his outlandish goals and put the entire livestock industry on its ear.

Something that Mark Jones hadn't accomplished, and something that Burke wouldn't, either.

Mark Jones. The missing ranger that no one would ever find. If luck would have it a second time around, Burke would go for a long ride in the wilderness and never return.

. . .

He continued to watch Gracie Hill work her way hesitantly through the timber. She was alone and afraid, and that's how he liked them. She would be an easy catch.

Yes, she would do, at least for the time being. His best catch was yet to come. The best woman he could ever hope to collect was home again, fighting with her father, weeping over her dying mother, and wandering the mountains like a lost child.

This was a woman he had dreamed of for some time, and she just might be the one to do him the special favor.

To collect her, the conditions would have to be just right. Charlotte Waddell would have to be dead, so that Cassie's disappearance wouldn't seem all that unusual. It was no secret how fundamentally tied to her mother she had become. It would come as no surprise to anyone that after her mother's death, Cassie would have tendencies toward suicide.

There had been rumors of her during her younger years, standing at the edges of cliffs, looking far into the bottom. That had happened when she had been jilted by Lincoln Prescott, and then again just before her departure for New York. Certainly after her mother's last days, she would be searching for a place to die herself.

Preston had already picked out the bull elk he would use for Cassie, a huge monarch with eight tines on each side, a massive animal that each and every fall was the ruler of a huge herd on Waddell Mountain. The bull was just waiting, ready to become part of the collection, ready to embrace Cassie Waddell.

There was no telling how long that would be, though, and he needed to make another collection as soon as possible. His yearnings had been increasing with each passing day, keeping him awake at night, making him shout at his mother again and again.

Once he had struck her, had knocked her, rolling, off the table and onto the dirt floor of his hidden cabin. But that wouldn't do. If he destroyed her, there could be no way that he could continue to collect women and make her watch, without speaking, while he did to them what he had wanted to do to her, over and over and over again.

It had been his most secret and his most delicious fantasy, to enter that special place with his mother.

Perhaps Cassie Waddell would be the utimate experience, but in time.

A few days back he had seen Gracie Hill wandering above the Eden ranch and had watched while Cassie had allowed her to ride down and then into town. He couldn't understand then, nor could he now, why Gracie Hill would be so far away from town, so far away from Bill Conrad, who would no doubt be wondering where she was.

He would have to harvest a bull elk. But that would be no problem. There were a lot of elk on the mountain. He was already feeling eager. It would work perfectly: He would add Gracie Hill to his collection and that would allow enough time for Charlotte Waddell to leave this world.

He suddenly realized there would be complications.

As Gracie Hill came closer, Preston scanned behind her to see if anyone was following her. Couldn't be too cautious. And it paid off. He noticed a rider, a good distance below yet well on his way, coming up the trail behind Gracie, headed toward his secret paradise.

17

urke dropped his saddle near the campfire and plopped down. Maynard and Lane settled nearby, blowing out their breath. They had hired no formal cook to prepare their meals and unlike the hands working for the big outfits, had to fend for themselves.

The day had been long and with just enough light left to work by, the cowhands from the various outfits were easing the herds onto a night bed ground.

Burke drank deeply from his canteen and looked toward the west, where the sun was a huge, gold-red ball headed over the mountains. He could remember roundups in Montana: At first it was tough, getting up early and working long hours. But after a couple of days, you got used to it. He felt odd being present at a roundup, doing something other than punching cows for the first time since his college days.

Though he felt like going right to sleep, he decided that eating something was a better choice.

"You two hungry?" he asked Maynard and Lane. "We'll cut cards to see who cooks."

"The hell with that," Maynard said. "We've got some beef jerky in our bags, Dean and me, and that will do for us. You want to start a fire, suit yourself."

Maynard and Lane began eating, discussing the day and the numerous things they didn't like about it. They had their backs to Burke, hissing like two adders, obviously disgusted with how the roundup was going.

Burke decided to get a good night's sleep and be ready when breakfast call was made.

Then Chick Campbell and Art Gilroy appeared.

Burke invited them in. "I'd offer you some grub," he said, "but I haven't even got a fire going yet."

"We didn't figure you wanted to cook any orange duck at this hour," Chick said. "Come over to the Rocker 9 camp and we'll feed you."

"I don't know," Burke said.

"You don't have to ask me twice," Maynard said. He and Lane got up and started the short walk across an open meadow to where the Rocker 9 cook fires burned.

"That's quite a pair to draw to," Chick commented. "Where'd you find them?"

"I was advised to bring somebody in who wasn't intimidated by irritated cowhands," Burke replied.

"Guess you found the right type," Art said. "And by the way they look at the stock, they seem to know good beef on the hoof."

"They came down from Montana, along the upper Missouri River country," Burke said. "They've been working some big outfits up there."

"They've got some tough hands up in that country, I'd say," Chick commented. "I hear some of them head for Canada when things get too tough."

Art laughed. "And they come back down across the line with horses and cattle they found running loose somewhere."

"Some do that, I guess," Burke said.

"These two friends of yours?" Art asked. "Do you know much about them?"

"Just enough to know that they won't get run over by Len Keller and the Eden boys," Burke said.

"They ever been in Canada?" Chick asked, grinning. "You sure the mounties didn't chase them down here?"

Sid Preston sat his horse in the trees, just off the trail that led into his domain. The rider he had been watching appeared on schedule, and Preston aimed his Sharps.

"What the hell are you doing up here?"

Len Keller jumped in the saddle and threw his hands up. "I didn't know where to look for you," he said. "You weren't down at the bunkhouse and no one knew where you'd gone."

"You know never to look for me here, but over where we introduced ourselves to Burke. We meet there all the time."

"Well, you didn't tell me where you'd be. But I needed to find you."

"What's so damned important?"

"Burke is bound to cut our numbers way back, just to spite us," Keller complained. "He's counting more stock against us than we've got. Way more."

"You mean he's running the numbers up on us?"

"He's out for us, I tell you."

Preston thought a moment. "Maybe it's time we make Mr. Burke uncomfortable."

"Then you're coming back with me?"

"Later. I've things to take care of up here."

"What things, Sid? This ranger is causing us real problems."

"I think you know how to handle him," Preston said. "I've got confidence in you."

"All the hands would feel better if you came down, Sid."

"You turn around and head back to camp now, Len," Preston said. "Tell everyone that you talked to me and that I left you in charge until I get down, maybe tomorrow sometime."

Burke finished his plate of beef and beans, smothered in green chile, and plenty of flour tortillas. He would take that kind of cooking over gourmet any day of the week.

During the meal, he had thought long and hard about his situation. Chick and Art—and who knew how many others— were very suspicious of Maynard and Lane. So what did they think of him, then? Could they possibly be wondering if he had any connection to the pair?

The more he thought about it, the more concerned he became. Chick and Art didn't seem to be treating him any differently, but they were watching Maynard and Lane very closely. They had to be wondering why the forest service would actually want two men so eager to start shooting.

Art picked up his fiddle and began playing a slow waltz. A couple of hands from the other camps had brought their guitars over and were strumming a rhythm.

Burke listened for a while, gazing into the twilight. The sky was filling with clouds and dry lightning was starting once again, distant strands of white netting that shot through the impending darkness.

He finished his meal and thanked Chick and Art and an old cook named Pecos, then retired back to his camp. Maynard and

Lane were still up, and didn't waste time challenging him about his policies.

"Why aren't you pushing these outfits to get their work done faster?" Maynard asked. "You give them all the time in the world to do their branding and sorting, as if it didn't mean a thing to you, one way or the other."

"It doesn't," Burke said.

Maynard threw his coffee cup across camp. "Well, it does to us! We're wasting good time here. Make them do the sorting after all the branding is done."

"I'm not changing anything here."

"You really want a load of trouble, don't you?" Maynard said.

"Oh, that's a bright thing to say," Burke told him. "You two have made it obvious that you enjoy gunplay, even though those days are long gone. When a pair like you come along, throwbacks without a good reason, people begin to wonder about motives. Does that make sense?"

"You're talking in circles," Lane said.

"Then I'll spell it out clearly," Burke told them. "Go ahead and start something with me. See if the cowhands don't come over here."

"We're not afraid of any of them," Lane said.

"Good. There's a lot of them and they wouldn't mind filling you both with bullet holes."

"So you think you can cozy up to these ranchers?" Maynard asked.

"I already have," Burke replied. "I've not pushing them and I'm taking a fair tally on all of their cattle. They've said so themselves. You two would be better off moving on."

"Oh, no," Lane said quickly. "We've invested to much time and the pickings are just far too good here."

Burke swirled his coffee. "As a forest ranger, I can't let you stay."

Maynard turned to Lane. "Looks like he's threatening us."

"Appears that way," Lane agreed. "Guess we'll have to write his daddy."

"Write whoever you damn well please," Burke said.

"I've got a better idea," Maynard said. "We'll advise the papers around here that their brand new shiny forest service guy with the brand new shiny new car got rich with stolen beef."

"They won't believe that," Burke said.

"But they'll look into it, and who knows what they'll find."

Lane was smiling. "He's right, Mr. Ranger Man. We're staying and you're going to leave us alone to do as we please."

Gracie Hill struggled to the top of the mountain, easing her way along a trail that skirted the edge of the cliffs above Eden Creek. She stopped once to look off into the distant bottom, the steep rock sides now coated with layers of purple and red and pink from the setting sun.

A short distance further she passed a huge fir tree alongside the trail. Tall and straight, it had survived a lot of years at the top of the world.

"What have you got to say?" she asked the tree. "Is there a paradise nearby, where my friend awaits me?"

She laughed and moved on, and soon entered a large burn area, a collection of lifeless tree trunks with sharp and twisted limbs. The sky overhead was alive with thunder and jagged light, the clouds churning and roiling like unsettled soup. A breeze blew across the top, slight, but gusty and unpredictable.

Gracie caught her breath and struggled to adjust her eyesight to her new surroundings. Twilight was nearly complete, leaving the burn area filled with odd shadows that appeared and disappeared with each flash of lightning, like lingering spirits trapped in the skeletal forest.

For a long moment Gracie thought of turning back down the mountain and forgetting her mission. But she had resolved to find her friend, no matter the challenges, and believed that this odd grove of destruction and regeneration to be the entrance to the paradise Lottie had been seeking. She would force herself to cross amidst the shifting shadows and would soon find herself united with her friend in the peace of the wilderness beyond.

She discovered a trail, well used, that wound its way through the scarred and twisted landscape. Her hopes rose, for with each jagged bolt, the way became ever more clear. But the shadows grew thicker and more active, like they were closing in on her.

She hurried her step, but a broken branch caught her dress at the collar, clutching her like a bony finger. She wheeled away, the fabric tearing free, and began to run.

She fell and hauled herself up, gasping for breath, trying to calm herself. Her heart hammered inside and her ears pounded. She leaned against a dead tree for support and quickly pulled away. A piece of nylon stocking had been wrapped around the trunk and adorned with strands of long, dark, braided hair, layered with something that felt thick and crusty to the touch.

Gracie stood on the trail and stared ahead at movement just ahead of her. A bolt of lightning revealed a form that appeared to be moving toward her.

She turned to run, but fell, crying. She stood up and looked behind her. The form remained in place, not having advanced toward her, and she noticed that it bore a resemblance to a woman's dress.

As she started toward the form, she noticed that the skeletal trees off to her right were filled with similar forms, some full and some partial, all hanging from charred branches, turning and twisting in the breezy darkness.

As she neared the form beside the trail, she saw what she thought to be a huge bull elk resting on its stomach. She quickly realized that the animal was not alive. She turned to seek her way in another direction and discovered another elk, situated the same way, its massive antlers arching up toward the night sky.

She was near the garment and saw that the sleeves and collar were lined with velvet—Lottie Burns's favorite dress.

Near the tree a huge elk rested, partially buried, alive with a foul odor. She noticed an arm protruding from between the ribs, and she knew instinctively that the arm belonged to Lottie Burns.

Gracie turned and vomited. After a moment she looked all around her. Movement was everywhere. The tattered garments moved and shifted and as the trees moaned and groaned in the wind, it appeared that the scattered garments were dancing with one another.

Gracie knelt down beside the elk's remains, blocking out the odor and the strange feeling that was welling up inside. She had a job to do and she must do it quickly, before something or someone from the shadows came for her.

She leaned over and looked under the elk, peering between two ribs. There she saw a head and a body and even with the flashing light, couldn't quite make out the face, only that the mouth was a gaping hole.

But the hair was quite long, just like Lottie's.

She pushed with all her might against the rotting elk corpse, working to move it onto its side. The skin slipped and she forced herself to grab under a rib, into the meaty part just behind the shoulder. After a period of intense labor, she had the elk moved partially sideways, just enough to extract the body underneath.

Gracie caught her breath. Her hands and arms and clothes were smeared with decaying flesh. She knelt down to pull Lottie free and heard a voice behind her.

"Who are you, little lady?"

She shrieked and jumped aside. A small man stood in the shadows nearby, staring at her.

"Did you hear me?" he said.

Gracie couldn't speak.

"Get out of here," the little man said. "Get away from here before he comes back."

With that the small man was gone, vanished into the inky shadows.

Gracie again knelt down beside her friend, trapped in death under the elk.

"Lottie, I can't leave you here like this," she cried.

Gracie took hold of one arm and jerked and tugged until she had pulled the dead woman's corpse partway from under the elk.

She released the arm and stood back, gasping. The entire body cavity was open, missing all the internal organs.

After vomiting again, she retraced her steps along the trail, back toward the giant fir tree. There was no sense in going on through the graveyard. There was nothing on the other side but the same thing. Lottie's paradise didn't exist; it never had.

She moved past the giant fir zombie-like, until she reached the towering cliffs overlooking the headwaters of Eden Creek. Gracie Hill stared straight ahead and, as if walking on an invisible trail that led out over the edge, stepped with confidence into open air.

Her fall was silent.

Resting on his ledge, watching the dancing light in the sky, he wondered at what form nature was taking on the mountain across from him. More and more seemed to be happening there, with the strange man who rode by himself and often led a pack mule laden with an elk.

He harvested too many elk in too short a period of time. No one ate that much.

Even at his age, his eyes were good enough to see the distances and his mind and body strong enough to feel the strangeness from afar. There were times when he brought his son with him, just to sit and feel and wonder at that strange mountain. But his son never stayed. He always got up and left.

He had hoped each time that his son might give him some answers. Though unable to speak well or to function as others normally did, he was nonetheless gifted in other ways and was capable of sensing that which most others couldn't.

And perhaps therein lied the old man's main concern: Did that mountain hold secrets too terrible to understand? What would become of a land where the unnatural occurred with frequency?

He believed that he was far too old to understand it yet still not old enough to avoid it.

18

Burke turned and twisted in his bedroll. The night was alive with dry lightning and rumbling thunder. Someone had ridden into camp earlier to report a fire to the north, somewhere near the Bear's Ears. Far enough away not to be a concern, but close enough to send a strong hint of burning timber down through the mountains.

There would no doubt be more fires as the season progressed. There had been very little precipitation throughout the late winter and spring, until the two-day rain that had extinguished the fire at the time of Burke's arrival. Since then the skies had been alive with thunder and lightning, but absolutely no moisture.

Burke had worried that the forest and dry grasslands near the roundup grounds would take a strike and begin burning, sending cattle scattering and cowhands chasing after them. Smaller fires might be controllable early on, but the grass and timber were so dry that even a slight spark would start a running blaze.

Though nothing major had happened, Burke's dreams were filled with disasters of every kind. The first few nights on the mountain, inside his tent, Sid Preston and his men kept coming for him with a rope. They wanted to put it just around his neck, not over his shoulders. They had already picked out a tree, a huge dead pine high along the cliffs, where they could push him out over the edge, let him dangle for a time, then cut him loose.

He would tangle himself in his bedroll and fall into the huge canyon, the rope flying out behind him in the wind. Just before hitting the bottom, he would jerk awake, sweat rolling down his brow.

He had not even gotten a chance to settle into his cabin before the start of roundup, and had worried about more dreams, which followed him into the darkness at the edge of the cook fires.

The previous night, his dream took him into the storm. Lightning struck within inches of him, exploding in glaring white, and he couldn't move, couldn't free himself from some kind of bond that trapped him while the tiny fires from each strike grew quickly into massive blazes that encircled him, bringing a wall of flame to his bed.

On this night he was trapped again, unable to move while the thunder built into a rumbling roar. But the tremendous pounding was not coming from overhead, but from all around him. He tried to rise while longhorn hooves flew in every direction around him. The hooves had eyes that glared red, streaming past him in huge waves.

Then the pounding stopped and the hooves left and the air suddenly filled with men, tumbling down and bouncing heavily on the ground.

Burke arose with a start. He jumped up, naked, and tried to run. He fell to the ground, tripping over Chick Campbell's bedroll. Chick leaned over and said, "You're not my type," and went back to sleep.

Burke was still gasping. He gained his feet and turned in circles, rubbing his face. There was no lightning, no thunder, and no wind. All was still and the darkness held only the drifting melodies of cowhands on the night shift, singing to the herd.

• • •

Sid Preston stood in the dawn light, looking over the desecrated grave site. His delicate work had been ruined. Someone had helped Lottie Burns escape her tomb. Her arms were sprawled over her head and her entire body cavity lay open and exposed to the sky. The bull elk had been turned onto its side, its head resting at an awkward angle.

He backed away from what he saw. He could never touch her or the elk again. That would be sacrilegious. He would never again come to this grave site or ever handle the garments and other trophies he had collected belonging to Lottie Burns. He could no longer consider her a true member of his collection.

She was different now. Tainted, somehow.

He must make up for it soon.

He wouldn't be using Gracie Hill, at least not until she reappeared. She had somehow disappeared from the area, as if into thin air. He had come back after his meeting with Keller and had been unable to locate Gracie Hill in the darkness. He had wondered how she could have found a place to sleep and remain so quiet and comfortable.

After a fitful sleep, during which his mother would not leave him alone, he had left at dawn for the top of the mountain, where he had discovered the horrible desecration of his sacred site.

Again he had searched everywhere for Gracie Hill. She couldn't have gotten off the mountain that quickly.

Unless someone had helped her.

• • •

He paced around the graveyard, his breath short, his veins bulging. He tried to think who might have come up here and deliberately ruined his domain. Ellis Burke came to mind. He would do such a thing. He could have even picked up Gracie Hill on his way off the mountain.

But he would've had to have left the roundup camp to do it. He would have been forced to travel a good distance in the darkness, along treacherous trails, and then gotten back to camp again before he was missed.

It would be very difficult, but Ellis Burke hated him enough to do something like this.

He would see to it that Ellis Burke paid for the desecration.

Burt Gamble washed his face and head in the creek. He looked into the near distance where the southern wall of the Devil's Grave rose into the air. A fitting landmark, he thought, for a trail that led past into the bowels of hell itself.

He didn't know how he had gotten to where he was, but the water was cold and pure and he drank deeply. Still, his headache just wouldn't go away.

He couldn't remember much about the previous night, except that he had gone high on Waddell's Mountain to look for Preston. He hadn't told Keller or Mason what he was up to; they would have discouraged it and likely kept him from going. He had discussed the issue of Sid Preston's obvious absence most of the time, but neither Keller or Mason had thought it important enough at this point to pursue it.

"He's coming into camp tonight," Keller had said. "He promised me."

But he hadn't shown up. Gamble had taken about enough

of Preston's laziness and he had meant to tell him about it.

He had wanted to find Preston, wherever he was, and ask him a few questions, like how did he think he deserved a full cut of the rustling profits when he didn't take part in any of the work. There had been a time when Preston was involved in everything. For some reason, that had changed.

Over the past two years, Preston had become more secretive. He spent less and less time with the other Eden hands and more off by himself. Finally, he had moved out of the main bunkhouse totally and had simply taken up residence in some secret location.

That had been the previous summer and no one had stepped forward to question him about it. After all, if Rube Waddell didn't care how Preston spent his time, why should anyone else? Preston and Waddell had always kept secrets, so another one didn't seem all that unique.

Len Keller had taken over most of the foreman duties, and that made it even easier to steal Eden steers. But even after the rustling had gotten going, Preston was still conspicuously absent. Even Keller and Mason had voiced their displeasure among themselves.

But nothing had changed and Gamble had gotten fed up. He knew all of the Eden range well, and the forested areas for a lot of miles around. The only place he had never been was to the private land behind Rube Waddell's ranch buildings, where he kept his prize Longhorn steers, or to the head of Eden Creek, way on top of the mountain. No one had any reason to go up there. All the work was done with the herds down below and in the high country to the north, across the canyon, on the forest summer range.

Gamble struggled to remember what he had seen. He had

suffered blackouts often when he was younger and a doctor had told him to quit drinking or die. He had quit, for the most part, falling back to the bottle when his pain became too much to bear, then quitting cold turkey when he realized his health was failing.

Now it had started again. Something had happened on that mountain that had caused him to remember a terrible scene as a child, something he had locked way back in his mind the night his adopted mother had been knifed to death in front of him.

He had been born in a Kansas City brothel and after four years, had been given up for adoption to a young couple headed west along the Sante Fe Trail. The husband had died in a shooting accident just before reaching Bent's Fort and the young woman had been devastated. Upon reaching the fort she had decided to go back to Kansas City with the next caravan headed that way. But a drunken trader had come into their tent and when she had refused him sex, he had ripped her open, raping her as he killed her.

Gamble had hidden under a pile of blankets and didn't speak to anyone for a month. The fort servants fed him and cared for him until a passing group of Catholic nuns took him to an orphanage in Denver, treated him well for ten years, and had wanted him to join the priesthood. Instead, he had crawled out a window and took to cowboying in the Fort Collins area, eventually working his way up the Cache la Poudre canyon and over onto the west slope of the Continental Divide.

In all the years he had cowboyed since that time, he had rarely thought about Bent's Fort or his adopted mother. The bottle had helped with that. But now something had certainly brought it all back.

In a way he wanted to remember. He wanted to know what

he had seen and what had happened after. It had to have involved Sid Preston one way or another. He knew that to be a fact.

He stood up and stared across at the Devil's Grave. He had a half-day's ride yet to the roundup ground, and he didn't know what he was going to say to Len Keller and Jeb Mason once he got there. If he didn't remember what it was he was doing on the mountain, he would appear silly.

The thought of the mountain bothered him. Perhaps he should ride back up and see if he could find what it was he had discovered.

Suddenly flashes of the night before came back. A strange kind of grave, with a bull elk resting on top; burned and jagged trees covered with women's clothes, all shredded and layered with dried blood.

And he was certain there had been a woman, a live woman, staring at him. Or had she been dead. There had been so many dead.

He walked over to his horse and rummaged in a saddlebag until he found a full bottle of blended whiskey.

Cassie had been out all night, riding through the forest, thinking, crying, wondering about the future. She had no choice but to accept the fact that her mother would be dying very soon.

The thought was terrible to bear, but the idea of what was happening with her father and Vivian Cross made it all that much harder.

During her ride, she had tried to think of ways to stop their union from taking place. Nothing logical came to mind. It seemed inevitable, beyond her control.

Her ride had ended with the first rays of sunlight over the

eastern mountains. She was pondering what she had seen a little earlier, a box canyon along Eden Creek that had been fenced off, holding some two hundred head of steers. They had been herded there within the past few days, it appeared, but there was no one around watching them.

Apparently they would not be counted at the roundup.

She wondered who had placed them there and why.

As she returned to the ranch, she caught her father returning to the house from somewhere up the creek, holding a bowl covered with a dishcloth.

"What have you got, there, Father?" she asked, riding up behind him.

"Cassie . . ." His surprise was evident. "You're up early."

"And so are you. What's in the bowl?" She dismounted.

"A surprise for your mother," he replied, holding the bowl close.

"Really?" Cassie closed in on him. "Why don't you want me to see?"

"I don't want you to spoil the surprise."

"What surprise would that be, Father?"

He didn't answer, but hurried into the house and closed the door. She hurried inside and discovered him pouring tea in the kitchen.

"Where's the bowl you brought in, Father?"

"What bowl?"

"The one you had covered with the cloth."

"Oh, this one?"

He pointed to a small bowl on the table. Cassie had no way of knowing if it was the same bowl or not. She walked over and examined its contents. Wild mint.

"Is there a problem, Cassie?" he asked.

"Yes, there is, Father," she replied. "I just don't know what to do about it."

Cassie mounted and rode up the creek in the direction her father had come from and discovered a small garden hidden among the trees along the creek. She noticed that someone had dug a small ditch that started a short distance up the creek and wound its way on the contour down to the garden, where irrigation water kept a number of plants very wet.

She dismounted and studied the garden. It contained a number of immature cucumber and squash plants, along with some onions and carrots and lettuce. At first she thought that the help had been tending a secret garden but dismissed the idea when she recalled that they had a large garden of their own that they tended not far from their quarters. This garden had to belong to someone else.

She had trouble believing that her father would go to the trouble of tending a garden. The whole idea baffled her. With further study, she discovered that though the ground seemed weed free, a number of small plants grew around the lettuce and cucumber plants, dainty plants with tiny white flowers.

She hurried back to the house and entered the back door. She discovered her mother sitting up in bed, sipping tea.

"Where's Father?"

"He didn't say where he was going."

"Did he give you that tea?"

"As a matter of fact, he did."

"Maybe you shouldn't drink it."

"Why not?"

"Because it might have poisonous plants mixed in with it."

"You father isn't a nice man, but he wouldn't do something like that," Charlotte said.

"Maybe he wouldn't have at one time," Cassie told her. "But he's gotten even worse. He's with Vivian Cross now, you know."

19

The sun rose, promising a very warm day. Bill Conrad rode up to where Burke sat on Lancaster. He waited until Burke had finished tallying a group of Rocker 9 steers before he spoke.

"Have you seen Gracie Hill?"

"I thought you came up to see if you needed to cut back on your numbers," Burke said. "You do."

"We'll deal with that later," Conrad said. "I asked you about Gracie Hill."

"Is she my responsibility?"

"One of your former employees, a Mr. Red Maynard, told me yesterday that she's been sleeping in your cabin."

"Is that a fact?"

"But I checked your cabin and didn't see her there."

"She came up looking for Lottie Burns," Burke said. "She stayed one night while I came over here to roundup camp. I tried to talk her into going back down, but then, I'm not her father, either."

"You could have taken her down yourself."

"She's a big girl, Bill. You can't tell her how to live her life."

"She *was* a big girl, Ellis. *Was* a big girl. I know something's happened to her. She's nowhere to be found. I shouldn't have let her go."

"Maybe you should have come with her," Burke suggested.

"This one time of being too busy, or stubborn, to do what she wanted is going to haunt you, isn't it? I hope nothing's happened to her but if it has, you can't blame it on me."

"Maybe you're right," Conrad said. "I should have kept better control of her." As an afterthought, he asked, "How long have you known Mr. Maynard and Mr. Lane?"

"Not very long at all," Burke replied. "Why?"

"I distinctly remember seeing them on a train about five years ago, a train between Cheyenne and Laramie, Wyoming. That train got robbed and there's some who think they were in on it."

Burke turned back to his tally sheet. "That's news to me."

Cassie rode with a mission. She intended to pay Vivian Cross a visit and to instruct her in the art of manners. Before the visit was through, Cassie had vowed to make her father's lover realize she wasn't welcome at the Eden ranch any longer.

She discovered Vivian watering the flowers on her husband's grave.

Vivian got up slowly and crossed her arms.

"I don't remember ever inviting you here," she said.

"And you've never been invited to our ranch, either," Cassie told her.

"I beg your pardon. You're father makes the rules there."

"My father is not always around, Vivian. If I ever catch you coming our way again, you'll wish you'd stayed home."

"Are you threatening me?"

"I'm promising you."

Vivian stood in front of her husband's grave, holding the pitcher tightly, staring at Cassie.

Cassie dismounted and approached her. "What are you hiding?"

"Time for you to leave, Cassie. Have you no respect for the dead?"

If Vivian wanted to play a strange game, Cassie thought, she had picked the wrong person to play it with.

She said, "Your husband told me that *you* have no respect for the dead."

Vivian stared at her. "What are you talking about?"

"I mean, after he died."

"What?"

"Yes, he told me how he's still so disappointed in you, for all the things you did to him. And don't for a minute think he approves of you and my father."

Vivian recovered from her shock. "Are you quite through?" she asked.

"Maybe we should talk to your dear husband, together, right now."

Vivian became noticeably more nervous. "You must leave, Cassie. Now."

"Oh, Vivian, you take such good care of the grave. Look at all the pretty flowers. You must spend a lot of time caring for them."

"I will call the foreman."

"No you won't. He's at the roundup. There's just you and me, Vivian. And of course, your dearly departed husband. What do you suppose he's thinking right about now?"

"Cassie, this is not proper."

"No, Vivian, what you're doing with my father is not proper. And I'm telling you, it's going to stop." Cassie was looking at the flowers again, noticing the small and delicate white blossoms mixed in with the larger blooms. "You know what, Vivian, my father has the same flowers growing in a little secluded spot along the creek. Do you know anything about it? Maybe the two of you have been tending it."

"Time to go, Cassie."

"What kind of flowers are they, Vivian?"

"Flowers like this grow everywhere," Vivian insisted.

"Maybe. I'll ask Ellis Burke."

"Cassie, it's time for you to leave. Now!"

Cassie reached down and plucked a stem from one of the plants. She noticed that another similar, white-flowered species was growing next to the first. She plucked one of those, also.

She also noticed a tube rising from the soil.

Vivian ran over and attempted to snatch the flowers. She became so forceful that Cassie asked her repeatedly to step back, but had to resort finally to pushing her, and hard enough to send her tumbling backwards to the ground.

"There's something about these little flowers, isn't there, dear Vivian?"

Vivian crawled on her hands and knees to a nearby tree and pulled herself to her feet, acting like a mother bird trying to distract a predator from her nest.

Trembling with rage and fear, she said, "I intend to tell your father about this."

"No, I'll tell him first," Cassie promised. "I intend to have some answers." She grabbed Vivian's handbag, sitting near the grave, dumped out its contents, and stuffed it full of plants.

"Cassie, you give me back my handbag," Vivian said.

Cassie climbed on her horse, clutching the handbag tightly. "I hope you heard what I said about coming over to the ranch. You'd better not dare show your face to me again. Ever."

.   .   .

They rode along the trail that led across the ridge to Cassie's special place among the aspens. Cassie had returned from Vivian Cross's, but had said nothing of her visit with her father's lover. Instead, she had merely suggested they take a ride. Charlotte Waddell had brimmed with happiness. They had not been together in this beautiful place for nearly three years.

It had been a difficult and very tiring ride, but well worth it. They had stopped along the way to rest and watch deer and elk returning from water to settle down for the day, and the ever-present marmots, big and fat and furry, running through the grass and flowers to their rocky dens along the mountainside.

At the aspens, Cassie helped her mother down from her horse and to a log, where the two of them sat and gazed over the wilderness.

"So, you brought Ellis Burke up here. Did he like it?"

"Very much so, Mother. He cares about all this, as much as you or I."

Her mother turned to her. "He wasn't born here, Cassie."

"That doesn't matter. He told me that everything in these mountains is connected to everything else in all other ranges of mountains—elevation, latitude, and longitude notwithstanding."

"I like that," Charlotte said. "When you were a little girl, a Ute woman used to come to the house to trade me berries and roots for freshly baked bread. Do you remember her?"

"Alice?"

"Her real name was Little Rainbow in the Eastern Sky. She was a wise lady. She once took two small bags of pine needles from her pack and opened each of them. She asked me if I could tell the difference between the two bunches of needles. Of course, I couldn't. She said one bunch had come from a big tree along the trail coming in and another had been brought down from Montana, by some relatives in the Shoshone tribe. She told me the same thing: 'Don't ever think that everything is not connected. It is.' I miss her. Maybe I'll see her soon."

Cassie's eyes welled with tears.

"Anyway," Charlotte continued. "I'm glad to hear that Mr. Burke has grown so fond of this country in such a short period of time."

"I think he liked it here the moment he arrived," Cassie said. "Sid Preston tried to intimidate him, but he's determined to keep this country from ruination. In fact, I'm afraid he wants much more than he can possibly attain."

"Wouldn't be the first time something like that happened," Charlotte said. She watched small birds flit about the aspens, singing songs and carrying food to their young. A large monarch butterfly flew past, landing on a large blanket flower. "It makes me sad that I took all this beauty for granted for so long."

"Mother, don't keep talking that way. You'll recover. You've got to have faith."

"Cassie, I'm getting weaker, not stronger."

"Why don't we move down into Glenwood Springs, or even Denver, the two of us, until you've fully recovered?" Cassie suggested. "We'll soak in the springs daily and we'll find a good doctor, not one of Father's choosing."

"Please, Cassie, let's not start that again."

"It would do you good to get away, and I wouldn't leave your side."

"Cassie, I couldn't stand a move like that. I'm in a lot of

pain. The only thing that relieves my pain for any length of time is my morning tea."

"You must promise me never to take morning tea from Father again. I mean, take it from him, but just don't drink it."

Charlotte frowned. "I'll ask you again, Cassie, what are you suspicious of? Do you seriously think he's poisoning me?"

"Honestly, Mother, I believe he's capable of it, but I want to be sure. I'll take some plants to Ellis Burke."

"And you saw the same plants at Vivian Cross's place, on her husband's grave?"

"She waters them like they were a prized peony, or something."

"Do you suppose she poisoned her husband, too?"

"It appears that way to me."

Charlotte took a deep breath. "Well, I guess I could see the two of them doing that to me, just to hurry me to the grave."

"I don't know anything about poisonous plants," Cassie admitted. "I would have thought they would have killed you sooner. More like a sudden death, something like what she probably did to her husband."

"Your father is probably giving me all small doses, in hopes of keeping me weakened against the cancer," Charlotte said. "If I died immediately, someone would wonder."

"What about Vivian's husband?" Cassie asked. "He didn't linger."

"That would be easier to do, since he already had a heart problem," Charlotte said. "She could easily make it look like a heart attack."

.   .   .

Cassie mentioned that she had given Vivian Cross a visit and had warned her against coming over to the ranch ever again.

"If only it were that easy," Charlotte said.

"I'll keep her away," Cassie insisted.

"What are you going to do, stuff her full of poisonous plants?"

They shared a laugh, but one that quickly ended in silence.

"Is the amount of land and cattle someone owns really all that important?" Charlotte asked.

"It certainly is to Father and Vivian Cross," Cassie replied. "They just can't wait to be together and join their fortunes, and it makes me so mad I just want to do something drastic right now."

"Now, Cassie, look at you. You're shaking."

"This isn't fair, Mother, not to you or me."

"The cancer would have taken me sooner or later, anyway."

"Mother, what are you saying? Are you saying that it's fine that Father has been poisoning you?"

"Of course not. Certainly not if he was truly trying to poison me."

"And you don't believe he's been truly trying to poison you?"

"Think of it another way," Charlotte said. "He may have been trying to do me in as quickly as possible by weakening me with the tea, but maybe he has been inadvertently holding the cancer back some."

"You don't believe that?"

"I'm not so sure. I do know that at times the tea helps the pain and makes me feel more alert. Of course, I don't tell him that."

"I'm sorry, Mother," Cassie said. "I don't know if I agree with all that."

"You don't have to agree, but wouldn't it be funny if it were true?"

Cassie helped her mother to another location that looked over a broad expanse of mountains and small lakes and meadows.

"I just want to remember this moment together, up here next to the clouds," Charlotte said. "I want you to think back on the times we came up here when you were a little girl, when we listened to the breeze in the trees and picked flowers together."

Tears again brimmed in Cassie's eyes. "Those were some of my favorite moments."

"And each time we came up here, there was something that I always told you."

"I remember, Mother. Always think of yourself as a butterfly, enjoying sunny days, always searching for the prettiest flowers. If you do that, you won't see the places where no flowers grow."

"Remember that now, Cassie, especially at this time. When I'm gone you'll still have the flowers, but not me here to remind you to look at them."

"Mother, I have something to tell you."

Charlotte took Cassie's hand in hers. "You don't have to tell me anything."

"Yes, I do."

"I already know, Cassie. I've known a long time. You even worked for Trixie when you were here."

"I don't intend to do that anymore," Cassie said. "I'll finish school and go on stage, just like you did at one time. You'll be proud of me."

"I'm already proud of you, Cassie. I always have been." She looked into the afternoon sun. "The sun is headed west. It's time to say good-bye to this place."

"Mother, I can bring you up again."

Charlotte was having trouble getting to her feet. "I'll be lucky to make it onto my horse and get back down. But when you come up here next time, after I'm gone, look for one of those big yellow butterflies and remember me."

Vivian stood in the newly finished mansion, gazing out the huge picture window that had just been installed in the living room. The view afforded a panorama of mountain vistas that stretched across Eden Creek to the divide and then beyond, a spectacular ensemble of wilderness peaks that spread as far as the eye could see.

"Rube," she said, "I'm tired of waiting for Charlotte to die." She turned to him and smiled, taking him in her arms, letting her hands roam freely to his crotch. "I want a wedding ring."

The papers had already been drawn up to consolidate Vivian Cross's holdings with Eden Land and Livestock. To make it legal, they needed to sign the documents as man and wife, and have them registered in county and state court—a mere formality.

The move had precipitated the resignation of nearly half of Vivian's ranch hands, who had all been wondering at Shorty Walsh's disappearance.

Vivian had decided to fire the rest of her hands and told Waddell that his hands could now keep track of her steers, as they would soon become part of a new empire, the *E X 12* brand.

"So why isn't Charlotte ready for burial now?" Vivian pressed.

"She's been hanging on," Waddell said. "I don't understand it."

Vivian led him to the kitchen, where she pulled a covered bowl from a locked cupboard.

"Let's go over it again. Two parts of this plant to one part of this one, mixed with the black Asian tea."

Waddell stopped her. "Two parts of which plant?"

She held up the smaller of the two species. "This one. Two parts. Haven't you been doing that?"

"I've been doing one part of that one."

"You fool!" Vivian cried, shaking. "No wonder she's remained alive so long. You've been medicating her, not killing her." When she recovered her composure, she said, "I should have asked you sooner. But you can count cattle. Why can't you count plants?"

"I've got it right now," Waddell said.

"I'm getting impatient, Rube," she said. "I want a lot of new things that I don't have now."

"How about Ellis Burke's automobile?" he said.

20

A long line of pink and crimson streaked over the mountains. Burke had been awake for two hours, checking and re-checking his tally sheets by lantern light. Maynard and Lane had moved their bedrolls a significant distance away and were having coffee beside their own fire.

Burke wondered how he would finish counting the cattle without them. Maynard and Lane had both told him that they intended to leave for good at first light.

They had cited the tallies as a waste of precious time that could be better spent relieving the cattle companies of their stock. Burke had argued repeatedly that his job was to count all the livestock using the forest reserves and that there was no way he could get out of that.

"Besides, it will give us a good way to see who has the most steers," he had told them.

"We already know that," Maynard had replied. "It's time to get busy."

Burke intended to see if they were really serious about leaving and walked over.

"If you think you can keep us," Maynard told him, "then you're a fool."

"What about the tallies? What about the appearance of working for the forest service?"

"We're tired of playing the game," Lane said.

"So you both intend to quit the country?" Burke asked.

Lane laughed and Maynard replied, "No, we're quitting you. We can do this on our own."

"Do you know what kind of problems this is going to cause?" Burke asked.

"Only problems that you decide to cause, Mr. Ranger Man."

Len Keller sat drinking breakfast coffee. A rider suddenly appeared in camp: Burt Gamble struggled to dismount and staggered over to the campfire.

"Where the hell have you been?" Keller demanded.

Gamble struggled to talk. "Been up there . . . terrible."

"What?" Keller said.

Jeb Mason was leading horses into camp.

"What's this?" he asked.

"I'm asking him where he's been," Keller said. He turned back to Gamble. "You're not making sense."

Both Keller and Mason smelled his breath.

"For hell's sake," Keller said. "He's dead drunk."

Mason checked Gamble's saddlebag and discovered a whiskey bottle with two swigs left. No one had ever seen Gamble drink anything stronger than coffee.

Keller and Mason helped the older cowhand to his bedroll. It appeared that besides drinking, he had also been in a fight. His nose was bloody and his face cut, and there was a knot on the side of his head the size of a hen's egg.

He was babbling again, this time slurring something about butchered women.

"Talk to us, Burt," Keller said. "What in the hell happened to you?"

Gamble was barely conscious. His face was slimy and the front of his shirt soaked with vomit.

"Who would have thought it," Mason said. "Maybe we should let him sleep it off and then get the story from him."

Gamble struggled to talk, but kept slurring his speech. They wrapped him in his blankets and left him passed out.

"I couldn't make out any of that," Mason said.

"Something about women and butchers?"

"Is that what you heard?"

"Something like that. Makes no sense."

Mason shook his head. "I would have bet everything I own that I'd never live to see him like that."

"The world is full of surprises," Keller said.

Burke rested on a fallen log. The branding was going well and the Cross 12 hands were separating the stock they wanted to sell from those they would leave on the reserves. The Eden hands were still branding Rube Waddell's steers and would finish close to nightfall. The word was that the two outfits would be running their cattle together.

That had caused a lot of speculation among the other outfits regarding the rumored union of the two ranches, based on the union of Rube Waddell and Vivian Cross. The talk was rampant and some of the hands from the other outfits had come to Burke for verification.

"That's none of my concern," Burke told them. "Take it up at your next stock growers' meeting."

That was a small problem compared to the backlash from the outfits when they learned that Red Maynard and Dean Lane had left, and that Chick Campbell and Art Gilroy had volunteered to help finish the tallies. Many of the other ranchers didn't trust Bill Conrad and even though Chick and Art had good reputations, cowhands were always very loyal to their brand. This could mean that their tallies of Rocker 9 steers might be low while the count on other outfits might be padded.

Burke had resolved the conflict by suggesting that other reps from other brands be present also, to help with the tallies and insure they were accurate. Most of the outfits were short of cowhands as it was and couldn't spare to have them doing anything but branding and sorting, so they grudgingly agreed to let Chick and Art do the work.

The two were gravely concerned about their relationship with the other ranches and their hands, and wondered if Red Maynard and Dean Lane hadn't wanted to cause problems.

They were hunkered down nearby, holding the reins to their horses and drinking from their canteens. Burke continued to organize his tallies.

"I wish those two would have stuck around until the branding and shove-up was done," Chick said.

"I did what I could to try and keep them," Burke told him.

"They said they were fed up?" Chick continued. "Just like that, up and gone?"

"I wasn't sure of them in the first place," Burke said. "I'm surprised they lasted as long as they did."

"I thought you knew them," Art said. "Apparently not very well."

Burke shrugged. "They've changed since I first worked with them."

"I can't say that I thought the three of you got along all that well," Art commented. "You forest service hands are a funny bunch."

"I won't need anyone now until the shove-down later this fall," Burke said. "That will give me time to find more dependable help."

Chick nodded. "Where'd those two say they say they were going?"

"They didn't," Burke replied. "They gave me an address in Montana to send their checks to."

"If you want my opinion," Art said, "You don't owe either of them one thin dime. They caused more trouble than they're worth."

Burke watched the branding operations going on not far away. "They're gone, and that's that," he said. "I'll just carry on, doing the range work and fine-tuning allotment numbers. I just hope nothing else goes wrong here."

"Once you get the Eden bunch done with," Chick said, "Most of your problems will be over."

"I hope so, but what's that I heard about one of the Eden hands?" Burke asked. "Burt Gamble, I think it was. Came in drunk and beaten?"

"Yeah, he came in drunk and they thought he'd gotten beaten," Chick replied. "But it seems he fell off his horse somewhere and took a bad fall down a hillside."

"That's what Gamble said?" Burke asked.

"He sobered up after a while, and said he'd fallen way up on Waddell Mountain," Chick said. "No one seems to know what he was doing way up there, least of all him."

"The crack on the head knocked him silly," Art put in.

"He kept saying wild things, like women are butchers, or butcher women, or something like that. But when he sobered up he didn't know what he'd said, or why."

"Well, there's a few women I wouldn't want to meet in the

kitchen," Chick said. He turned to Art. "You don't have that problem."

"Nope, all my women want me back for more. Makes for a hard life."

Burke was thinking back on his first night on the job. Burt Gamble had been the only one not sucking from a whiskey bottle the night he had met Preston and his men. Gamble had seemed quiet and reserved, disgusted at being a part of it all. That he would suddenly start drinking seemed out of character.

Chick was saying, "Gamble used to drink a lot in his younger days. It seems he stopped for a long time. Must have taken it up again."

"He couldn't have been all that neighborly in the first place, to be part of Preston's bunch," Art added. He looked to Burke. "He's not one of your good friends."

"No, he's not," Burke said. "But he wasn't a crazy man, either. Something must have really gotten to him."

Cassie rode her horse into roundup camp and searched everywhere until she found Burke watering his horse in the creek.

She dismounted and said, "Must you be so hard to find?"

"I wasn't hiding from you," he said.

"When you take a job, you stick to it until it's finished," she said. "I'll give you that much."

Burke nodded to her at the comment, but wondered to himself if he could stick around after roundup. If Maynard and Land didn't leave the country, they could cause serious problems. And if he caught them rustling, he knew it would be them or him.

"It's been harder than I thought," Burke said. "I lost two men who were working for me. It's slowed things down."

"I'll just be a minute," she said.

"Well, I've got at least that much time for you," Burke said.

"So, you are glad to see me?"

"Certainly. Where's my favorite dress?"

"This isn't that kind of visit, Ellis," she said. "Besides, you're too busy to take off somewhere with me, and let me take off your clothes. Right?"

"Unfortunately, that's correct," he agreed. "How can I help you?"

She showed him a small handbag filled with plant material. The name *Vivian Cross* was stitched on one side in gold lettering.

"I presume you borrowed that," Burke said with a smile.

"Permanently," Cassie said. "Do you know what kind of flowers these are?"

He studied them. "One is nightshade. It's poisonous. I'm not certain about the other. Why?"

"Vivian Cross killed her husband with a combination of those two plants, steeped in hot water as tea," Cassie replied. "My father is doing the same thing to my mother."

"That's quite an accusation."

"You don't believe me?"

"I don't doubt you at all. But you should have hard evidence before you start accusing someone of something like that. Did you see your father steeping these plants in hot water and then pouring tea for your mother?"

"He's been careful not to do that in front of me," Cassie said. "None of the servants ever serve her tea, though, like they used to. Just him."

"It does sound suspicious," Burke said. "But he would have to know how to mix the two plants just right not to cause a strong reaction and kill your mother outright."

"Don't you see, Ellis? He's trying to get mother out of the way as quickly as possible by using the poisonous plants in her tea. She'll die sooner, but everyone will believe it was the cancer that killed her."

"Yes, I can see that reasoning," Burke said. "But poisonous plants are funny: They mix differently with different plants, even other poisonous ones. I'm not a toxicologist but I do know that mixed in the right doses, they can be medicinal. But get it wrong and they're deadly."

"You sound just like Mother," Cassie said. "She believes he's been holding the cancer at bay by giving her the tea. That's why she's been going along with it."

"You're saying she knows that your father has been trying to poison her?"

"Maybe she just wants to die."

"I don't know what to tell you, Cassie," Burke said. "You're likely right about your father, but you've got to have solid proof."

"As long as you believe me, maybe you could see your way to help me get at my father." She studied him, seeing immediately that he wasn't sure he wanted to go along with any plan like that. "You could stop all grazing by my father on the forest reserves. While he's dealing with that, I can get mother out of the house and down to Glenwood Springs. She doesn't think she could stand the trip, but I think she could. Especially if it means saving her life."

"Cassie, she's not going to survive the cancer. You can make her life more comfortable, maybe, but you can't stop the inevitable."

"You don't care, either, do you?"

"Cassie, it's not that at all."

"But you won't call my father's cattle off the reserves. . . ."

"I can't do that. I can insist that he cut back, which I will do, but I have no legal grounds to terminate his grazing privileges entirely."

"Even if it's proven that he's trying to kill my mother?"

"Those are two separate issues, Cassie."

"Then how about his precious longhorns that are overgrazing the reserves behind the ranch?" Cassie asked. "And there are some two hundred head that are being held in the box canyon at the head of Eden Creek. Isn't that grounds to end his grazing privileges?"

"Those issues will be brought to his attention in writing and he will have to deal with them," Burke told her. "It's a process."

"And a damned long one," Cassie said.

"Unfortunately, you're right. But I have to go by the book."

"I thought I could count on you." She threw the handbag at him and climbed back on her horse. "I guess I should have known better."

"We should talk more about this," Burke said.

"I think we've talked quite enough," Cassie said. "I'll find someone willing to help me, you wait and see."

He sat on the ledge, by himself this time, at his father's request. He had made it clear to his father, a man old and so very wise for one of his kind, that he would be in no danger climbing out on the ledge and just sitting, trying to gather the information that his father had wanted from him for so long.

He didn't know what good he could do, or if the information would even come to him, but he had vowed to himself and to his father that he would try.

He had come to the ledge with his father before but had not been able to remain there. His father had told him what he had seen, wondering, wanting an answer from him. He had no means of describing his mental turmoil at gazing across the expanse toward that mountain, feeling something he couldn't understand. So he had just left, and his father had wondered.

His father and mother had both been so very good to him, even though they were much older than ordinary parents with offspring his age, so they certainly couldn't understand some of his ways. His mother, particularly, thought of him as so very special, and took care of him in such a way as to go beyond spoiling him, with what meager means they had, so far from anywhere.

They would never, ever set foot anywhere besides this secluded area where they had lived for so long, and for that he was eternally grateful.

As he rested on the ledge, the uneasy feeling again overwhelmed him, coming on so powerfully that he felt like bolting. But he didn't want to disappoint his father so he remained in place, fighting the urge to scream.

As he endured, he remembered times in the very recent past when he had felt similarly, times when he had been led to danger spots and had worked with his parents to take care of the problem and save their place of seclusion. This, he realized, was such a time, and he should see it through, no matter how difficult it became mentally.

And then his mental anguish was suddenly over and he smiled. He could see the outcome.

He sat for a time, enjoying the fulfillment, giving thanks for the answer, in his own particular way.

When he finally left the ledge, he rejoined his father. In his own particular way of expressing himself, he smiled and drew a picture in the dirt, a picture of a large circle enclosed within a number of jagged lines that spread out in many directions. At one time in his life he might have been able to communicate enough with his father to explain the diagram. But not today.

So his father smiled and nodded and clapped him on the back, pointing to the picture, asking if he was sure of it. He nodded. The answer, as he knew it, had come to him on that ledge, making him feel warm inside, making him feel safe, and insuring that anyone who stayed with him would be equally as safe.

21

Len Keller and Jeb Mason had arranged to meet Sid Preston at the edge of the roundup camp, after dark. They had met earlier in the afternoon, when Preston had finally made it down off the mountain.

They sat listening to Preston while he discussed the plans for the newly branded Eden livestock.

"I don't care if Burke tells you there are too many. You push them up onto the reserves anyway."

"I told you what happened last time we tried to do that," Keller argued. "He'll just charge us a high number and get a bunch of help to push the stock back down. I don't think he's afraid to use a gun, if pushed hard enough."

Preston was pacing back and forth, drinking coffee. "I believe that," he said. "I've been thinking about where I know him from."

"Did you figure it out?" Keller asked.

"It'll come to me," Preston said. "Those two he had working for him. Where'd they go?"

"No one seems to know," Keller replied.

"I never got to meet them," Preston said. "I understand they were a couple of hard cases."

"They would rather have used their guns than their ropes," Mason said. "But I wasn't afraid of them."

"Are you afraid of anybody?" Preston asked.

"No one I've met so far," Mason said.

"Really?" Preston said. "You're a special man, aren't you?"

Mason frowned and studied Preston. "I suppose you're going to ride out again."

"You heard my instructions, didn't you?"

"You expect us to just watch you head off and come back again whenever you damn well please?"

"You expect me to stick around and hold your hand?"

"I expect you to do your fair share," Mason shouted. "You're gone way too much. That doesn't add up to a full cut of the profits."

Keller walked over to Mason. "Let's not be unfriendly. We're making good money, all of us, working together."

"We're the ones doing the work, you and me and Gamble," Mason pointed out.

"Maybe," Keller said. "But Sid's got Rube Waddell in his back pocket."

"He's right," Preston said. "That counts for a lot. Who else do you know that would allow you open access to his cattle herd?"

"The point is, you don't do anything but shoot elk," Mason persisted. "I can't figure that."

"Are you ready to move to another outfit?" Preston asked.

Mason smiled. "You wouldn't fire me."

Keller broke in. "Jeb, you know what happens to any one of us who tries to break out of this."

"You can't call me a rustler, any one of you, without bringing it on yourselves."

"It's our word against yours," Preston said. "Why don't you ever use your head?"

Mason frowned. "I don't like the way you treat me, Sid. You're always calling me stupid."

"I've never said you were stupid," Preston corrected him. "Reckless, yes. Bullheaded, yes. But you've never made a stupid move."

Mason relaxed a bit.

"Yet," Preston added. "You haven't made one yet. You've talked about it but you haven't actually followed through. Just don't let it happen."

Preston noticed someone watching from the shadows. Burt Gamble staggered forward and took a drink from his bottle.

"I heard you ran off night before last," Preston said. "Where'd you go?"

"Into town for a drink," Gamble replied.

"Into town? For all that time?"

"That's where I was."

"I've never known you to drink, Burt," Preston said. "But, then, I've never known you all that well."

"No, we haven't known each other all that well," Gamble said. "It's a surprising thing what you don't know about somebody."

"What is that supposed to mean?" Preston asked.

Gamble stumbled and fell forward.

"He's drunker than he was last night," Keller commented.

"Lean him against that tree," Preston said.

Keller and Mason propped him up. They stood back while Preston lowered himself to one knee and whispered into Gamble's face.

"Where'd you go the other night?"

Gamble spat in his face.

Preston wiped the spittle from his jaw and touched the knife at his side. Keller tapped his shoulder and said, "That ranger's standing over there."

Preston came to his feet and Burke met him.

"Hard to find you, Preston," Burke said. "Do you want to finish your count in the morning?"

"First thing," Preston said.

"You going to be here, to sign off on the tally?"

"Keller will do that."

"Another thing," Burke said. "I don't see Waddell's prize longhorns anywhere here."

"Don't know anything about that," Preston said, obviously impatient.

"Waddell needs to have everything counted, or sell them. His choice."

"Yeah, sure."

"Also, I understand there are some two hundred head of steers fenced into a box canyon near here. I don't want to have to go looking for them."

"Then don't," Preston said.

"Tell Waddell he will be getting a letter addressing both issues."

"Sure, Ranger Burke," Preston said. "Send all the letters you want."

•　•　•

Preston watched Burke walk away toward the Rocker 9 cook fire. He turned back to Keller and Mason.

"Are you two doing all you can to cause a ruckus about Burke using Chick and Art to help him?"

"We've got all the camps in an uproar," Keller said.

Preston was nodding. "Good. That should make it easier for us. I want all of our steers in the forest reserves. None of them go back or get sold. Got it?"

Keller shook his head. "Sid, I told you, Burke won't go for that."

Preston leaned into Keller's face. "I guess I'll have to have a word with Rube Waddell. He wants to know who's doing a good job and who's not. Do you want a cut in pay?"

Keller stepped back. "What is this? First, you threaten Jeb and now me. What the hell's gotten into you?"

"I've got a lot of things on my mind, Len," Preston said.

"Don't we all," Keller said. "But that don't make the impossible possible."

"I don't want Burke getting his way," Preston pushed. "I mean that."

Mason stepped forward. "We'll get it done."

"That's what I wanted to hear," Preston said.

Keller stared at the two of them. "How do you expect us to push all the steers onto the forest when the other outfits are being forced to cut back? They'll all be watching us."

"Stop complaining, Len," Mason said. "We'll get it done."

Keller studied Preston and Mason. "Do you two want to tell me something I don't know?"

"Mason will fill you in," Preston said.

Mason pointed over to Gamble. "What are we going to do with him?"

"I'll pack him on his horse and set him loose," Preston replied. "I don't think he wants to remain an Eden cowhand."

Burke sat drinking coffee with Chick and Art. A silence had ensued some five minutes earlier and no one had yet broken it.

"I suppose a man is judged by the company he keeps," Burke said. "But I would hope not to be hanged until I was caught red-handed."

"I won't call you a rustler, because I don't think you are one," Chick said. "But I know the Rocker 9 is missing just over a hundred head of steers and like I said, the tally you ran yourself shows that."

"I don't steal from friends," Burke said.

"But you didn't rule out enemies," Art observed. "Maybe Rocker 9 stock would stay put, but Eden steers are fair game. Is that what you're saying?"

"I don't have time to rustle stock."

"How long were Maynard and Lane in the country?" Art asked.

Burke swirled coffee in his cup, looking into the bottom, as if hoping for an answer to surface.

"I couldn't tell you," he finally replied. "They showed up at my cabin the night before roundup started."

"Maybe they'd been around for a while before that," Chick suggested. "Long enough to make off with those steers."

"I won't say that didn't happen," Burke said. "But I didn't know about it."

Chick poured himself another cup of coffee.

"We don't mean to trouble you about this," Art said, "but

we just want to know what happened to those steers. We were hired to watch out for that sort of thing."

"It won't happen again," Burke promised. "After roundup I'll be out every day mapping the reserves."

"What would you do if you caught those two rustling?" Chick asked.

"I'd do what I'm paid to do," Burke said. "Report it."

"Even if it was Eden stock?"

"It wouldn't matter whose stock it was."

Chick sipped his coffee, peering over the rim at Burke. "I saw you cleaning a pistol in camp the other night," he said. "A Smith and Wesson? New gun, good brand."

"Yes," Burke admitted. "I had it with me, but didn't think I needed it."

"Maybe you decided you needed it after Maynard and Lane showed up," Chick suggested.

"The Eden boys aren't exactly hospitable folks," Burke said. "They've made that plain. And they've gotten a few of the other bigger operators riled up as well."

"You're right, there could have been some trouble," Art put in. "And maybe in some way those two helped you avoid it. But if they're still around these parts you can mark my words, something bad is going to happen."

Sid Preston rode toward the Devil's Grave, rising huge and naked and stark into the late evening sky. His mind was on Cassie Waddell, as it had been all evening, making his meeting with Keller and Mason difficult. They couldn't possibly understand what it was like to want something so badly—to *need* something so fulfilling that nothing else could possibly matter.

He had been thinking about Cassie ever since Gracie Hill had disappeared. Gracie's whereabouts were still a mystery, but she didn't matter any longer. It was time to bring Cassie to his paradise.

Getting her there would require some planning. He couldn't just ask her to ride up and find his cabin; he had to take her up there for some reason, a reason that would seem logical to her.

He rode, thinking, not paying attention to his surroundings, when she rode up from behind.

"Sid, could I have a word with you?"

Preston was as unbelieving as he was startled. He had been fantasizing, and wondered if she might not be real. But as she came closer, he realized that she was, indeed, before him in flesh and blood.

He touched his knife, feeling exciting sensations run through him.

"I need to talk to you," she said.

"Sure. What about?"

They rode together along the shadowed trail past the Devil's Grave, turning up toward Eden Mountain.

"You're certainly aware that my father and I do not get along. . . ."

"Who isn't?"

"Then you can understand that I'm having some major problems with him. You see, Mother will be gone soon and I stand to be left out of the ranch ownership completely."

"Would he do that?"

"Yes, because he plans to marry Vivian Cross, and join their two operations together."

"I've heard that rumor," Preston said. "But I can't stop that from happening."

"No, but you can let me help you destroy my father's empire."

"What do you mean?"

"Sid, I know that you've been stealing his cattle." She was taking a chance. She had a good idea that Keller and Mason and Gamble had bunched the steers in the box canyon, because no one else would have that kind of access to land so close to the Eden headquarters.

And Sid Preston owned those three men.

"So if you don't like my father, either, then let's work together," she said.

Preston stopped his horse. "Why would you say something like that?"

"Am I wrong?"

"Your father has been good to me, has given me everything."

"Sid, I know that Keller and Mason and Gamble are never with the other cowhands. They're always off doing something separately, and I know that it's taking steers from Father's herd. Now, are you going to keep stalling?"

"We would have to plan it very carefully."

"Of course."

"You and I would have to go somewhere, be out of sight where no one could find us."

"Yes, that's correct."

Preston studied her. "I'll set up a time to talk?"

Cassie smiled. "You tell me when and where."

22

Burke awakened from a sound sleep to a heavy rumbling. At first he thought it was another dream, accentuated by the ever-present night thunderstorms. There was another storm overhead, but what had actually disturbed him was the fact that the ground was literally shaking.

The campfire was out and in the lightning storm he couldn't focus long enough to see where Chick or Art had thrown their bedrolls. Everything was a mass of flashes followed by distorted outlines, images that swirled in and out of focus with each burst of light.

What he knew to be real, though, was the steady, heavy rumbling, coming ever closer.

He pulled on his pants and boots, and stood up. The air was filled with the smell of crushed sage and dust, and the pounding was nearly upon him.

He ran as fast as he could across the bottom. A longhorn steer crossed just in front of him, running wildly in the darkness. More followed. He dug in and churned as fast as he could, dodging two more as he started up the slope toward safety. He grabbed shrub branches and tufts of grass, anything he could to gain a better hold as he climbed.

At the top of the hill, he sagged to his knees, fighting for breath. Overhead, the storm worsened and the sky rolled with thunder, adding to the noise of the heavy trampling just below.

He heard Chick and Art yelling, but he couldn't see them. Their cries were quickly swallowed up by the drumming sound of the herd, their hooves pounding the small draw into fine dust.

Burke sat down, helpless to do anything but remain where he was, and watch the herd of stampeding cattle go on and on just below him, a rolling mass of horns and dark backs in the flashing light of the storm.

The herd passed and the dust hung thick, darkening the sky even more, and turning the bolts of lightning into giant filmy webs of white. Burke remained seated on the hillside, afraid to go down. He could hear cowhands yelling to one another. Many of them had already mounted their horses and were after the stampeding herd.

Burke started down the hill toward a group of hands who had surrounded something. One of them had a lantern.

"It looks like a shirtsleeve to me," the cowhand was saying. "It's wet."

"That's blood," another one said.

Another one knelt down and said. "Isn't that part of a hand?"

Burke had trouble with what he was seeing, powdered pulp that had been human flesh and bone, sticky globs of mud that had once been a man's lifeblood.

"Ellis Burke, is that you?" a cowhand asked.

"Yes," Burke replied. "I was camped down here but got out."

"Who was with you?"

"Chick Campbell and Art Gilroy. I didn't have time to find them."

"Yeah, it happened pretty fast," the hand said.

As they looked further, more body pieces were located, and

the trunk of someone, with one leg attached, shattered, trampled into pulp.

"Who is it?" the cowhand with the lantern asked.

Burke couldn't answer. He turned away to be sick.

"We'll have to gather everyone from the Rocker Nine," another cowboy suggested. "That's the only way we'll know."

As light broke in the east, Burke wandered the bottom, numb with shock. The segment of the herd that had stampeded through the draw was mainly Eden steers, with a few steers and cows that belonged to Bill Conrad's Rocker 9. All the loose stock was now scattered throughout the high country, all through the reserve, and would be impossible to round up again without spending at least another four to five days.

For the time being, Eden Land and Livestock would be grazing more cattle than their allotment allowed.

What remained of Art Gilroy had been gathered in a grain sack and rested at the bottom of an open grave at the edge of the Rocker 9 camp. Chick Campbell lay unconscious and covered with blankets, in the back of an empty cook wagon. His lower left leg was badly broken, but he had managed to climb a tree and save himself. Burke had discovered him doubled over a large limb, his arms and legs dangling. He would have never noticed him except for the dripping blood.

Some of the hands were taking turns telling stories about Art and how well they had liked the man. Some said prayers for him, while others stood with their heads bowed, their hats in their hands. They took turns shoveling soil into the grave.

Burke had constructed a wooden headboard and had branded the words:

ARTHUR JAMES GILROY
October 10, 1869–June 14, 1905
Killed by stampede
A fine man to ride the trail with.

Burke wished Chick was able to take part in the burial, but his condition was worsening and the cook was eager to get him down to town, to Doc Simmons.

Though the stampede had been sudden, it hadn't been totally unexpected. The storms had kept the stock on edge all during roundup. There had been a small bunch of horses that had taken off the first night, but they had run up into the reserves, not through the draw.

This led Burke to wonder why the steers had gone through the draw and hadn't scattered in different directions. It seemed to him that they had been herded, and kept close together, so that as many as possible would stampede through the area where he and Chick and Art had laid their bedrolls.

The more he thought about it the more he became convinced that the stampede had been orchestrated. But that would be difficult to prove, and he couldn't keep the cowhands from returning to work. The roundup was close to over and despite the tragedy the branding had to continue.

After Art Gilroy was buried, Burke announced that the tallies were finished for the time being and another would be done during the fall shove-down onto the winter pastures. Everyone sensed his pain at having lost a good friend, and some even offered to help him finish his work.

But Burke decided he wasn't putting anyone else's life in

danger. He politely declined the offers and offered a regular job with the forest service to anyone who wished to help during that fall. In the meantime, he would complete a series of range and forest surveys, compiling an accurate assessment of the grass and timber cover on the reserves that he could check against the work already done by the still-missing Mark Jones.

Everyone had pretty well given up on the idea that he was still alive. He had yet to reappear anywhere and there had been no correspondence by him to anyone, not even the forest service.

Burke thanked one of the Rocker 9 hands for lending him a saddle and prepared to leave camp. He intended to catch up with the cook's wagon that was taking Chick Campbell to town.

As he climbed on Lancaster, he heard a hand yelling as he rode back from the lower end of the draw.

Another body had been discovered.

Once again, there was little left to identify. But one of the Eden hands discovered a hat that had somehow escaped trampling and declared that it belonged to Burt Gamble.

"Must have gotten drunk and fallen off his horse," Jeb Mason said. He laughed. "Picked a bad place to pass out."

Though few of the hands from any of the outfits knew Gamble that well, another grave was dug. Len Keller and Jeb Mason were absent when the dirt was shoveled in.

As the branding and sorting got underway once again, Burke scouted the area above the draw. He decided to postpone catching up with Chick Campbell for another hour or so. He began his search without knowing what he was looking for until he found it: An empty peach can with the lid still partially attached, filled halfway with small pebbles.

Rattling a can of small pebbles during a lightning storm could set off the most tranquil herd.

He took the can and stashed it inside a saddlebag that had been loaned to him by one of the Eden hands, a longtime friend of Art Gilroy. His own belongings existed as small remnants somewhere within the dusty mass of soil and vegetation left behind by the herd.

Burke had then quietly met with a few of the cooks for the various outfits—the Eden cook first. In discussing the disaster, he had noticed that the supplies inside the wagon contained a case of canned peaches, produced by the same manufacturer.

But the Rocker 9 cook had a few cans of the same variety, as did one other cook for another brand. Apparently the general store in Eden carried that brand of peaches exclusively.

A short discussion with Len Keller and Jeb Mason had proved a waste of time, as he had envisioned it would. Only dark frowns from these two, who wanted to know why he hadn't been sleeping in the draw.

Despite his inability to officially pin the disaster on Keller and Mason, or the absent Sid Preston, Burke made a promise to himself: He would be sticking around and Art Gilroy's death and Chick Campbell's terrible injury would be a major factor in his decision on how to manage the new allotments on the forest reserves.

23

Red Maynard and Dean Lane tied their horses within the cover of the trees and crept to the edge of the box canyon. They had been scouting the area for the past few days, doing most of their searching late in the afternoon, when the shadows were longer and the hiding places easier to hide in.

The day before, they had split up, each one taking a different direction, in order to cover more ground. Dean Lane had discovered something and couldn't wait to show Maynard. He didn't want to wait until dusk to bring Maynard to his find. They would have to move quickly if they were to take advantage of their luck.

"I told you," Lane said to Maynard as they peered down into the canyon. Trapped behind a fence were two hundred steers, just waiting to be escorted out.

"We can't take them all at once," Maynard said. He smiled. "Half of them now, half later."

"It's a good holding area," Lane said. "We could move more in here over time."

"It's been used for a while," Maynard observed. "There's not much grass left." He smiled. "It doesn't matter. There's plenty of beef to go around."

•   •   •

As the sun set over his secret paradise, Sid Preston continued with his plans to have Cassie Waddell come for a visit. He had already dug the grave, had already decided when he would kill the huge trophy elk. It was all coming together. He just had to get her to the cabin.

She was desperate to destroy her father's empire and would apparently go to any extreme to accomplish that goal. How could it be so easy? Was it possible?

He couldn't force things, though. She was far too intelligent. He would have to work on her gradually, get her to trust him first.

But he worried about his own patience level. His urges were difficult to deal with now. His fantasies kept him awake at night and although his concerns about Ellis Burke were growing as well, they could not compare to his wild yearning to have Cassie join him.

Of immediate concern was Keller and Mason, and where they would be during his time with Cassie. He had already made plans for them as well and prepared to meet them over at their regular rendezvous location, the place they always complained about.

Very soon, he wouldn't have to hear any more of their sniffling. He would send them off to do their duty for him and it would provide ample time for his union with Cassie.

He rode to the meeting place and started a fire, then set up his table. After resting his Sharps rifle against a nearby tree he placed his knife on the table and got his deck of cards out. He was busy with solitaire when they arrived.

"You're late," he told them.

"Why didn't you tell us you were going to dump Gamble in that draw?" Keller asked. "We had a tough time with Burke over that."

"You don't have to answer to Burke for anything."

"He didn't see it that way. Especially since he saw Gamble with the three of us not two hours before it happened."

"That doesn't mean anything," Preston said. "He saw Gamble drunk. We didn't pour it down him."

"Drunk or not, he was alive," Keller pointed out.

"And what was all that about women and butchers?" Mason asked. "Did you get that?"

"I had never seen him drunk before, so I had no idea what he was rambling about," Preston replied.

"He seemed to hate you the most," Mason said, watching Preston's expression.

"He always hated me the most," Preston said. "That doesn't matter now. The roundup is over and it's time to move those steers out of the box canyon. First thing tomorrow, before Burke starts on his range surveys and finds them."

"We can't handle that many all at once, just the two of us," Keller protested.

"Just move them, damn it!" Preston said. "Sell fifty at a time and just keep moving them from place to place."

Mason stepped forward. "You know, with Gamble gone now, we're shorthanded. You need to be working with us more."

Preston stabbed his knife into the table. "When are you going to figure it out? You don't give the orders."

"Sid, it's only fair," Keller put in. "After all, we can't do it all by ourselves any more."

Preston took a deep breath. "Let's do it this way. Move the steers way up to the Bear's Ears. It will look to anyone like you're pushing them to market in Wyoming, like some of the other outfits will be doing. Take fifty head on up and come back down here. I'll let you know what to do after that."

"We can't do it, just the two of us," Keller said.

"I'm telling you to do it," Preston insisted.

Mason turned to Keller. "It's time to tell him."

Preston looked up from his cards. "Tell me what?"

"I thought you told us you were keeping watch on those steers in the box canyon," Keller said. "When was the last time you saw them?"

"What the hell is this all about?" Preston asked.

"Half of them are gone, Sid. Where'd they go?"

Preston stood up. "What are you trying to say?"

"I'm just saying, they're gone," Keller replied. "What do you suppose happened to them?"

"This had better be a joke."

"No joke," Mason said. "The fence was tight and the gate shut. Someone took half and left half."

Preston paced in front of the fire. "We'll do it this way," he finally said. "Don't take the rest of them to the Bear's Ears. Just sit tight and watch them. See who comes along."

"Do you think there's someone invading our territory?" Mason asked.

"Has to be," Preston said. "Where did those two that worked with Burke go? Are they still around?"

"Hard to say where they went," Keller said. "But that's a possibility. Word was that they worked the Canadian line out of Canada."

"So get to the box canyon and set up a watch," Preston said.

"What if Burke shows up?" Keller asked.

Preston stabbed his knife into the table again. "Then it will be time for him to disappear."

Burke stood over Chick Campbell, adjusting the lantern light in the room, assuring him that having lost his right leg from the knee down wouldn't make him any less of a man.

"I'm of no use any longer," Chick insisted, "not to nobody."

"How can you say that?" Burke asked him. "You'll still be able to ride."

"Who are you trying to kid?"

"What would stop you?" Burke asked.

"You ever try cutting steers from a herd with a bum knee?" Chick asked. "Then try no knee at all."

Doc Simmons, who had left his office to bring in some firewood, arrived in time to tell Burke, "Don't get him upset."

"Too late," Chick said. "And don't stoke that fire no more. I'm cooked as it is."

"Can't let you get chilled," Doc Simmons said. To Burke he said, "What are you bothering him about?"

"I'm trying to convince him that his life isn't over."

"That's all well and good," the doctor said, "but maybe you should wait a few days, when he's stronger."

"Is that what you intend to do?" Burke asked.

"Neither one of you can make me believe I'll ever be the same," Chick said.

"Of course you won't ever be the same," Simmons said. "A lot has changed, but that doesn't mean you can't lead a productive life."

"I don't intend to be no store clerk," Chick said.

The doctor came over to the bed and filled a little glass with liquid. "There's a lot that you could do besides that," he told Chick. "Sit up and drink this."

"I want to cowboy. That's all I've ever done," Chick argued. He made a face as the liquid went down.

"Think of this as a new beginning," Simmons suggested.

"New beginning, my ass," Chick said. "Or what's left of it."

"You're upsetting him," Burke told Simmons.

"I suppose you're right," the doctor said. He took Chick's chart from the table beside the bed, along with a pencil. "Let's allow him to rest."

Burke followed Simmons from the room into his office and took a seat at the front of his desk. He noticed a handbag resting on the desktop.

"Cassie Waddell gave that to me," Burke said. "There's some poisonous plants in there. Can you have them tested?"

"I'll send them to Denver," Simmons said. "Is it important?"

"Cassie thinks it is," Burke replied.

From the other room, Chick Campbell yelled, "Open the damned door! I'm cooking back here!"

"Just endure it," Simmons said. "The heat will help kill any infection in you."

"The heat will kill me first," Chick said.

"You'll be up and at 'em in no time," Burke yelled.

Simmons leaned across his desk toward Burke.

"We can't push him too quickly," he said. "Even if we're successful in getting his spirits up, they'll fall again when he tries to walk on his own."

"I just don't want him giving up," Burke said.

"That's not likely." Simmons scribbled on the chart. "He'll do a lot of complaining, but he won't go any farther than that."

"How can you be so certain?"

"I've seen men like him before, with similar injuries." He tapped the pencil against the chart. "They detest their condition and they're so angry they could shoot somebody, but they don't call it quits. It's the quiet ones you have to be concerned about."

"You sound like a psychologist."

"I could practice that if I so wished. I have a degree that allows it."

"Why don't you?"

"Nobody out here believes they have any problems." He began to chew on the end of the pencil.

"So you fix them physically and hope the rest takes care of itself?"

"I do what I can for them physically and do a little work on their head at the same time. Illness takes its toll out here but a great many of the injuries are caused by spills from horses and carriages, train-yard accidents, together with some shootings— and I've had a lot of experience with the psychological trauma of violence."

Doc Simmons explained that he had worked with police officers in Boston for a number of years before leaving for the West, treating mainly injuries caused from gunshot wounds, knives, blunt instruments, and burns from fire.

"You would be surprised how many of those officers had difficulty coping with their jobs after that," he said. "But the wounds they suffered themselves were far less devastating mentally than the wounds they saw inflicted on others."

He went on to describe the life-altering scenarios experienced by the officers, and how many of them coped.

"Alcohol and opium were drugs of choice, followed by a lot of various combinations of things. I worked with a number of cases, the worst ones being those who saw women and children in death."

"That would be hard to deal with," Burke said, recalling his inability to deal with his younger sister's death.

"Discovering the aftermath of a horrible crime can leave an emotional scar that can't be erased," Simmons continued. "All you can hope to do is work with them, to help them cope with it."

"Sounds like it's affected you pretty deeply as well," Burke observed.

"I thought I'd left that all behind," Simmons said. He toyed with the pencil and stared out the window into the darkness. "Then Burt Gamble arrived in town the other night."

Burke straightened in his chair.

"He was very disoriented when I first saw him," Simmons continued. "He was babbling and stumbling in the street, and though he hadn't been drinking yet, he was psychologically devastated." Simmons chewed the tip of his pencil. "I tried to talk to him, but he wanted nothing to do with me. Later, I tried again and as soon as I entered the saloon he covered his face and went under a barroom table with a bottle."

"Acting like a frightened child, in some way," Burke said.

"Precisely," Simmons acknowledged. "He saw something that brought back horrific childhood memories. But I really don't know what it was."

The doctor went on to describe how he had kneeled down next to Gamble, working to calm him. Gamble had said, "They're gutted. . . . I saw it, I swear on my mother's grave."

"What was he talking about?" Burke asked.

"I don't know for certain," Simmons said.

"He didn't say what he saw gutted?"

"When I asked him to come with me to the office, he refused," Simmons continued. "I couldn't get him out from under the table. Who knows, he might have been hallucinating. It bothers me."

"I guess we'll never know now," Burke said. "He was killed in the stampede, you know."

"Did he say anything to you?"

"He was too drunk." Burke stood up. "I've got a lot of work to do. If you get some results back on those plants, let me know."

24

Burke stood in his cabin doorway and looked out across the mountains. A lot was happening and he didn't know what to make of any of it. There seemed to be no way that he could rid himself of Red Maynard and Dean Lane, and the matter of the poisonous plants also troubled him.

There was no question that Rube Waddell and Vivian Cross were conspiring to unite themselves and their empires, at everyone else's expense. But that was a matter for authorities, if and when the time came anyone could prove anything.

He returned to his table to finish a long overdue report that he would be sending to Washington, D.C. He hadn't initiated any correspondence for some time and they would be wondering.

His report had remained within the boundaries of his job. He had documented Art and Burt Gamble's deaths and Chick's leg injury, and had included the latest tallies taken during the roundup. He had noted that almost all the cattle that would be using the forest reserves, with the exception of those steers that had stampeded through the draw, had been included in the inventory.

He had also mentioned that the majority of the steers not counted in the tallies belonged to Eden Land and Livestock.

As he sealed the envelope, he considered the two other conditions that had emerged.

After returning from roundup, he had discovered two items

in his mail: A badge that he was instructed by official memo to carry attached to his vest during his work on the forest, and a letter from the Pinkerton detective agency in Denver.

He had known that badges were to be issued to each ranger, but didn't expect the letter from the Pinkertons.

The subject was Sid Preston, who had once worked for them.

Burke knew all too well that Preston had once been a Pinkerton. That was something he had been wishing he could forget. It was only a matter of time until Preston remembered their meeting of five years past. But the letter requested his reply regarding any interactions with Preston. It seemed he had been dismissed from the agency for an indiscretion they didn't describe in the letter.

In the letter, the agency was requesting that he forward, through his superiors, any information he might have regarding Preston's present position with Eden Land and Livestock. They had written Rube Waddell several times, but had never received an answer.

The agency's main concern had to do with a Wyoming train robbery that had taken place five years earlier, during which Preston had established a stakeout on the train and had been injured in a shoot-out with the robbers. During Preston's attempt to stop the holdup, he had pulled the mask off one of the outlaws, but had passed out in the process from excessive blood loss.

Burke had noted in the letter that the agency had reason to believe that two of the three outlaws involved in the robbery were somewhere within the Routt National Forest. A man named William Conrad had written them a letter stating emphatically that he had seen them during the recent roundup, and that he thought they should be aware.

Now the Pinkertons were interested in closing an open case. He had to find Maynard and Lane as soon as he could.

Burke went over his list of supplies that he would need for the next week. He had included plenty of bullets for his Smith & Wesson. He didn't know how Maynard and Lane would greet him.

His thoughts were interrupted when Cassie Waddell rode up and quickly dismounted.

"You seem a little edgy," she said. She noticed the Smith & Wesson holstered on his belt. "I was hoping to see your pistol, but not necessarily that one."

"There's a lot going on, Cassie," he said. "But I am glad to see you."

He took her in his arms and they began immediately to kiss passionately. She reached down and commented, "My, but your pistol certainly is ready for action."

Inside the cabin, she and Burke took turns undressing one another, touching, caressing, kissing one another all over.

"It's been a long roundup," Burke said.

"It would have been nice to have warmed your bed a few nights for you," she said, pulling him on top of her.

"I thought about going to look for you," he said.

She gasped when he entered her. They surged together, rolling off the bed in a tangle of covers, laughing, exploring one another, coming together again, and finally reaching fulfillment together.

"So let's not wait so long for this next time," she said. "I'm getting spoiled."

. . .

She watched Burke get ready for his trip to do range surveys. He hadn't fully unpacked everything since roundup and his sleeping gear was piled in a heap. But instead of hauling water from the creek, heating it, and getting out the soap, he decided that the smoke smell in his blankets was there to stay.

Cassie offered to wash his clothes for him and he thanked her. "Just the uniform and an extra shirt and pants," he said. "I've got some other clothes and I'll take care of the rest when I get back."

While Cassie worked, she thought of the following week. She was torn between wanting to go with him and needing to return to her mother's side. It was so difficult, watching her gradually shrink in size, yet never complaining, always willing to smile.

Her father had stopped giving her mother tea and had tried to start once again. But Cassie had convinced her mother that drinking anything that she didn't get for herself wasn't a good idea.

Cassie had come to see Burke at her mother's request. "Tell him he can't give up his work here, no matter the pressure put to bear against him," she had said. "And take him this, as a present from me."

Cassie went to Burke and handed him a small yellow pin in the form of a butterfly.

"Mother wanted me to give you this," she said.

Burke studied it. "I'll pin it to my vest, next to the badge."

"She'll be glad to hear that."

"Tell her thank you for me."

"Why don't you tell her?"

"I would do that," Burke said. "If your father wasn't around."

"I believe he'll be leaving for Glenwood Springs toward the end of the week," Cassie said. "Another stock grower's meeting."

"I'll be surveying by then. But I could come back."

"She would appreciate that," Cassie said. "And after you see Mother, then what?"

"There's a lot of work to do, and I will say that I'm going to target your father. I had a short meeting with Preston one night during the roundup and I'm certain he's behind the stampede."

"So you think he caused it?"

"He wasn't there, but either Keller or Mason rattled a can of pebbles. I found the can."

"That sounds like something Sid Preston would instruct them to do," Cassie said. "He's certainly not to be trusted."

"That's an understatement."

Burke was going to continue, but Cassie told him something he hadn't imagined.

"Preston told me the other night after leaving roundup that he's been stealing Father's steers for some time now."

"You saw him?"

"I was angry at you and approached him to help me ruin my father's empire. I told him I knew that I suspected that he'd been stealing cattle and he as much as admitted it."

"That is truly unbelievable," Burke said.

"I guess I'll have to tell him that I won't be needing his help, if you're going after Father yourself."

"Cassie, the best thing you can do is stay as far away from him as possible," Burke said.

"I know I made a mistake," she agreed, "but I don't know how to tell him I don't want his help."

"If he shows up, just tell him that I'm helping you now. If he wants to know any more than that, have him come see me."

"I don't think it will be that simple."

"You have to make it that simple, Cassie."

"I'm beginning to wonder about him," Cassie said. "I saw him again briefly at the corrals the other day. I was saddling my horse and he just appeared. We talked about stealing Father's cattle. He stared at me for the longest time, and he loves to fondle his hunting knife."

"I'm telling you, stay as far away from him as you can," Burke repeated. "There's more to him than anybody knows."

Sid Preston walked naked in the night fog, holding his hunting knife, circling the burial ground. He had located the huge elk and would bring it down at first light, but only if the fog had lifted. Right now he was praying to the forest to send the fog away, then bring it back again once he had the grave dug and the elk tied in place.

Nights were fine for his pleasures with knives and women, but fog added a special dimension. The smooth and silky feel of it highlighted the event, made the screams more pronounced in some way, allowed them to roll out into the dense atmosphere and remain there forever.

That was what had him so excited. Cassie Waddell was almost his, and the forest was glad.

After he was through talking to the fog and the forest, he would take a ride down to the ranch and meet with Rube Waddell. The stock growers' meeting began in Glenwood Springs on the weekend and Waddell would surely have some instructions for him regarding the ranch and its management. He always did.

Tonight, Preston suspected that Waddell would have some

plans about what to do with Ellis Burke. Everyone knew that Burke was beginning his range surveys and there was no doubt that he would target the Eden brand, especially after the roundup. Something had to be done about Burke, and he would convey that to Keller and Mason.

Then, with Waddell gone and his two men dealing with Burke, he would have ample time to bring Cassie up to his private paradise.

Len Keller and Jeb Mason ate steak and beans at an open campfire. Mason had staked out the box canyon ever since they had discovered that half the steers had been stolen, while Keller rode the area, looking for riders he couldn't identify, or Red Maynard and Dean Lane.

"I say we just take those steers and sell them," Mason said. "They're losing good weight penned up like that."

"I don't know that Sid would like it," Keller said. "I mean, what if whoever took the steers rustles some more while we're gone?"

Keller thought a while. They could easily move the steers out without being detected. The fog made for excellent cover. By the same reasoning, anyone else with the same idea in mind could round up enough to make a good sale and a lot of extra money for themselves.

"I don't like it that Sid hasn't come to check on us," Keller finally said. "I know we talked at one time about finding out what he's up to, but I think it's time now that we do just that."

Mason was surprised. "I never thought I'd hear you say that. You're always defending him."

"Well, it's true that he's got a good connection with Waddell and that's good for us, but if he don't ever come to help us, then we can't get anything done, either."

They decided to wait another day. If Preston didn't show and neither did Maynard and Lane, they would ride together up into the headwaters country of Eden Creek and see what was keeping Sid Preston's undivided attention up there.

25

The old man and his son sat in the firelight, eating cuts of deer mixed with roots and berries. The old woman sat nearby, sewing porcupine quills onto a buckskin dress and singing an ancient song.

"You know what that means," the old man said to the boy. "She sings that song when something bad is about to happen."

The son knew what it meant. He always listened but seldom spoke. He spent most of his time with a small knife, whittling animals and birds from pine and sometimes oak. He had a large collection of carvings that he kept neatly arranged, in families of a sort, and each new carving had a special place among the others.

"But you believe we'll be spared from anything bad," the old man said to his son. "You learned that the other day. Right?"

The son nodded once again. It disturbed him that his father couldn't relax and enjoy himself. Yes, the bad thing was about to happen. The beginnings of it were already starting, and it would carry on for a while.

The boy didn't want them worried about the bad things that were about to take place, for as he had already told them, they would be spared, along with some others.

. . .

Sid Preston stood in the new mansion with Rube Waddell, discussing the roundup, the stampede, and Cassie.

"I thought you should know," Preston was saying. "I followed her for a while today and she rode straight over to that ranger's cabin. That can't be good."

"It's not good at all. I'll speak to her about it," Waddell said.

"I thought you two were having your troubles."

"We are."

"Maybe I should talk to her," Preston suggested.

Waddell stared at him. "What?"

"You know, mention that Burke is an enemy of the Eden ranch. Let her know that you care about her but would rather she kept the best interests of the family at heart."

"Sid, I never saw you as a politician."

"It was just a suggestion, since you two have your troubles and all."

"It should be me," Waddell said. "I'll get it done right away."

Cassie stood at the window in the old house, looking out into the fog. It had rolled in so quickly and silently, blanketing the mountains.

No hint of rain, only dense fog. The year was a very strange one.

She walked back into the bedroom with the chopped steak and potatoes and diced green peppers that she had rustled up at the stove for her mother.

"The fog is getting thicker, Mother," she said. "How strange is that?"

"Certainly strange for this time of year," Charlotte said. She allowed Cassie to help her up and place a pillow behind her back. "That looks good."

"I'm glad you're feeling better," Cassie said.

Midway through the meal, Rube Waddell came barging into the house. He tottered into the bedroom, a cigar in one hand and a glass of brandy in the other.

"I need to speak to you," he said to Cassie.

"Can't you see, I'm helping Mother with her dinner?" she said.

"She don't eat as much as some stupid bird," Waddell said. "I want to see you now."

Charlotte glared at him. "I'm feeling significantly better, Rube, thank you very much," she said. "What's the occasion for your drunkeness?"

Waddell ignored her. "Cassie, in the living room. Now."

"You can tell me here, Father," Cassie said. "Or just forget it."

Charlotte smiled. "By all means, Rube, lay your wisdom on both of us."

Waddell reddened. He cleared his throat. "I understand you've been seeing Ellis Burke."

"And what if I have?"

"I don't want to be accused of consorting with the forest service for special favors."

"I didn't know you had been," Cassie said.

"Cassie, don't be flippant. I'm talking about you, here," he said. "You're my daughter and how you behave reflects directly on me."

"What I do and who I see is none of your business."

"It is as long as you live on my property."

Charlotte said, "Come now, Rube, you're crossing the line."

Waddell stepped closer to the bed. "I wasn't talking to you."

"Cassie and I are united here, Rube. Believe that."

Waddell blew smoke from his cigar. "Woman, you don't even know what you're saying. Who knows if you'll even see tomorrow."

"She'll see plenty of tomorrows," Cassie said.

Charlotte studied her husband. "Maybe you'd like to just shoot me. Is that it, Rube?"

Waddell glared at her.

"But that would be too messy, wouldn't it, Rube?" Charlotte continued.

Cassie took her mother's hand. "Mother, relax. He's not worth it."

"There's no point in discussing this any further," Waddell said. He drained his brandy. "Just remember what I said about Ellis Burke."

"So, you think you've had the last word?" Cassie asked.

Waddell blew smoke from his cigar. "My word is the last word."

Cassie laughed. "Tell it to Ellis Burke."

Waddell threw his brandy glass into the dresser mirror. "I will tell it to Ellis Burke, don't think I won't."

"Seven years, Father." She pointed to the glass on the dresser and the floor. "Or should I say, seven *more* years of problems."

Waddell started for the doorway. Cassie watched him, laughing.

"I'll take your regards to Ellis," she said. "I'll whisper in his ear."

Waddell turned in the doorway. "The two of you won't last," he said. "This whole thing will all be over soon."

"You are already over, Father," Cassie said. "Your time has passed. People are watching how you manage your grazing and your cattle now."

Rube Waddell took a deep breath. He looked around the room.

"Enjoy yourselves while you can. I'm having this building torn down first thing tomorrow." He smiled and savored the shocked expressions on Cassie and Charlotte's faces.

"You can't do that," Cassie said.

"Just watch me." Waddell threw the old cigar across the room and lit a new one. "And there will be no wagons or horses for transporting your mother anywhere. She can walk if she wants to leave."

"She can ride with me," Cassie said.

"I'll see to it that my men watch you," Waddell continued. "I'll have them pull her off onto the ground. If she wants to leave, she walks. I'll have a tent erected for the two of you, so get your valuables out tonight." He puffed hard on his cigar. "Good-bye, now. I'm going to join someone who truly knows my worth."

As he clomped drunkenly out of the house, Cassie turned to her mother.

"Is he serious?"

"He would do anything to get back at you and me," Charlotte said.

"Can we stop him?"

"I don't see how."

Cassie thought a moment. "Didn't Father just say that he was going to join someone? Someone who 'knows his worth' as he put it?"

"Cassie, don't."

"And I'll bet that someone is right up the hill, pandering him in the new mansion."

"Cassie, let it go," Charlotte said.

But Cassie was already gone.

Cassie stood outside the new mansion, clouded with fog and late evening shadows. She could hear Vivian and her father inside, talking in heated tones. Their voices were muffled but she could understand enough of it to realize that the conversation related directly to her and her mother, and what a burden they had become.

She tried to enter the front door. It was locked. She asked to be let in. Silence from inside.

She went around to the back. Locked. More silence.

She hurried around to the front and yelled, "Father, it's important that we talk. Please."

Silence.

Cassie went back into the old house and found a piece of paper. While her mother called for her to remain there, she wrote a note and then found a string and, once in front of the mansion, tried calling to her father again.

Continued silence.

She found a good-sized rock and after attaching the note, hurled it through the picture window that faced the valley. That brought her father to the window.

He peered into the fog. "Cassie, what in the hell do you think you're doing?" he yelled.

"Did you read the note?" she replied.

He held the note up. "It says, 'Can't you hear me?' "

"Well, can't you hear me? I asked to be let in."

At that moment Vivian Cross appeared in the window next to Waddell. She said something to Cassie about growing up and acting her age and leaving them alone and returning to her mother's side, where she belonged, and staying away from their beautiful new house, yelling out into the fog as if she would tolerate no more of the nonsense.

But Cassie heard little of it. She was prepared for Vivian's appearance and had been holding another rock in her hand.

She let it fly and it crashed through an unbroken segment of the window, whizzing just over Vivian's head, missing her by inches, but spraying her with shards of glass.

She screamed and slumped to the floor.

"Cassie! For God's sake!" Rube Waddell rushed through the door and onto the porch.

Cassie held another rock. "Come on down here, Father. I have one for you as well."

Rube Waddell, beside himself, only stared at Cassie. Again she taunted him, daring him to come toward her, just one more step.

He went back inside.

As soon as he faded from sight, she sat down on the ground and wept.

Doc Simmons stitched the cuts and gashes in Vivian Cross's face, assuring her that the scars would eventually vanish. He knew better but he needed a way to get her to stop complaining and gesturing with her hands.

It was bad enough that they had wrested him from a sound sleep, but Waddell had told him payment would come when and if Vivian healed unblemished.

There were days when the Hippocratic oath seemed hypocritical.

Rube Waddell paced the floor nearby, puffing heavily on a cigar. He had intended to take Vivian to Denver following the meeting in Glenwood Springs, so they could test out a few of the new dining rooms, and reacquaint themselves with the older, well-known ones. Now he would be taking her not for socializing, but to see a different doctor, one who could hopefully undo the quackery practiced by Simmons.

"Do you want me to finish this or not?" the doctor said to Vivian.

"You're hurting me."

"Yes, Vivian, I'm using a needle to close some cuts that I would think must be very painful."

"Just finish," Waddell blurted. "Finish and be done with it."

"I believe I have finished," Simmons said. He turned to Vivian. "And before you leave, I have something to show you."

He reached into his desk and pulled out some small flowers. Though they were shriveled, Vivian recognized them immediately.

She said, "What have you got there?"

"Flowers, Vivian," Simmons replied. "I understand you're a gardener."

"Yes, but I can't help you with those. Sorry."

"Surely you can. They're from your garden."

"You must be mistaken, Doctor," she said. "Why would you say a foolish thing like that?"

"They came to me in a small brown handbag," the doctor replied. He took it from his desk drawer. "See here? It reads 'Vivian Cross' in gold letters along the side."

26

Cassie heard her mother's voice and got out of bed in the darkness. She wondered why her mother was calling her. When she wanted something, she usually got it herself.

Perhaps she was too tired, or as Cassie feared, had gotten sick.

Cassie lamented the aftermath of her father's earlier visit. Had she the opportunity to do things differently, she would do so without hesitation.

She shouldn't have gone over to the mansion. She felt guilty for having made her mother so upset with the assault on her father and Vivian. The whole thing had exhausted her, and Cassie worried that it might set her back.

On the other hand, Cassie wished her aim at Vivian had been truer.

"Cassie, can you hear me?"

She reached her mother's bedroom and lit a lantern.

"What's the matter, Mother?"

"Cassie," her mother said, "someone's in the house."

"What?"

"In the house. Someone's in here. I feel so groggy. So tired."

Cassie took a cold cloth from a bowel on the nightstand. She began touching her mother's brow.

"You're getting fevered again, Mother."

She brushed Cassie's arm away. "Did you hear me?" she said in a coarse whisper. "Someone's in the house!"

Cassie listened. The foggy air outside was black and still, the air inside the same.

"I don't hear anything, Mother."

"I swear I heard something."

Cassie and Charlotte both listened intently.

"Maybe it was nothing," Charlotte said. "I wish I didn't feel so awful."

Cassie wiped her mother's brow.

"I don't need that, Cassie. Get me some water, please."

Cassie returned from the kitchen with a glass of fresh water, which her mother sipped, then laid back down.

"Okay, then go back to sleep, Mother. I'll stay up a while."

At her mother's request, Cassie left the lantern burning and stumbled back into her room. She slid into bed and lay with her eyes focused overhead on the black ceiling. Everything was so still, so calm. Nothing moved and there was no sound but an occasional mosquito, one of the rare specimens that had survived the drought.

She suddenly heard creaking, but then she always heard creaking on occasion. The house settled for the most part, but little groans often came from the upper level, where the roof was never at ease.

She felt herself drifting . . .

"Cassie . . . Cassie?"

Still drifting.

"Cassie?"

She jerked awake and sat up. There was no sound.

In her dream, she had been in her mother's room, her

mother's eyes round and wild. Her mother had her arms up, shielding her face from something—a shadow that hovered just inside the doorway.

The shadow had gleaming white teeth and held a large knife that gleamed even brighter.

"Cassie!"

The voice was real this time. She sat up quickly in the darkness.

She swung her legs around to plant them on the floor. She felt the soles of her bare feet touch someone's bare back. She shrieked and pulled them onto the bed, shrinking back against the headboard.

"Hello, Cassie. I was just trying to get a little rest."

Sid Preston sat cross-legged on her floor, just back from the bed. His face was a shadowed outline against the lantern light that seeped in from across the hall.

There was enough light to tell that he was naked, and that he toyed with a knife between his legs.

She pulled the sheets up in front of her.

He tested the knife's edge against his thumb, grunted, and sucked both the blade and his thumb.

Cassie struggled to speak. "What are you doing here, Sid?"

"Getting a little rest. You don't mind, do you?"

"This is highly unusual. You know that?"

"Maybe, but we're getting to know one another better, aren't we?"

"On a business level, Sid. Just a business level."

From the other room: ". . . Cassie?"

"I don't think she's sleeping very well," Preston said. He laid the knife between his legs and stretched back against the wall.

"I'd better go see what she wants," Cassie said. She waited for him to leave. "I need to get dressed."

"I had a meeting with your father tonight," Preston said.

". . . Cassie, can you hear me?"

"Your father told me to be sure your mother gets a double dose of tea every day while he's gone," Preston said. "That woman, Vivian? She was with him. She showed me how to mix the plants for the tea."

"You were over at the mansion?"

"I was there when you stoned the place. Interesting. Old Vivian got some bad cuts."

Preston uncrossed and then crossed his legs, keeping the knife in front of his genitals.

"Did you hear me about the tea?"

"Yes, I did."

"I thought to myself, I could add something to that tea that will make it even better, if I wanted to.' "

Cassie sat still, still shrunken against the headboard.

Preston continued. "Your father also said that after your mother dies—and he figured it would take three or four more days at a double dose—then I was to haul her into town and leave her at the doctor's office, then come back up here and tear this place down. Find the biggest horses in the valley. Buy them. He said do whatever it takes, but level this place."

"I can't believe you were in the mansion," she said aloud.

"I can't believe this is happening!" she thought to herself.

From the other room: "Cassie? Please, can you hear me?"

"You know what, Cassie? Your father wants me to do all

that, but I won't do any of it. You know why? Because we're partners."

"Can we talk about this another time, Sid?"

"What's the matter, Cassie? You don't act like you want to be partners."

"Sid, I do . . . it's just that I don't want to meet here, with my mother and all."

"Next time we'll meet at my place. How's that? We'll become true partners, and then we'll truly join," he said.

"Cassie . . ." Her voice was growing weaker.

"Sid, please," Cassie said.

"We can meet at my place?"

"Maybe. We'll see . . ."

Preston sat silent for a moment. "Go see to your mother."

Cassie pulled the sheet off the bed and wrapped it around her. In her mother's bedroom, she said, "Mother, are you all right?"

"I heard someone in my room a while ago, just after you left. He whispered, 'Cassie is mine. She's all mine.' He said it over and over. Then he was gone."

Cassie sat silent.

"I'm sure of it, Cassie. I think I might have heard the voice before."

"I won't tell you that you were dreaming," Cassie said. "But do you think that you were?"

Cassie noticed a shadow move across one of the side windows. The shadow stopped and a face appeared, then disappeared.

"Cassie," her mother said, "I wasn't dreaming. I only wish that I was."

.   .   .

Burke had started his surveys the previous afternoon, working his way into the high country above the devil's grave, venturing south, above the forest boundary. He had decided to spend the initial time locating areas where he wanted to sample the vegetation and then map them for future reference. After designating all the sample areas, he would return later, possibly with an assistant, and begin the documentary phase of his work.

During these first few days, his main intent was to roam the headwaters of Eden Creek, the area where Sid Preston lived in private seclusion.

It bothered him to think what he would likely find there. If Doc Simmons was right—and Burke had decided that he definitely was—then something beyond human reasoning existed there. So he had packed even more ammunition for his new Smith & Wesson, and had also purchased an older Colt's navy revolver with ammunition while getting supplies in Eden.

But he hadn't anticipated the fog, now a thick blanket that impaired his vision to the extent that he had remained in his first camp much longer than he had wanted, waiting for the sun to burn through.

But it didn't appear that the cold front would leave any time soon and Burke decided to break camp and work his way higher into the mountains. With any luck the following morning would arrive with open skies.

Cassie stood outside the house, holding a rifle she had taken from the mansion, peering out into the fog. If someone arrived they wouldn't see her before she saw them and regardless of their numbers, she would make them pay.

"You're not thinking right," her mother said from a rocker on the porch.

"There are a lot of us in that condition, it would appear," she replied.

Even the servants, who had once known her as calm and practical, wondered at her behavior. They watched with concern from within the mansion, pointing and talking. She held nothing against any one of them, but had warned them against interfering.

Though the doors had been locked and the servants had told her they couldn't allow her entry, she had knocked out more of the broken picture window, climbed in, and taken the rifle, along with enough ammunition to hold off a number of people for a long time.

She continued to stand in the yard, holding vigil.

Her mother sat on the porch, feeling better, but disturbed at the possibilities of Cassie's decision.

"Shooting everyone won't solve anything," she said. "Besides, you don't really believe he'll tear the house down."

"You should know him well enough to believe that he will," Cassie argued. She argued further that, even with the heavy fog, her father was crazy enough to send a wrecking crew.

"It will take him a good number of days to locate a team of horses big enough to pull the logs apart," Charlotte reasoned. "He will have to go out of the valley."

Cassie finally agreed, but still didn't want to take any chances. She worried that he would want them out of the house immediately, regardless of when he planned to destroy the building.

He could come at any time.

"Let's just take our chances with riding out of here now," Charlotte suggested.

"After last night," Cassie said, "you need to regain your strength."

Though Charlotte had awakened much stronger than the night before, she still felt groggy.

"Did you drink some tea?" Cassie asked her.

"As a matter of fact, I did," she said. "It tasted sweeter than usual. I thought you were just trying to be kind."

"Mother, I didn't mix any tea for you," Cassie said. "Don't drink anything anymore unless I'm with you."

"Who would have made it then?" Charlotte asked.

"I don't know," Cassie said. "Maybe one of the servants?"

"They're not allowed over here any more. Your father has seen to that."

"Just don't drink any more tea, then," Cassie said.

They discussed other ideas regarding getting away, like having Charlotte hide somewhere nearby, under the fog's cover, while Cassie rode for Doc Simmons.

But, they reasoned, what if Doc Simmons wasn't there? He often made house calls outside of town.

"I tell you, let's just go," Charlotte said again. "We'll get away."

Charlotte maintained that nothing was more important to Cassie's father than seeing that Vivian had good medical care, and he would go to Denver for that.

So neither of them really had any idea where he was or when he would return, only that he would sooner or later and that they didn't want to be there when he arrived.

"I'm not going to allow myself to stand here and waste time," Cassie finally said. "I've got a plan."

Even as Cassie was helping her into the house, Charlotte fought to get an answer.

"You'll only call me crazy, Mother."

"Too late for that."

"It will work and I will come back, and then we'll go. This will insure us of a passage. I don't know how safe, but it will be a passage."

Sid Preston drove Burke's new Buick down the wagon road into Eden, whistling "My Darling Clementine" as he negotiated the last turns. He was so grateful to Burke for having gotten the headlights repaired; it made such a difference in seeing through the fog.

After their meeting the previous night, Rube Waddell had instructed him to hurry over to Burke's cabin with one of the hands and take the car. He had ridden over with Len Keller and had sent him back to the ranch with the two horses, while he drove on down into Eden. Upon arriving in town, he was to park it in front of Valley Bank and Trust, where Lee Miller would greet him.

Lee Miller was to be the best man at Rube Waddell's wedding to Vivian Cross, as soon as they got word of Charlotte's death.

They would drive the car down into Glenwood Springs for the stock growers' meeting, and on into Denver for the wedding ceremony.

Vivian Cross didn't seem to mind that her wedding pictures would feature her with a face full of stitches. The simple fact of having Rube Waddell at her side was all that mattered to her.

But Preston's mind wasn't on any wedding. He couldn't keep his mind off Cassie. He hadn't even considered that his midnight visit might have bothered her. In fact, he thought she might have been excited by his visit, the display of modesty with the sheets being just that, only a display. Because, he reasoned, whores didn't have a sense of modesty.

And he had managed to get a sound cup of tea down Charlotte, laced not only with the poisonous plants, but his own special blend of laudanum.

The same blend he always used on the women.

It always worked very well.

27

Instead of burning off, the fog had thickened. Burke continued along the treacherous trail, allowing Lancaster to pick his way among the rocks and fallen timber.

The deeper he got into the back country, the more certain he became that he was very lost. He decided to locate a place to camp, someplace other than in heavy timber, and wait for open skies to return.

He found a small meadow that abutted a rock ledge. The swirling fog made the rock face appear and disappear before him so that he had to stop and look closely to be certain he wasn't imagining it all.

As he neared the ledge he discovered a cave, and the air smelled of wood smoke. Before he could dismount, he was confronted by an old man, dressed in skins.

"I can't figure how you found your way up here," the old man said. He carried a Hawken rifle, pointed straight at Burke.

"I mean no harm," Burke told him. "I'm lost."

"Turn around and get your lost self out of here."

Burke studied him. "Ah, yes, old Buck Gentry."

The old man was taken aback. "How in hell do you know me?"

Burke dismounted. "Everyone knows you."

The old man raised the Hawken.

"Damn it, I told you to stay on your horse."

"Go ahead and shoot, Mr. Gentry," Burke said. He took the bit out of Lancaster's mouth so that the horse could graze.

"You don't think I mean business?" the old man said.

"I suppose you do," Burke replied. "But if you shoot me, someone else will take my place. Maybe not tomorrow or the next day, but one day for sure. And I'm too damned tired and hungry right now to turn tail."

"What are you talking about, someone else?"

"I took the place of the man before me," Burke replied. "I'm a forest ranger. Should I disappear also, there'll be another come along soon."

"And I'll take care of all of you, each in turn," he said. His eyes were alive with rage. "Just like that last one."

Burke stared at the old man. Mark Jones came instantly to mind.

"Did you say there was someone up here before me?"

"He tried to run me off, too."

"Who said anything about running you off? I just want a place to sit out the fog."

The old man lowered the rifle. He continued to study Burke.

"I figure you to be pretty straight," he said. "Any man not afraid to meet his maker's got to have a good pair of balls."

"You didn't really want to shoot me, did you?"

"You saying I've never shot a man before?"

"I'm saying I don't see you as one to shoot men for fun."

"What makes you the resident know-it-all?"

"I'm finding out that the back country holds some strange people," Burke replied. "But the ones who appear the most normal are the ones to watch out for. Now, tell me about Mark Jones."

"First, I need to know your name."

"Ellis Burke, and I'm right in calling you Mr. Gentry, aren't I?"

"No, just call me Buck. All my friends are well gone under, a long time past. They all called me Buck. Ever tasted root coffee?"

At first, Burke had trouble keeping the dark liquid down. Thick and boiled from chicory roots, it settled into his tin cup like molasses in February. He discovered that slipping a little clear water into the mixture when the old man wasn't watching made the taste moderately bearable.

Old Buck Gentry didn't get a lot of opportunities to visit and took advantage of Burke's good nature.

"You remind me a little of Darlan Evans," he began, "a man who could hold his own with anything born, excepting maybe that grizzly bear which took him out on a cold spring day, while it snowed as soft as you please. That bear drug him off and I never bothered to go looking for him. Best friend I ever had. Ain't you got nothing to say?"

"I'm sorry about your friend. Do you know what happened to Mark Jones?"

"You wouldn't believe me if I told you."

"Try me."

Buck led him into an adjoining cave where a young man with long hair sat whittling wood. One corner of the cave was filled with small horses and eagles and bears and mountain goats, nearly every kind of bird or mammal that frequented the forest.

Burke looked into the man's unusual eyes.

"Mr. Mark Jones?"

"He don't know what you're saying," Buck said. "Or if he doesn't he won't let on."

"What did you do to him?"

"He did it to himself. Fell from a rock ledge his second day up here and laid still as you please. I was set to bury him but she wouldn't have it."

He pointed into the corner of the cave where an old Indian woman sat, tanning a mountain lion hide.

"She said he had the 'near-death sleep' but would be back, so I let her tend to him. Must have been four months before he came to. But he didn't know who he was or even what he was all about. She's seen to his care ever since."

Burke studied Mark Jones, who looked at him seldom, and with sideways glances.

"Were you a ranger up here?" Burke asked.

Jones whittled in silence.

"Like I said," Buck told Burke, "he's not the same person. Not even close."

Mark Jones examined his work, a small bird in flight.

"The first time I met him, he got the drop on me. I was washing, bare-assed naked in the creek. He told me I had no right on the forest reserves. I asked him what the hell that meant and he showed me a map and said I was inside the boundary and would have to move. He stepped out on yonder ledge to tell me where the line was and fell about twenty feet downslope and slammed his head. He stood up and walked back up and collapsed in my wife's arms. Damnedest thing you ever saw."

Burke sat down in front of Mark Jones. "Can you understand me?"

Mark Jones handed him the bird and made a sign.

"He says that's for you," Buck said. "Hold it to your heart if you accept it with thanks."

Burke held the bird to his heart.

"Do you want to come back with me and try to recover?" Burke asked Jones.

The woman got up and crouched between Burke and Jones, protecting him.

"Best let well enough alone," Old Buck said.

Buck introduced the old woman as his wife, Little Bird Running, a Ute whom he had married many years ago. Neither of them had wanted to leave the area to go with the tribe to a reservation, so they had lived by themselves high in the back country, where no one ever came, until Mark Jones arrived and had threatened to make them leave, since it was now forest service land.

"Why didn't you take him down below?" Burke asked.

"I told you, Little Bird Running wouldn't have it."

Burke frowned. "She wanted to save a stranger who had threatened to force you from your home?"

"You don't savvy Indian ways at all, do you? Little Bird Running and I never had any kids, so she figured the creator sent him to her and wanted her to look after him. Besides, I don't ever go down below, not for any reason."

"Things have changed that much?"

"Let me count the ways," he said.

"You don't think Mark Jones will ever improve?"

"Hs name is From the Rock now."

"Does he ever speak?" Burke asked.

"On rare occasions, but only when something's going to happen. A few nights back, during one of them lightning storms, he took us through the dark to an old tree. Each of us carried a jug of water, just enough to put out the fire when the tree got struck by lightning. Otherwise this whole area would have burned up."

Burke stared at the man who had once been a ranger, who continued to whittle and lick his lips, as if he were all by himself.

"My wife says the spirits are with him and that he's come to help us get by in these changing times," Buck said. "This morning, early, he drew a stick man in the dirt, with a big hat and a big star that covered his chest. What's that you're wearing?"

"It's a forest service badge," Burke replied.

"Want more coffee?"

"I need to be going."

"Thought you were going to wait out the fog."

"I've got a feeling that I should get back," Burke said. "How do I get down from here?"

"Where do you want to end up?"

"That big mountain with the rock walls at the headwaters. They call it Eden Creek."

"Eden's not anywhere near that place," Buck said. "Take my word for it."

Burke rode Lancaster along a winding trail that took him through patches of dense timber and out into open meadows. The fog remained thick and swirling, and darkness was coming on quickly.

He had to ride slowly, as Buck Gentry had directed, or he would find himself taking a trail that led down toward the bottom. To reach the headwaters of Eden Creek, he had to stay to the right at all times, no matter what he thought he should do.

"The fog can fool a man," Buck had said. "When you coming back for more coffee?"

"Maybe I'll bring up some of that newfangled stuff from South America," Burke suggested. "You feel like something new and different?"

"I don't mind new if it's not *too* different," Buck said.

Burke thought about old Buck and his wife, and Mark Jones, who had become their adopted son. They would have to be left out of his report. Even if he included them, the Washington boys would think he'd been drinking while creating official business. They would be right.

Upon leaving, he had said to Buck, "Maybe I'll be back for a visit someday."

"You'd be welcome," old Buck had responded. "And maybe you could see your way clear to bringing up something for my eyes, so I could see up close, and some reading material."

Sid Preston prepared to field dress the huge bull elk. He was elated at his good fortune, for the bull had wandered into the graveyard and he had discovered the massive animal by accident in the fog. Even so, the elk had been difficult to bring down and even more difficult to finish. It was still kicking and trying to get back up.

Avoiding a front hoof, Preston tied the front legs together and tossed the rope over a tree limb, then pulled the animal up with a team of three horses. The huge bull grunted and groaned and worked to free itself, but was helpless.

Preston then spread the two hind legs apart, tying them to opposite trees. He plunged his knife into the elk's middle and ripped downward. The big blade sliced through skin and muscle and stomach lining. The stomach and entrails rolled out in a huge, squiggling, bloody mass.

Only the heart and lungs remained.

But the huge bull refused to die.

Perhaps this struggle was a sign, Preston thought to himself, a sign that he needed to take strength from the bull. After all, Cassie Waddell would be the ultimate prize and he would need all his strength when the time came for them to unite.

But to gain the strength, he would have to do everything just right.

He stripped naked and walked circles around the still struggling elk. The animal was nearly dead now, but still showed amazing strength.

Preston then reached up into the body cavity and found the heart. Still beating, it coated his hands in warm blood as he cut it free. He held it high over his head and screamed, long and loud, then held the organ to his own breast, allowing the last of the blood to pump out onto his chest and down over his stomach and legs.

He smeared himself from head to foot with fresh blood, and circled the elk. He ripped a chunk of heart loose with his teeth and swallowed it whole, feeling the strength and power surge through him.

He screamed again, much louder, and raised the shredded heart to the sky.

He smiled to himself; the sounds that came from him were the sounds of power coming to him, sounds much stronger than even the last screams of the women he had given to his private paradise.

He was ready for Cassie Waddell.

He now had the power.

Burke made camp at the edge of an aspen grove, where a trickle of spring water fed a little pond. He chewed on fresh pemmican that old Buck had given him, savoring the juicy mixture of deer meat and wild berries. He watched deer drink their fill for the evening and listened while owls discussed the odd weather. More fog, even thicker, rolled in with the last rays of light.

It wouldn't be so discouraging, Burke thought, if some rain would precipitate from the clouds. But nothing of the sort was going to happen. Just dense fog, with its swirling array of eerie, ghostly patterns.

He settled in for the night, wondering how he was going to write his report and not include Mark Jones. He decided that it didn't matter and had just taken another bite of pemmican when he heard a strange scream, coming from the near distance, followed by a second, louder and even more macabre.

The sounds were primitive and harrowing, unlike any animal he had ever heard before. The closest thing would be a mountain lion, but it wasn't that, and it certainly wasn't a howl.

It was primeval in nature, but it wasn't animal and it wasn't human.

And he was far too close to the sound to get a good night's sleep.

28

There were birds in the dawn, but they were few and far between in the fog. A huge raven pecked at his saddlebag and Burke tossed him a small chunk of pemmican, which the bird instantly swallowed, then lifted its wings and spread its feathers, its beak open, as if taking over the bag for himself. More ravens arrived and when Burke finally got Lancaster saddled and Jarvis unhobbled, a convention of black-feathered squawkers had filled the trees in the immediate area.

As he swung into the saddle they took wing, soaring out into the dense morning, leaving Burke to wonder how they planned to find their way through the wall of mist.

He had waited so long for dawn to arrive. He had listened all night for the scream to come again, but it hadn't come. In some ways he had been glad; in others, very disturbed. At least, had he heard it again, he would know where it was coming from and not coming for him.

Burke decided that maybe he had made too much of the sound. Maybe it had been a cougar: They could sound awfully strange. But something instinctively told him that whatever had made the sound was something that enjoyed blood on a deeper level than just ingesting it to survive.

He rode through the continuous bank of fog, keeping his eyes to the trees and the trail to avoid confusion, especially while negotiating the steeper twists and turns that were bringing him closer to the headwaters of Eden Creek.

He kept thinking in the back of his mind that he was riding toward the source of the screams.

When he arrived at his destination, he peered out into the gloomy vastness from an overlook. He couldn't see the other side of the canyon and could only make out the bottom when the swirling mist would open for a few seconds at a time.

Lancaster and Jarvis had become noticeably nervous and Burke also reacted to the sound of trampling hooves nearby. He thought about the night of the stampede and reacted by turning his horse and riding along the edge of the steep cliff, leading the mule behind.

The thundering sound behind him left nothing to Burke's imagination, the heavy bawling and the snapping and cracking of timber under trampling hooves. He kept urging Lancaster ahead, negotiating the twisting trail along the canyon's rim, certain the herd would be upon them in moments.

He turned up a trail that led along a hillside and breathed a sigh of relief, realizing that the stampeding herd would not climb uphill. He watched below as they came into sight, Rube Waddell's prize longhorns.

They roared past, hurtling themselves through the fog and out into the vast space over the cliff. They trampled past and never stopped, until the last few steers that trailed behind veered to one side and found their disoriented way along the trail that paralleled the canyon.

Burke stared over the canyon's rim. The muffled bawls of injured and dying cattle sounded from the bottom, a steady pattern of

deep guttural moans that echoed through the floating veil of
heavy fog.

He looked to the side and noticed a rider emerging from the
gloom. He held his Smith & Wesson ready until he recognized
Cassie Waddell.

"Is this your idea of an early morning outing?" he asked.

"I wanted to disrupt things," she replied.

"I believe you've done just that," he said. "We're going to
have to go down there."

Cassie sat slumped in the saddle and covered her face. She
sobbed quietly, shaking her head from side to side.

"I had to do something," she said. "I didn't know what else
to do."

"You hate your father a great deal," Burke told her.

"If you were me," she said, "you would, too."

They wound their way down a steep game trail, dismounting
often to help their horses negotiate the slippery twists and turns.
Along the way, Cassie explained the events of the preceding few
days, including her father's threats to tear down their home and
set them out in a tent.

"And I don't even want to begin regarding Sid Preston." She
reluctantly described Preston's visit, feeling guilty that she had
somehow lured a psychotic man into the same house with her
mother. She admitted that Preston posed a much more serious
threat than did her father.

"Why are you blaming yourself?" Burke asked.

"Because if I hadn't approached him he never would have
come to the house."

"How can you be so certain?"

At the bottom, they discovered the steers in a jumbled mass.
Protruding legs kicked spasmodically, as if hooked to an elec-

trical generator; flopping heads turned and twisted among the thrashing legs, huge round eyeballs rolling wildly in their sockets. The earlier quiet of the morning was shattered, the layers of rocks and scattered shrubs at the water's edge stained a glistening red, the water itself filling with dark and heavy rivulets.

Burke's morning visitors, the ravens, plus numerous crows and magpies, were already arriving on the scene, darkly winged shadows descending through the curtain of haze, pulling strips of flesh from the dead and the still living alike.

"I don't know how you did this alone," Burke said.

Cassie stared at the carnage, silent, her face tear-stained.

"It's amazing what you can do when you're driven to it," she said.

"I don't have enough ammunition to even begin to take care of this," Burke continued. "I'll have to pick and choose which ones to put out of their misery."

Here and there around the edges of the pileup, a few of the steers had somehow managed to escape the fall unscathed. They meandered awkwardly away, splashing through the shallow current. Some turned their heads to watch Burke stick the barrel of his pistol behind the ears of less fortunate herd members and pull the trigger. Many that had managed to survive, but were badly injured, stumbled on shattered legs and hips. Some tried to escape Burke's advances, hobbling on jagged stumps.

When he was finished, Burke holstered his pistol and joined Cassie where she sat under a large spruce.

"I can understand your rage," he told her, "but there's no sense in this kind of waste."

"I don't want to hear any sermons," she said. "Besides, I can't stay here."

She stood up and started for her horse.

Burke followed her. "You're not listening. Do you realize that I should report this?"

"Do what you have to do."

"Why don't you tell me what this is all about?"

"I don't have time."

A short distance away, two men appeared on horseback, filtered shadows in the heavy fog.

"Who are they?" Cassie asked.

"Ex-friends of mine."

Cassie watched while he walked over and discussed something with them. He returned shortly.

"Things are getting complicated," he said. "You'd better get out of here."

Cassie mounted. "I'm glad to see that you're so supportive."

"I just don't know why you would do this."

"Go talk to Doc Simmons," she said. "He'll fill you in."

When Cassie was gone, Burke returned to Maynard and Lane. He pointed out to them that the fog was beginning to lift.

"The best move you two could make is to hightail it out of here," Burke said. "I'm serious. The Pinkertons are on their way."

"How would they know we were here?" Maynard asked.

"Bill Conrad was on that Wyoming train we robbed," Burke replied. "He saw you at the roundup."

"Them coming and getting us are two different things," Maynard said. "Besides, we've got you to front for us. Remember?"

"I told you, you're on your own."

"We never did mesh too well," Maynard said.

"It could have worked, but you two should have been happy

with the stuff in the strongbox. You didn't have to go through the passenger cars."

"Why leave all that money behind?" Lane asked.

"It doesn't matter now," Burke said. "If you want to stick around, you can expect to see a number of Eden cowhands before long. If you get past them, expect the Pinkertons."

Len Keller and Jeb Mason hurried to saddle their horses. They had heard unusual sounds from a distance up the creek, toward the headwaters, something that reminded them of terrorized cattle.

They rode through the fog, noting that it was breaking in places and would likely be completely gone within a few hours.

After realizing that the bawling was coming from the bottom, they angled onto a trail that led them around the cliffs.

On the bottom, they rode directly into two men herding steers together, getting them ready to drive away in a group. One of them pulled a pistol and fired. Keller heard the bullet whistle past his ear.

"I think we found our rustlers," he said.

Maynard and Lane turned their horses and rode upstream, but their escape was blocked by the mass of fallen steers. They dismounted and climbed in among the fallen cattle and sought to hide themselves. They heard the sound of gunshots all the while, and the *plunk* of bullets smashing into the flesh of the dead and dying steers.

"We've got to figure something out," Lane said, "otherwise, we can say good-bye to this world."

Maynard didn't argue. He had nearly been struck by a bullet as it smashed into a dead longhorn he had chosen to take cover behind. He cursed as he pulled splinters of horn from his neck and the left side of his face.

"Maybe this will work," he said to Lane. He called out to Keller and Mason to stop their shooting. "I've got some information that you might like to know. It concerns Ellis Burke."

Burke sat in Doc Simmons's office, listening closely as Simmons talked with Chick Campbell.

"Chick, you need to give that leg a lot of rest," he was saying. "Stick to the bunkhouse and bone up on your poker skills."

"Bad pun," Chick said. "But I'll give you credit for trying."

Chick was still having a difficult time with Art Gilroy's death. He didn't say much; but earlier Simmons had told Burke outside the office that Chick's grief was playing a part in the healing process.

"He's angry and sad at the same time," Simmons had said. "It's tearing him up. Maybe he'll talk to you about it."

"Maybe I can get him to come to work for me," Burke had suggested.

As Burke listened to the present conversation, he awaited an opening to offer Chick a job.

"I don't fancy sitting in some bed any longer," Chick was saying. "I belong on a horse."

"Maybe you'd like to be on a horse," Simmons said. "But just try mounting one and see what your leg tells you."

"I own my damn leg," Chick said. "It does what I tell it."

"Want to make a bet?" Simmons said.

Chick cursed and stood up. He hobbled to the window and

peered out. He had been experimenting with crutches and had found it awkward, but better than sitting around.

"It's clouding up again," he announced. "I'll be there's no rain, though. Don't matter one way or the other. I won't be riding for Bill Conrad any longer, anyway."

Chick explained that Conrad had come into the doctor's office with Jackson and announced that he was moving his cattle south to a different range and selling his hotel to a consortium that had connections with a Denver hotel.

"He said he'd start fresh down around Montrose, where he could have a girlfriend and not have to see her vanish into thin air. I'm not able to ride down with them, so that leaves me without a job."

Burke got up and joined him at the window. "I've got an idea, Chick. You can help me map the forest reserves."

Chick continued to stare out the window. "I'm just a cowhand, Ellis."

"When you're ready, you can ride with me. Until then, you can transcribe information I bring in to you onto maps."

"I don't know nothing about maps."

"I'll teach you."

Chick turned from the window. "You just trying to be nice?"

"I need the help, Chick."

"Only if I can go with you after Preston."

"What do you mean?" Burke asked. He turned to look at Doc Simmons, who was equally as perplexed.

"I overheard you and the doc talking about Burt Gamble the other night." He hobbled over and sat down at Simmons's desk. "I know what Gamble was trying to tell you. I remember, a few years back, when I worked for Waddell and Art and me and Burt Gamble and some others we were rounding up steers.

Gamble talked in his sleep one night and when I woke him, he said that when he was a kid, he'd seen some bad stuff, something about knives.

"When you two were talking about Gamble the other night, I remembered that and wondered what he'd seen around here. You know, Sid Preston carries a big knife and there's a lot of women missing."

Simmons threw his hands down. "I should have known all along. The signs were all there. I've seen Preston's kind behind bars in Boston—psychotic killers, some of the worst specimens of humanity. They live in secrecy and they prey mostly on women."

"So he's the reason Lottie Burns and Gracie Hill are missing," Burke said.

"There are more missing than just those two, and no clues as to where they went," Simmons said.

"What kind of crazy man is Preston, anyway?" Chick asked.

"He's most likely the same sort of beast that some friends of mine in Boston were chasing—a sadistic killer with a strange fantasy. He uses knives on women, but has a real desire to die the same way he kills his victims—by evisceration. I talked to him after they caught him. A cold-eyed man, so cold. He wanted a woman to stick a knife into his middle at the same time he was stabbing her. He told me it would allow them to come together, to join and become as one, by mixing blood and entrails. Of course, every woman he kidnapped couldn't handle that and said no, so he murdered them out of rage."

Burke got up from his seat. Cassie Waddell was coming into the office.

"Why is your car parked over at Lee Miller's place?" she asked Burke.

"What?" Burke replied.

"Oh, I meant to bring that up," Chick said. "Conrad said that Waddell and Vivian Cross are going to get married, just as soon as Cassie's mother dies. Your car is Vivian's wedding present."

"We'll see about that," Burke said. And he was out the door.

"I'm going back to the ranch," Cassie said.

"Wait for Burke to get back," Doc Simmons said.

"Can't," Cassie told him. "Mother's all alone up there."

"I wanted to take a wagon up there, and pick her up," Doc Simmons said.

Cassie turned in the doorway. "You can catch up."

29

B urke got on his horse and decided what his course of action would be. Doc Simmons had just left for the Eden ranch, driving a wagon with Chick Campbell in the back.

Burke decided he would catch up with Simmons and Chick later. First he wanted to pay a visit to Lee Miller's place.

He rode through town, mysteriously quiet as people gathered indoors to wait out the storm. The skies continued to darken and in the west, lightning shot into the forest, followed by heavy rumbling.

There was something in the air, some kind of strange and strong charge.

Whatever it was, Burke was catching it.

Lee Miller lived a couple of blocks from his bank, in a new wood-frame home built with French tower designs at both ends of the two-story structure. The house was totally dark and Burke wondered if they weren't at the bank, finalizing paperwork.

His Buick was parked in front, big as you please. Apparently they thought he would be surveying the forest for some time to come and wouldn't miss his car.

Or, more likely, they just didn't care.

Burke tied his horse a distance away, in the cover of the trees, and made his way to his car. He found the crank and once the engine was started, he hopped in and drove to the bank. He could see them through the window—Miller, along with Waddell and Vivian—laughing over drinks in Miller's office.

Burke aimed his Buick at the front picture window and pushed the pedal to the floor. The automobile roared up to full power and Burke quickly discovered himself inside the bank, trapped in the driver's seat, while a kerosene lamp exploded amidst the debris on the hood of his car.

He frantically dug out from under wood splinters and shards of glass as flaming kerosene spread across his hood and onto the seats.

Vivian was screaming, while Miller and Waddell tried to get a clear shot at Burke. He thought about drawing his pistol and returning their fire, but decided instead to duck behind the car and escape out the huge hole he had created by the crash.

Lee Miller attempted to follow, just as the car blew up.

Burke rushed for the edge of town and untied his horse. He mounted and turned in the saddle to see Miller, aflame from head to foot, running and yelling through the street. Waddell had his coat off and was trying to catch him while Vivian stood and watched.

Burke looked farther down the street and noticed that two riders had appeared, dressed similarly. Burke guessed that they both carried the same Pinkerton detective credentials.

"I'm so tired, so very tired."

"You should rest, Mother. Don't think about anything."

"I'm afraid rest won't help," she said.

"No, rest won't help her."

Sid Preston stood just behind Cassie, where she knelt beside her mother's bed. He was naked, covered with elk blood, holding his knife, rolling the handle over and over in the palm of his hand.

"So, are you ready to go with me?"

Cassie turned back to her mother. Charlotte Waddell had turned her head sideways and after a deep breath, lay very still.

"Mother?" Cassie said. "Mother, don't go . . . don't . . . please."

"She's gone," Preston said.

Cassie shook her mother. Preston put his hand on Cassie's shoulder.

"We have to go, Cassie."

She turned, struggling to keep her composure.

"Sid, I have to take her to town. Surely you understand." She pulled the sheet up over her mother's head.

"Is she really dead?" Preston asked. "Let's see."

He pulled the sheet down and pressed the blade of his knife against Charlotte's throat. She arched her back and gasped.

"I thought so," he said.

He turned and flipped the large knife in his hand, so that he was holding the blade and not the handle, then suddenly rapped Cassie soundly along the side of her head. She slumped to the floor.

Charlotte sat up, her eyes huge and round.

"What's the matter with you?" she asked.

"I think we'll not play dead any longer," Preston replied, "unless, of course, you really want to be dead."

He gagged her with a handkerchief from one of her dresser drawers and tied her hands to the headboard.

"Just sit still and watch," he said.

He dragged Cassie onto the bed next to her mother and tied

her in a similar fashion, but omitted the gag. Then he left the room and returned with a canteen.

"A little sustenance for your daughter," he told Charlotte.

Cassie was returning to consciousness when she felt a rough hand pry her mouth open and force the lip of a canteen between her teeth. The liquid was nauseatingly sweet but she swallowed it rather than choke.

In less than a minute, she began to feel tired and dizzy.

"Don't worry," Preston said to Charlotte. "I'll tie her on her horse."

When Burke caught up with Simmons and Chick Campbell, they had but a few miles left before reaching the Eden ranch. Once there, Burke realized immediately that something was wrong. Cassie's horse wasn't tied in front.

Inside, they discovered Charlotte tied to the bed. When they untied her, she slumped forward and wept.

"Where did he take her?" Burke asked.

"He didn't say," Charlotte replied. "I'll never see her alive again."

"I believe we will," Burke said.

"I'm going to take you back to town," Simmons told Charlotte. "You'll lay still under the blankets and sheets I've got in the wagon."

"I already tried that," Charlotte said. "Preston almost killed me."

"He's not here now," Simmons said. "I'll get you to town, where you're safe, and leave the rest to Mr. Burke."

"Where do I fit in?" Chick asked.

"You'll be under another set of blankets," Simmons said. "If someone stops us and wants to see if Charlotte's really dead, you'll shoot them."

Vivian Cross and Rube Waddell waited on a bench outside Doc Simmons's office. The earlier crowd had dispersed after the fire had destroyed the bank and burned Lee Miller so badly that he was now close to death.

Many were watching the smoke clouds in the distance, wondering how close they would come to town. Others were already packing their belongings.

The Pinkerton detectives had asked about Burke. Waddell had said that Burke was responsible for the fire, but they hadn't believed him and had started toward Burke's cabin, needing him to help with their search for the two train robbers.

"I wish they hadn't been so hardheaded," Waddell was saying. "We could have gotten rid of Burke right away."

"Well, I'm tired of waiting here, Rube. I want to go to Glenwood Springs and on to Denver."

Waddell looked out into the sky. "It's too late to go now. We'll wait until tomorrow, when the storm has passed."

Vivian touched her stitches. "I need to see a good doctor real soon, Rube."

"We'll wait for Simmons to get back and take care of Miller," Waddell said. "Then we'll discuss it."

"It's a good thing we got all the banking papers in order before all this happened," she said.

Miller lay on the boardwalk in front of the doctor's office, wrapped in blankets, his face red and swollen. His breathing was difficult to detect.

"Rube, why are we sitting here? There's nothing we can do

for him now." Vivian stood up and paced. "Maybe we should go back to his house until the storm passes over."

"And just leave him here?"

"What else?"

"That will seem strange," Waddell said.

"No stranger than just sitting out here by ourselves in the storm," she said.

They were getting ready to leave when they noticed Doc Simmons returning in his wagon. They watched as he pulled to a stop and jumped down.

"What happened to Lee Miller?" he asked.

"That ranger drove his car right into the bank while we were conducting business," Waddell replied. "Burned the place down."

"How come neither of you were injured?"

"We got out quickly," Vivian replied. "Can you save him?"

Simmons knelt down and examined Miller carefully.

"I'm afraid there's nothing I can do," he said. He stood up and addressed Waddell, "I'll take him to the undertaker, along with your wife."

Waddell was momentarily shocked. He asked to see her.

Simmons led them over to the wagon and lifted the blanket. Charlotte lay still and in the stormy twilight, appeared very dead.

Waddell peered in at his wife, a shadowed, haunting figure to him. He was feeling strange and waved Doc Simmons to lay the blanket back down.

"Too bad," Simmons said. "She was a good woman."

"We have someplace to be," Vivian told Waddell.

After she had led him away, Simmons drove the wagon around to the back of his office. Chick and Charlotte emerged from the blankets.

"Where do you suppose they're headed so quick?" Chick asked.

"My guess is to the justice of the peace," Simmons replied. "But now they don't have a best man."

Vivian led Waddell up the steps into Lee Miller's house. She was beaming. The justice of the peace had found a man and woman in a local saloon who had agreed to stand up as best man and maid of honor, for a good fee.

"We've done it," Vivian said. "Together we own half the cattle in the valley."

She was pouring wine and Waddell said, "Why don't we rest a while? We can celebrate after I take a nap."

"No time for naps," Vivian said. She was pouring them champagne.

"I feel bad about not having Burke's car for you. That man is strange."

"Think nothing of it, Rube. We'll get another one." She pointed out the window. "Is that hillside burning?"

Waddell went to the window and said, "I'll be damned if it isn't. That could come down here." But somehow he felt that he didn't care one way or the other.

"Let's celebrate," Vivian said. "Then we'll go."

She joined him at the window and handed him a glass of champagne.

"Here's to us," she said.

They toasted their joint holdings and she set her glass down.

Waddell drained his and was asking her for a refill when his tired feeling suddenly escalated and he became very dizzy.

Vivian was smiling. "I'll need your money as well, Rube. I have to find a doctor who can fix my face."

Waddell was trying to make it to a chair, but quickly lost control of his muscles and fell against the wall. He should have wondered at his drowsy feeling all day.

He struggled to hold himself up, but slid to his side.

He said, "You . . . bitch . . ." and rolled over on his face.

Vivian took what cash he was carrying and his pocket watch, then hurried out the door and down to the livery stable, where she had a wagon waiting for her. She had to be certain that the flowers on her husband's grave were well watered before she left for Denver.

30

Preston untied Cassie from her horse and pulled her off, letting her fall to the ground. She stared up at him, his naked body glistening with each strike of lightning from above. He had freshened the coating on his body from a bowl of blood and water that rested on the table with his mother's head, and seemed to be on some crazed journey deep into his own mind.

As she worked to revive herself, Cassie realized that she smelled smoke.

"Fire," she told Preston. "There's a forest fire nearby."

Preston ignored her. He took her by the arm and dragged her toward a huge bull elk that lay upside down in death, spread wide open from neck to crotch. In his other hand, he held the sack with his mother's head, waving it around and chanting something.

He had shown her the head earlier, at the remote cabin he lived in alone, telling her that his mother was ready to see them be joined forever.

Initially, Cassie had fought him, but the drug had robbed her of all her strength. He had stripped her almost completely, having torn at her dress while calling her vile names.

She had asked for a drink of water and he had refused at first. When she had mentioned that she could die and rob him of their joining, he had obliged her.

Now, slowly, her senses were returning. As she watched him do his crazy dance, she realized that the smoke smell was growing stronger.

Burke rode past the headwaters of Eden Creek, around the pile of dead steers at the bottom of the cliff, a jumble of legs and horns that had attracted every wolf and coyote in the area, all feeding in a frenzy as the lightning and thunder grew more intense.

He rode on, into the high country south of the creek, beyond the trail he had taken out from old man Gentry's cave, farther still into the lost area where he believed he had heard the strange scream.

The entire forest was alive with the storm and scattered pockets of flame were growing in every direction. Here and there he heard cattle, elk, and deer crashing through the timber. Smoke began building a haze above the forest, reminding him of the evening he had first arrived in the area known as Eden.

He rode further into the forest, heading higher toward the top of the mountain. The storm was tremendous and the higher he climbed, the worse the lightning became.

Finally, he reached the summit and looked across a broad expanse, illuminated by the storm. In the distance he viewed what he knew to be a burn site from an earlier storm, a large expanse of jagged trees that looked like skeletons reaching into the thunder overhead.

Preston finished his chants and lifted his mother's head from the table. He kissed it on the lips and set it back down, arranging the shrunken eyes so they were trained on the grave.

"She can see everything from there," he said.

He took his Sharps rifle from the scabbard on his horse and rested it against a tree. "Never be without it," he had told himself many times.

He rolled Cassie onto her back and began untying her, straddling her from behind as he worked. She struggled to throw off the effects of the laudanum. When he had finished he dragged her to the elk by one arm, then tied her left wrist to the elk's left leg, just below the knee joint. He tied her left ankle to the elk's left leg. He tied her right wrist to the elk's right leg, and stood up.

"I'm going to finish tying your last foot," he said, "and then I'll take your tongue."

As he took her ankle in his hand, he heard a horse approaching and a man's voice rise over the storm.

"Sid, you up here?"

Len Keller's voice.

Preston lowered himself to Cassie's ear. "Not a word, or my blade goes into your brain."

Len Keller tied his horse to a burned pine and dismounted. The lightning had grown worse and it looked like extensions of a huge and jagged spider web across the darkening sky. He also smelled smoke and knew a fire was burning nearby, one of the many that had broken out in the forest since the storm began.

He called again for Preston, trying to understand what was going on and why the Eden ranch foreman would be up on a lonely hilltop in the middle of a dangerous storm, with fires breaking out everywhere.

Then he saw the dangling clothing and what he thought to be rags, floating like tattered ghosts. He soon realized they were pieces of women's garments, stained with something dark. He didn't want to touch anything, but looked closely at them and struggled to comprehend it.

In the flashing light he began to see the burials, numbers of huge bull elk placed upright, halfway into the ground, and the bony human arms that protruded from between the ribs.

He dismounted and led his horse further, calling for Preston again. It all seemed like a strange dream to him, confusing him deeply.

Just off to his left, a short distance away, Sid Preston stood facing him, beckoning him over.

The foreman stood naked, glistening, like he had painted himself.

As he approached Preston, Keller realized the man was covered with blood.

He thought immediately that the woman tied to the butchered elk must be dead.

"What's going on here, Sid?" Keller asked.

Preston stepped forward, waving the knife in front of him.

"I told you never to come up here. Never!"

"My God, Sid, that's Cassie Waddell you've got. And all those clothes hanging everywhere . . . the human bones. And look at you . . . what in the living hell?"

Preston grabbed him by the collar with his free hand and shook him. "Why did you come up here?"

"I had to find you." Keller was choking on the words. "Those two thieves—we caught them. They said they work for Burke."

Preston still had ahold of Keller's collar and was pushing him backwards, away from Cassie. His entire evening was spoiled, his fulfillment interrupted. His mind raced and turned and churned. The new information—Burke and the two thieves—entered his mind, but he couldn't concentrate.

"What am I going to do with Keller?" he thought.

"They said they robbed a Wyoming train with Burke and that you got shot and passed out. You were a Pinkerton then. Right?"

"You're never supposed to come here, Len. I've told you over and over."

"Sid, I thought you would want to know," Keller said. "Why didn't you come down when the steers got pushed over the cliff?" He stared at Preston, whose eyes were dull and blank. "Sid, didn't you even know about that?"

Preston released him. "Where are Maynard and Lane now?"

Keller stepped nervously from foot to foot and rubbed his brow, trying to comprehend what he had discovered. His mind wouldn't work right but he knew full well that he had to get away, and fast.

"The thieves, where are they?" Preston repeated.

"Not far below. They're set to hang."

"Mason's watching them?"

"Yes. But I said I'd bring you right down. But if you're not ready to go . . ."

Preston frowned. The train memory was coming back. Yes, he remembered Burke now as the thief who had stopped Red Maynard from finishing him off. He had been nearly unconscious. It was the voice that had triggered his memory. Yes, Burke's voice. "Don't kill him. We just want the goods," he remembered Burke saying.

The ranger had once saved his life.

For what?

. . .

"I'm leaving," Keller said. "Come down when you're ready."

Preston took his arm. "Wait."

Keller tried to pull away, but Preston held him firmly.

"I want to talk to you, Len," Preston said.

Keller reached for his pistol but Preston held his wrist, at the same time driving his knife toward Keller, intending to gut him.

But Keller was yelling, twisting away. The blade entered his upper hip area, grating on bone.

Keller yelled and swung, catching Preston across the side of the head, knocking him backward, dazing him momentarily. Keller stumbled and turned for his horse, but Preston was upon him.

Preston cursed. He had lost his knife.

The two struggled, falling over Cassie, kicking and swinging and cursing.

Preston had Keller by the throat with one hand, slamming his fist into Keller's face with the other. Cassie swung her free leg around, whacking Preston flush across the bridge of the nose.

Keller rolled out from under Preston and struggled to his feet, gasping, disoriented, slurring curses. The feeling in his right hip and down the back of his leg was fuzzy and he stumbled repeatedly.

He finally reached his horse, gasping for breath, fighting against the intense pain. He tried to calm his horse, taking the reins, pulling himself into the saddle.

. . .

Preston came to his feet and staggered, shaking the cobwebs from his head. Keller's horse was running wild through the burned trees, on an angle for a trail that led across an open ridge.

Breathing heavily, Preston grabbed his Sharps and began to run.

"Got to stop him!" he thought. "Got to!"

As the lightning flashed overhead, he could see Keller, riding low over the saddle, bouncing, holding on with all his might.

The horse burst from the burned trees and started up the ridge. Preston's only chance was to drop the animal before Keller spurred it over the top.

It should have been an easy shot for him, even with the storm and flashing shadows from the lightning.

But his nose was bleeding and his eyes were watering.

And the rifle was a single shot.

He took aim and pulled the trigger. The horse kept going, nearing the top.

Preston cursed, fumbling to open the breech, to load another bullet. He tried to calm himself for a steady shot, but his head was ringing and his brain was throbbing.

He fired again, thought he saw the horse stagger.

But it was still on its feet. Still running, nearing the ridge top.

Preston reloaded and ran headlong through the shadowed grass and brush. His feet churned and his left arm swung wildly, his right arm rigid, cradling the Sharps.

He stopped and gasped for breath. Smoke filled his lungs and he coughed.

A ways ahead, he saw that Keller's horse had reached the ridge. Riderless, it surged across the open, silhouetted against the lightning-filled sky, stirrups swinging freely.

Preston shuddered with anticipation, filled with new hope. He peered into the darkness around him.

"He's close by. I'll find him . . ."

Cassie struggled with her free foot to reach the knife, just out of reach. She stretched with all her might, her toes just inches from the handle. But the elk was tied fast and her bonds wouldn't give enough.

She lay back, frustrated, exhausted. The smell of smoke was growing ever stronger and she knew the fire had to be getting close.

This was no time to give up, she thought, and reached her foot toward the knife once more. She stretched and worked and exhausted herself once again.

It appeared hopeless.

If it had to be either the fire or Sid Preston, she would take the fire.

Vivian stared at the flames that roared through the tops of the trees just beyond her corrals, coloring the night sky with orange. She had stopped in front of the house and had jumped out just as the horses bolted away with the wagon, running wild across an open meadow. She considered herself lucky to be able to have held them and kept them from running off earlier.

She had passed two separate fires on the way up and realized that this one would soon consume the property. She had seen numerous cattle running in every direction. It seemed that the entire forest was ablaze.

She hurried up the hill to her husband's grave site, where she coughed and touched her stitched face. The air was so dry and so smoky. She had to hurry and do the watering and get down to Denver. She couldn't bear to have her face ruined.

She struggled to find her pitcher in the stormy darkness, then rushed off the hill and through a grove of trees to the creek to fill it with water. She thought she saw a man standing nearby, silhouetted by the approaching flames, watching her closely.

"Byron? Is that you?"

"He's come back for me. I should have kept the plants watered better," she thought.

She rubbed her eyes and when she looked again, all she saw was fire, rolling through the trees in her direction.

She coughed again and tried to brush her stringy hair away from her face.

Again, the man in the flames appeared.

"Byron? Please . . ."

The pitcher fell from her shaking hands and she started to run, then returned to the creek and searched, crying, until she found it. She filled it and stood up.

The man was standing there again, his hand outstretched to her, flames all around him.

"He wants to take me with him to hell."

She hurried from the creek through the trees, desperate to reach the grave and fill the tube with water. She ran, yelling, looking behind her, rushing from the vision of Byron Cross.

She didn't see the fire surge into the trees overhead, the flames crackling and popping, exploding, sending showers of burning wood down upon her, lighting the tinder and the grass and everything around her, except the man who stood nearby, waiting.

31

H e's got to be here someplace. . . ."
Preston worked his way along the trail that led up the
ridge, crouching, searching for any sign of Len Keller, his
Sharps ready to fire. The gusty wind and the lightning and the
thunder and the increasing smell of smoke was distracting, but
he had to keep his concentration.

Keller had no doubt fallen from his horse and could be anywhere, either dead or still alive, waiting for a clear shot at him.

Preston neared a grove of dead trees along the trail. They
moaned in the hot, windy darkness, their bony branches reaching, creaking.

Preston's breath caught in his throat as he heard something
in the grass.

He turned as a covey of sharp tail grouse rose, clucking
noisily, into the sky. Then something else moved on the ground.

Lightning flashed and for an instant, Preston viewed Keller's
terrorized face, his huge eyes, and the barrel of his pistol aimed
straight at him.

They fired simultaneously. Keller's pistol flashed and Preston fired as he dropped, hearing Keller's loud grunt. Another
bolt of lightning showed Keller writhing, his right arm blown
loose at the shoulder.

Preston left him.

He had to hurry back to the graveyard.

Cassie was still waiting for him.

Cassie felt all her muscles pulling as she tried to lurch free of the ropes. She had managed to touch the knife handle once with the tip of one toe, but worried about knocking it farther away.

She laid back to regain her strength, certain that Sid Preston was nearby. She hadn't heard gunshots for a while and knew that either Preston or Keller was dead.

Somehow she knew it wouldn't be Preston.

The skies continued to come apart overhead, sending bolts of jagged white into the forest everywhere. She closed her eyes and took several deep breaths, trying to regain her strength and keep from panicking.

When she opened them again, she was looking into a man's face.

She screamed.

Ellis Burke reached down and touched her.

"It's me. It's all right," he said.

"My God, Ellis. Get me out of here." Burke began to struggle with the ropes and she said, "No, no. His knife. It's right there."

She pointed with her foot. Burke began to pat the ground carefully in the darkness, trying to avoid cutting himself on the razor-sharp blade.

"Hurry, Ellis," she hissed.

With a burst of lightning overhead, he said, "I see it."

"Don't touch it, Ranger Man. Mr. Outlaw Man."

Sid Preston stood behind him, pointing the barrel of the

Sharps at the back of Burke's head. He slipped around and picked up the knife.

Burke could hardly believe what he was seeing: A man covered with blood and gore and dirt, whose eyes looked like white marbles with small dark patches in the light of the storm, the craziest man he had ever met.

"Glad you came, Burke," Preston said. "I remember you from that Wyoming train. Or is that your little secret?"

"There's fire everywhere," Burke said. "We've all got to get out of here."

"No, we don't. We're going to do this thing together."

"What thing?" Burke asked.

"You'll see. Take off your clothes, all of them. I'll instruct you."

"I won't be doing that," Burke said.

"Do it or die right now," Preston said.

Following Preston's instructions, Burke first slipped the holster holding his Smith & Wesson off his belt and tossed it aside. He waited for Preston to pick it up. But he didn't. He was preoccupied with Cassie, rubbing watered-down blood on her from a bowl, forcing her to drink from it.

Burke thought about rushing him, but Preston looked up. He rose and stepped forward, jabbing the Sharps into Burke's midsection.

"Have any kind of an idea what sized hole this could make?" he asked. "First, your shirt."

Burke complied and Preston handed him the bowl.

"Smear yourself with this." When Burke hesitated, he again

jabbed him with the Sharps. "I'm not going to ask you again."

Burke smeared the slimy mixture across his chest and over his stomach.

"Slop some over onto your back," Preston ordered.

Burke did as he was told. As Preston then instructed, he set the bowl down and started to unbuckle his pants. From the shadows came Chick Campbell's voice.

"Preston, you son of a bitch!"

Preston turned and fired the Sharps. Chick's horse reared, mortally wounded and throwing him to the ground.

Burke took the opportunity to lunge to one side and grab his pistol from its holster. But Preston had dropped the Sharps and had ahold of Cassie's hair. He jerked her head back and placed his knife against her throat.

"You'll drop that pistol, won't you?" Preston said.

"You won't kill her," Burke said. "That would spoil your plan."

Preston pulled Cassie's head back farther.

"Do you want to see her bleed?"

Burke stepped over to Preston's table and picked up his mother's head by the hair and jammed the barrel of his pistol into one ear.

"I guess I'll just pull the trigger," Burke said.

Preston held his breath. "Don't do that."

"No, let Cassie go or I'm going to spill her brains."

"If you must," Preston said. "Then I'll take Cassie's head."

Preston turned to pull the knife against Cassie's throat, taking his eyes off Burke for a fraction of a second. Burke turned the pistol and fired at Preston, who jumped up like a wounded animal and began to spin in circles, wailing and screaming, holding his side.

.   .   .

Burke found Preston's knife and cut Cassie loose. They hurried to where Chick had fallen. He was lying on his side, semiconscious.

"I don't know how you got here," Burke said, "but I'm glad you did."

"I borrowed the horse from your corral, Cassie," he said. "Then I set the others loose. I'm sorry Preston shot him. I'll replace him."

"You don't have to replace anything," Cassie said.

Burke caught Lancaster and hoisted Cassie up, and then Chick on behind.

"I'll find Preston's horse," he told them. "Get out of here."

Cassie and Chick both protested but Burke argued that they were wasting time. He slapped the horse on the rump and turned to look through the smoke for Preston's cabin.

It was impossible to see anything and he headed in the direction of the creek. His only chance to escape the flames was to immerse himself totally in the water.

He splashed into welcome freshness and, finding his way on his hands and knees, discovered a sinkhole that he could fully immerse himself in, allowing only his nose and mouth to surface from time to time.

As he prepared to go under, Sid Preston crossed the creek a short distance away, a naked, staggering, man screaming at the top of his lungs, holding his side with one hand and cradling his mother's head with the other.

Then he vanished into the smoke and fire like a bloodsmeared ghost.

.   .   .

Cassie and Chick sat in the dawn light with their backs against a rock wall, enjoying the sudden rainstorm. An old man stood nearby, holding a Hawken rifle in the crook of his arm, standing vigil over the edge of a cliff, peering into the smoky distance.

Chick was drinking a brew that an old Indian woman had given him, and his leg now felt much better.

Cassie had figured out that the old man had to be old Buck Gentry, the legendary mountain man who had secluded himself from society a number of years earlier.

He told Cassie that he had been expecting her, along with Chick and maybe one other.

"I have a son who can forecast events," he said proudly.

But he hadn't been expecting the two men he had tied to a tree nearby. One was tall, the other short, both wearing similar clothes.

"They say they're detectives," Buck told Cassie. "But they won't tell me what they're looking for. So, why are you here?"

"Trying to escape the fire," Cassie replied. "And we're looking for a man who was with us."

"Getting to be a lot of people up here," the old man said.

Buck Gentry was then joined by his son, who pointed downhill through the smoke and smiled. Buck smiled also.

"That the man you're looking for?" he asked Cassie.

She rose to her feet. "It sure is."

Burke was blackened with soot from head to toe. He had walked the entire distance from Preston's private graveyard, getting a good view of the devastation. Cassie ran to his arms and they embraced. He told her about his two hours in the stream and the terrible aftermath of the fires.

"There weren't so many elk or deer," he said. "But the cattle were everywhere. I stopped counting at two hundred head. There's a lot more and there's more fires burning. This storm won't put them all out."

"A good time back there was a fire that burned all summer long," Buck put in. "Damned near burned up the whole forest."

That answered one of Burke's questions regarding the trees he had taken note of since his arrival. The lodgepole pine and quaking aspen, particularly, were indicators of fire and regenerated regularly after a blaze.

In walking up from Eden Creek, he had spent some time looking around for Sid Preston. But there was so much burned flesh in the forest, much of it unrecognizable, that he gave up.

He met with the Pinkertons who told him they had ridden up to his cabin to look for him.

"No fire in that gulch at all," the taller one said. "You're lucky."

"But the Eden ranch didn't fare as well," the shorter one added. "It all went up in smoke except the big old log house. The new mansion was leveled."

"That's too bad," Cassie said. "I loved that place."

Burke smiled.

"I imagine there'll be a lot of changes in the valley," the tall one said. "Being the whole town burned to the ground."

"You two did a lot of work in a short time," Burke told them.

"We did a lot of homework before we came," the taller one said. "We learned there were three outlaws at that train robbery, not just two."

"Maybe he got burned up, too," the shorter one commented. They had come across the charred bodies of Red Maynard and Dean Lane, with the burned remnants of the ropes around their necks. "It appears that somebody beat us to them," he added.

"I'll keep looking for the third one," Burke said. "Just in case he's still around."

"We'll be going then, just as soon as the old man unties us," the taller one said.

Burke talked old Buck into releasing them and they stayed for a meal of serviceberries and roasted elk, then left with a tip of their hats.

When they were well down the mountain, Cassie and Burke adjourned to a nearby stream and began cleaning one another up.

Cassie rubbed Burke's chest with a yucca-root soap she had gotten from the Ute woman. She smiled and said, "I want to hear the story of outlaw man."

"Who?"

"I heard what Preston said."

"Another time," Burke said, pulling her down beside him.

Afterword

Historical conflict is always an interesting study, and a theme that is perpetually in motion. The history of the early conservation movement in western Colorado provides enough fodder for anyone's curiosity.

Though a large number of the ranching operators welcomed the changes, a well-documented few fought the intervention tooth and nail. A great reference in understanding their feelings firsthand came from *History of Routt National Forest, 1905–1972*, a U.S. Forest Service publication. This document is a compiled account of the changes through letters and histories submitted by the people who lived in the area at the time.

In my story, Ellis Burke represents a composite of the early forest ranger, a dedicated individual who struck out into, quite often, dangerous territory to save a resource desperately in need of assistance. I saw clearly through the eyes of one such man while reading *Forty Years a Forester* by Elers Koch (Mountain Press Publishing Company, Missoula, Montana, 1998).

The conflict itself was presented very clearly in George Michael McCarthy's *Hour of Trial: The Conservation Conflict in Colorado and the West, 1891–1907* (University of Oklahoma Press, 1977). Among the other volumes that provided added information was *Hoof Prints on Forest Ranges* by Paul H. Roberts (The Naylor Company, San Antonio, Texas, 1963), another good study of the turmoil that comes with change.

In addition to the original turmoil, when you learn just the fragments of an old secret, there is an added edge that cannot be measured.

The history of the landmark called the Devil's Grave is difficult to track clearly. Though there are documented shootings and a few murders in the area, no one is certain just how the mesa came by its unusual name. However, the fact that some women working in the brothels in Glenwood Springs left and were never heard from again is not a matter of dispute. As that was often the case among transient individuals, no one questioned their motives.

Sid Preston is based on a mystery, a faint hint of something that could have actually *been*, but could never have been accepted, especially in those times along the far reaches of a wilderness where most everyone lived in harmony with nature and one another.

Such a man was never documented as ever having been discovered, caught, or brought to justice. But the feeling of such a possibility remains behind in the vast reaches of timber and rock.

—Earl Murray
Fort Collins, Colorado
Spring, 2000